THE
BOOK OF VLAD

ONE

THE

IMPALER

THOMAS ARTHUR

THE IMPALER
by Thomas Arthur
The Book of Vlad, Book One

Editor: Sylver Foley
Cover illustration: Manthos Lappas
Cover and interior layout and design: Suzanne Fyhrie Parrott

Library of Congress Control Number: 2016931458

Paperback: ISBN 978-0-9914804-6-3
Hardcover: ISBN 978-0-9914804-9-4

10 9 8 7 6 5 4 3 2 1

PENMAN
PRODUCTIONS

Published in the United States by Penman Productions,
P.O Box 400, Gleneden Beach, Oregon 97388
www.penmanproductions.com

CONTENTS

PROLOGUE
A Message from Vlad

GOOD EVENING, MY FRIENDS,

My name is Dracul. I have been known by other names, and I will let you discover them as you read. Now, the little you have heard of me is not the entire truth, but is instead gross exaggerations of real events. Some scholars will say that I am the foulest person to have ever lived. That might be true, but all that you should take from that statement is that I had, indeed, lived. I am not a figment of someone's imagination that has been fabricated into stories, lies, and tales to tease children. I am, in fact, a truth, an existence that cannot be denied.

There are other things, besides names, that many people know me as: a monster, a legacy, a tyrant and something to be feared. I am much more than what they realize; for I am, in part, each one of them, each one of you. I am a trial of humanity. I am the essence of one that is tested in life and in death, one that was brought through the journey with absolution and dismay, and one that walks forth in eternal darkness, because he has seen such beautiful, brilliant light. That is who I am, but my story has never truly been told.

The historians and the scientific minds have hidden the plain facts because they have become too otherworldly to believe. The heretics and the religious are too fearful to listen, because my story is not a simple one and it cannot be processed by a simple mind. My story stretches on, and will continue stretching for eternity. No simple set of actions made me how I am; no, that is a fool's thought. It is as if these fools see the universe as a simple pebble that they found in a garden, unware of the jungle that surrounds them. No, my story is complex and holds forth a series of events that will lead me to my path, to my demise, and much more. It is a journey that must be taken from the start to understand, a journey that is riddled with pain, fury, redemption, and savage loss. This is what I have to say you.

But before you go on reading, I must warn you. I will say things you will not want to hear. If you are a hopeful being, I have no wish for you to listen to my story, because everything that I say is unkind, raw, shameful, and disdainful. You will question my words, my thoughts, and my actions. You will wonder about my sanity, as you should, for I can concur that I have none. You will wonder about my premise, and you should for it is anything but holy. You will wonder and contest all of the words that I put in front of you, that is to be certain. However, I will tell you this: everything that I say to you is real to me. It's what is in my mind, what I have felt, and what I feel.

To utter anything else would be nonsense, a lie, and I will not lie to you. I won't tell you what you want to hear, but what you need to hear. Listening to what I have to say is a choice that I leave to you, for I hold no law or power that dictates your will, or your soul. Instead, I give you a choice that consists of listening to truth, or being deaf to the reality that surrounds the essence of life. This choice is yours and it always will be, and it is one that I will never take from you. Therefore, I leave it up to you whether to continue or not, whether to hear more words of truth or to put me back on the shelves with the unheard revelations of so many others. You may do this at any time you feel the truth becomes far too real to handle. However, I must tell you that once we begin the journey, it will never end.

Now, shall we begin?

~Vlad

CHAPTER 1
An Unhallowed Birth

I WAS BORN A COMMON MAN, in the common woods, in a common land. For the mere mention of anything grand, anything rich, anything other than *common* would be an insult to reality. It was in these harsh times that I bore my first name, a name given to me by my mother and father, although I was not fortunate enough to have both, and only had one. It was my father's hand that passed the name down to me upon the death of my mother. It was a name that I knew too well, a name that I lived and felt. *the name of, Bastard.*

I was known only as this because I was a killer at birth. I had taken the life of my mother for the selfish reason of living my own. In doing so, lost my father as well. As I came out of her womb, she became lifeless. Her strength had been given away in return for mine. Even before I learnt to breathe, I had become a murderer, heartless and cold, screaming of my glory as my father wept for losing his. I had come to this earth without their blessing; I was a curse that took away everything he had in nine months of torture, concern and worry, and in an instant I stole his hope and his dreams.

In the eyes of my father, I was such a dreadful being that I did not deserve the right to live. Yet, he had no desire to kill me then and there, at the moment of my birth, for he knew that I was the last gift left to him by my mother. I was the last connection he had to her heart. And it was this truth that made his heart burn, that made his anger grow, and made his hate rage.

I must say, it was a mistake to let me live beyond that first turmoil, beyond that first step into the light of this world. It was a mistake to have plagued all those that came before me, and those that have died after me. It was the beginning—a beginning of grim times, and a beginning of my dark journey as I took the first step in the light. But, we will come to that later.

As a child, I had not known much except that I was to be the receiver of dried fruit, of ravished nature and deserted plains. I was the end to the element of life, the last morsel of tainted essence. I was the soot. I was the dirt. As such, I was discarded like the most unwanted, the most unwelcomed, the most undeserved things in life. I was no more significant than rotten cabbage or soiled, festered meat. I was more those things than I was a son or even a man, both of which I could not claim to be.

I was no more my father's offspring than that of a slave, which would have garnered more respect than I did. I was no more his child than I was the child of the pests and nuisances that plagued the farms every day. I was unnecessary, unloved, unneeded, and a blight to the land. This was what my father had come to accept.

My father would have traded a thousand of me for only one short glimpse of my mother. Nevertheless, it was a trade that he could not make, a proposition that he could not undertake, and he knew it well. The diviner of life had denied him the pleasure and love he had once felt, the task of raising a child of respectable nature was replaced with a villainous monster that was to be his burden of a son.

And a monster I was; I had been the scissor that cut the thread of his perfect life, his perfect wife, his perfect existence. A monster I was, because I only knew evil, only knew self-interest, and one's self wants to survive. I was to be treated as the flaw that I was, and would be denounced like all things crucial to vitality. Hope. Love. Compassion. All things lost.

It was a wonder that my father did not abandon me. I would have thought it to be as easy as that. He could have taken me some place far away and let me go, set me on a cart and sent me to ride lost in the unknown, or barter me off to a man, sentencing me to live my life in servitude. However, each of those options would have caused interaction and the recognition that I was his son. For that reason, I was not to be abandoned. Yet, now, when I look back, I realize that maybe he already had abandoned me in his own way, but I was too young and of little mind to have realized it.

We slept in the same hut, even bathed in the same streams. I followed him as he performed his daily tasks. I followed him as he performed his daily rituals. From foraging to working the fields, I followed in the darkness, in the shadows, watching, learning from what I witnessed, and so understanding how to survive and thrive. All this I did, always at a distance.

It was if he knew of my existence but showed no sign of it. Not a single word he had spoken to me, not a single glimpse did he send in my direction. Only silence, only remorse, and only hate. Yet I did exist to him, for I could sense in his spirit the haunting plague of desecration, destruction, and devastation that I brought to his pristine life. I saw myself in his misery, in his hate, and felt his loathing towards the woeful distaste of my life. His grim expression and downturned face was the symbol of my presence, for without that I would not have believed that I was an actuality.

I would have indeed thought myself as a ghost, a specter, an apparition that crawled the lands, except that I saw my confirmation of existence in the people of the village. On those rare occasions, when those 'others' saw me and pointed in my direction, I knew that I was real and not a phantom. Yet the only response from my father was that of disgust, if there was a response at all, which made me further question my convictions of reality.

I was determined to change that fact, to be noticed, to be confirmed. I had made all efforts to harbor attention but each time I failed. I had cried. I had screamed. I had broken what little we had. I had even stolen from others in order to be caught, all in the vain hope of acknowledgment from my father. In all that, I failed.

No reaction came, no difference of opinion, good or worse, had I felt. It was that emptiness that was most haunting; it was the void and abyss that I felt instead of emotion. I was not lectured for the evil I had done. I was not scolded for the filth that I was. I was not even punished by the stinging of the flesh, for even that would have been something to show that I was a son, a human being.

No, I did not even receive the decency of pain. Instead, I was left alone, ignored, out of sight, invisible and forgotten to the eyes of my father. I was a mere fairy tale, a haunting nightmare that plagued his thoughts. I was an illusion of a child, no more and no less.

The bitterness in my heart and in my soul grew. It was born as a foggy shade until it went dark grey, and with time it had become black until all I had become was a nightmarish abyssal haze. O that darkness bellowed in my stomach and churned in my heart. It twisted in my eyes, and stung my soul, if a soul I did have. If I was not born a monster, I had become one. A monster only brought forth to cause misery, which I did every day from the ongoing sin of my mere existence.

I believe it my right to say that I was born motherless. Although my mother had no remorse for my birth, she never had the possibility to see what my father saw. I had not given her a chance to hate me, for I was cruel enough to take even that away. For sure, I can truly say that I was fatherless, for how can one be a father if he has never seen his child? No, I can truly say that I was an entity brought into this world by a being of divine light or putrid darkness, but nurtured by none, only raised by the harshness of neglect and disdain, and harbored by all the wretchedness of humanity. No mother, no father. I was to be left alone, left to see the world with childlike eyes, left to see what the world truly was and truly is—pain.

* * *

Yes, pain is what existed as the basis of my world. O and how magnificent and mysterious was this pain. If the world was broken up and examined at its bitter core, in its smallest dissection, then they would only find one answer, and that would be pain.

Pain was truly the only thing that stretched to every fiber of the world, for it was everywhere and it made its presence known in the oddest of places. Striking in the pits of the stomach when I was hungry, to the back of the mind when no sense was to be made, and when I suffered a gash or a wound, pain was there, always. However, my pain had a home, where it always returned to no matter where else it briefly resided. The place I felt it most often and at its most severe was in my heart. Pain was my first companion as a child and the only one to never abandon me, for I would feel it infinite times and in infinite abundances and it would guide me through life as I grew.

I grew very quickly in those times. Left alone by everyone and shunned by everything else. I thought I was at my weakest and at my worst in those times, but looking back I miss those times the most. Life was simple for those of immaturity, those with simple answers and simple thoughts. Sadness filled my mind and cleared all else. How easy life would be if it was only that way, but life has a way of surprising you, of taking you to places you do not expect. I would have thought anything to be better than where I was, but I did not realize one important thing, one important fact that life knows all too well and does its best to teach you: The fact that you cannot fall if you have already fallen, and you cannot go any lower when you are at the bottom. Life knew what it had to do, and it was simple. It took me higher; let me soar higher than the mountains, the clouds, and even the gods. Then life did what it always does; it takes you to the very top, and pushes you off the edge.

CHAPTER 2
Illyana

HER NAME WAS ILLYANA, my first true love, my only love. I did not know then what it meant, for I knew not what love was. I only knew anger; I only knew pain and loneliness. She was the first to look in my direction and not see a monster, but to see a man that was just a boy and not a curse brought onto the land. For my father had spread the word that I was evil incarnate, that I brought doom to one's life. In those superstitious times, it became truth to the land. For what is truth but the common belief that something is certain? And when something is certain, anything else becomes a lie.

So, the truth was that I was a monster, a grave-maker, a herald of death. Still, she did not see me as such. Instead, she looked at me as she looked at everyone else. She saw me as no more intimidating than the rising sun, the coming night, or a cool breeze. She saw a man, a mortal, a mere being left alone on this earth, standing amongst many of its equals.

O, I did not know the power of sight until that moment. I, for the first time, knew I was not evil. I was not a terror. Instead, I was a simple tortured man, one with regrets, one with pain, and one with an empty heart no longer.

She said not one word to me that day, but I knew. She went to her tasks, pulling the wheat from the land and placing it in her hand-woven basket, as was done in those days. She went through her daily routine, and I watched. It was one of the few times I had truly known peace, a quick second or two of content, fullness, and serenity. Yet as she walked away, something else took its place—a hunger. A hunger for more, a desire that was unending, a sorrowful need to feel that calmness and peace once more that I did not know I needed until I had it.

I realize now that love is a hunger that is bitter to the taste. It brings as much sorrow as it does joy, as much pain as it does pleasure. It is a yearning that is unrelenting, and a desire that is a gruesome torture hidden in a mirage of pleasantry.

And that hunger possessed me to my very core, 'til I could not think, I could not eat, I could not drink, all I could do was to hope for that moment to come again, to be a quick cure to the poison of the heart. How I dreamt of that moment. How I fantasized about a life that I would never live, lusted for a moment that would never occur, dreamt about a time that I would never travel to. Still, I dreamt. O, how I dreamt with open eyes of all the futures that were not to be.

That hunger drove me to the grounds daily, to watch her as she passed. I watched her to gain a bit of that feeling that I had never felt before. That content was prestige, elegant, pure, and a fantasy so serene that it was untainted by the cruel world of truth. I would see her every day, every hour that she was out, and every second that passed, I relished. I took those moments into my soul as a gift.

I knew the movements of her demeanor, the motions of her hands when she worked, the way she took each breath with softly curved lips. Every facet of her I saw, and I memorized, carved it into my heart so that no tool or force would be able to rid me of the feeling and of the sight. I knew of the marks she wore on her arms and her neck, the bruises she had occasionally, that appeared and disappeared with the passing of time. All the details of her façade, I saw in real life, and then saw again and again as I dreamt. O, how I wished my dreams were true, the magnificent and benevolent dreams that held the freedom that I wanted. Instead, I got the stark reality that the world was so sure to show me.

I remember that day clearly, although the skies were anything but. They were stormy and dark as if they knew what was to follow, as it should be with all things that occur in nature. It was on the verge of winter and the leaves were giving way to the ground, a slow, freezing death. Like the discarded leaves, so would my dreams come collapsing down. For like those leaves, my dreams were about to be trampled on, beaten into the dirt, forgotten by life and left to decay. My illusions would be broken, and the fantastically woven tapestry that I had created started to be undone.

I remember seeing her that day. Walking out of her little hut, tears flowing down her cheeks. She wiped them away as quickly as she could, but the sight did not escape me. She picked up her basket to run to the fields, yet it was not the season for the fields to harvest, or for the bushes to bear fruit, all of which I found odd. She went to the fields to most likely sit in solitude, but I could not bear to not see her, so I snuck behind anyways.

I saw her there as I foxed through the fields to get a glimpse of my spectacular beauty. A glimpse that would incite those feelings and appease that wretched hunger once more, and in fact it did, the moment I saw her.

She sat in the middle of a clearing, down on her knees in the dirt, with a stick in her hand. She scraped it against the dirt, making some sort of picture that I could not decipher from my vantage point. I moved closer and closer until I could smell her magnificent, wonderful scent on the wind, but still I could not see the picture, and I had not the heart or courage to get any closer.

"I know you're watching me," she said.

To my surprise, she had detected me. I had always thought myself as a stealthy man. I had seen myself as a man that prided himself being hidden from society and not bothering other souls, an eternal watcher of those around but never a participator. Yet she had seen through that. She sensed my presence, and to my relief, she was not vexed, disgusted or repulsed. Instead, she was not bothered at all.

"You don't have to be scared," she said. "Come out. I'm not angry."

It was a strange invitation, for I had never been asked to join company of anything or anyone, and it held back my reactions even if that was all I wanted. The air brushed against the grass as waves crashed on the shores. It flowed through me as a chill does through a bone, making every fiber of my being shudder. I did not know what was to come, how I was to face her, or what to say, so I stood there, silent like a fool. She did not look. She did not even turn. She played in the dirt with that wooden stick of hers, until I finally drew up the courage to move. Finally, I did what I was told and made my way near her until I stood out of the grassy field, in the clearing next to her. The closest I had ever been.

It was as if one of my dreams had come to life and I was living in that false reality that I wished for. In response, my heart was beating through my chest in such a furious nature that I thought it might burst out.

"Why do you watch me?" she asked.

I had no choice but to answer, for it would have been rude not to. Any word I would speak would have been a chance to speak to my love. Words that I could confess to her about, what I wanted to give her but I could not, for I had nothing.

Yet, when I opened my mouth to utter even a simple answer, no words came out. Instead, I stood silent, hushed by the hand of fear. There was a pause as she waited for an answer but afterwards, she sighed a reluctant sigh.

"Is it because of my shame?" she questioned.

I did not know what she spoke of for I saw her in nothing but brilliant light. Eventually, my curiosity overcame my fear and I spoke my first words to her.

"What shame?"

She turned around to face me. Her eyes were as beautiful as the heavens. Her light blonde hair blew past her face in the cold wind. "My father."

I looked down, unable to keep her stare. I had heard he was a drunk, that he did little but stay in his cot, and was ruthless to anyone who entered. I had heard the shouting. I had heard the screaming. I heard the dark words he spoke and I had heard the stories he bolstered. Without needing me to speak my thoughts, she read them in my face and went back to her picture in the dirt.

"I have heard that he is a drunk," I finally spoke, revealing the truth that she already knew.

"He doesn't mean it, you know. He just can't help it," she said looking back at me.

"When he beats you?"

"No," she turned back to the dirt, "...when he touches me." She continued scratching away the face she drew in the dirt.

In my naivety, I did not know what she meant at first. Then, the pain of life reminded me, the misery that is to live blew away the haze that covered those delightful thoughts and became all too dreadfully clear.

The marks on her arms and the bruises on her legs and ankles. The reddened eyes from when she left her hut, even down to her accepting me and not shunning me away. It made sense; there was no need to look at me as a horrid being because she was tarnished as much as I. The perfect, pristine pedestal that I held her on was blemished to its very core.

"Does that disgust you?" she asked, not able to return my gaze.

In fact, it did not disgust me, not the slightest bit. Instead, I loved her even more. I felt closer to her than ever, for I had found a kindred spirit in the torture of life, and that spirit too endured against all odds.

"I'll be thirteen, next week," she continued. After a much hopeless pause, "My father said that he wants to give me a baby."

I was shocked, for I knew what it meant. I knew how the act was done. I had used my stealth to sneak into places that weren't meant for childish eyes, for I had never been a child. I had seen what lurked in the hearts of men—it was evil to its very core, and I hated being one.

"I don't want it," she cried. "I don't want another child brought into this miserable world. How could I bring a child to suffer like this?"

I do not know if it was fear that once had silenced me or if it was the misfortune of not having a cure to her plight, but again I had no words to say. In all my uncertainty and my unpracticed experience, I moved to her.

I did what I had seen other mothers do to their child to comfort them, those that were like them, such as we were like each other. I had wished for that moment so many times in my time of need. A touch from another being to tell me that it was okay, that life was going to change. In her time of need, I had no other offer to give. So, I tried to give her that gift, to hold her in my arms. I did not know how, but that was all I could do. I reached out to her, to place a hand on her shoulder if nothing else.

"Don't touch me!" she screamed the moment my hands touched her.

She pulled away immediately and got up. Even my touch had become corrupt, as if death had sprouted its reach into my fingertips and all that I imagined to be embraced was not to be.

"I'm sorry," she said frantically, "I...I don't know why I told you all that. I have to go."

Then, she quickly ran back to her hut, back to her hell hole, back to suffer what nightmares the demons could conjure up for her to endure. Back to a suffering that seemed better than to be with me. How hellish of a world this was, and how vile it was every ruthless moment of its existence.

It was at that moment that I felt something uncanny, for it was a feeling that I had not known existed in such a way. I felt true hate for the first time. Hate like I had never felt before, because I had never truly felt hate. I had always felt that humanity's thoughts, blames, accusations, worries, neglect, contempt, and disdain were justified towards me, for I was guilty. But that fact did not apply to her. She was innocent; she had not committed a crime or an atrocious act such as I had. No, she had done none of it and that made me hate. But this was a different sort of hate. It was a hate not for humanity's feelings or desires, but a blame for their actions. And I blamed something far greater than just humanity, far more powerful, far more scornful for allowing such deeds to occur at its footsteps and not taking any actions. I blamed Him, sitting on His throne like a coward, looking down at what conspired in front of His eyes, not moving His hand to even motion for it to stop. I blamed the lack of action, the lack of spirit, the lack of God in the world. I blamed and I blamed until I could blame no more, for sitting and watching a world go by without any intervention was not what I would do. No, I would take action of my own.

CHAPTER 3
Wrath

IT WAS A DAY LIKE ANY OTHER, a day like all before, a day that I was not to understand what the day's end would truly unfold, for I was to take a new step. This step would lead to a new life, to a new death, to a new rebirth. I was to become the man I was destined to be and it would take a single act of justice, a single act of will, a single deed that would lead to many more like it.

On that day, I wanted to see Illyana as I did all days before, to satisfy my heart that always wanted more. I ventured forth to the market in the center of the town to see if I could spot her. I did not, for she had not visited the market that day. I walked to the edge of the grounds where children played, where she stood and watched but never took part. Instead, I watched with a wishful heart, but she had not visited the playgrounds that day. I embarked on the trails that she traveled to pick up berries on some days, but she had not and did not walk on those trails that day.

Again, I embarked on another trip, and yet another to see if I could find her, but I could not. I ventured far and wide, roaming the town like a vanguard, searching, but I did not see her. I only knew of one other place to check; the one place I did not wish to go since I had failed so miserably there before.

The once gentle fields that were no longer ripe for plucking were dying and waiting for winter to wither them away, just to be brought back to life after being scorned by nature once again. A field that was to be raped over and over again of its gifts and left to die so a cycle of a new harvest could begin. A cycle that would never end.

The high grass stalks were full of yellow and orange that day, a yellow that creeped on its edges, showing signs of winter. Yet they had not withered yet, and were tall enough to hide our shameful past when we managed to retreat there to find peace.

I went to that place, the sacred place where I first heard her words. The place where I first felt her touch, her heart, her pain, her loneliness, and realized we were the same. I went to that place to share in her misery that day, to see her like all the days that she hid it away, only in shared secrecy with the feeling of my own. I went to see what I wanted, but I found what I feared.

I saw Illyana in the grass, laid out on the dirt, her legs covered with fresh bruises that traveled up her thighs. I saw what made me rage, made my stomach turn, my heart burn and made my vision turn red. I saw blood.

The fear that I knew had come to realization. I could hear a thousand blares of thunder in my head, a thousand roars of a lion, a thousand piercings of a spear, all strike within my mind at once, like the clanging of a giant bell that would not stop ringing. It bellowed in my mind until my mind screamed. The hatred I felt burst through my veins, my blood boiled, my senses shut. I only saw fury. I only saw pain.

Illyana was the love of my life, the spark of purpose for my existence, a light in the dark void of my misery. I know now that it is the greatest lights that cause our darkest shadows, and in that miserable void, I had found a light of my own. A light that gleamed brighter than any sun, burned stronger than any fire, and raged as deeply and violently as the one in my heart.

It was that light that created my darkness, and the light was being snuffed. I would have done anything to save it, taken any unjust action to bring forth justice, and chosen any path that would right that wrong. It was then that I sealed my fate, and set my destiny in stone—an unmoving stone that would travel with me for the rest of my life, that would always be my outcome for every action I was to take and those to come that need not be taken.

On that day, at that moment, I was to be what I was told I was at birth. I was to be what I was always cursed as by others as I grew. I was to be what I was always to be, to become a murderer once more. I had taken my first life at birth in the name of survival, and I would take my second life in the name of love.

I know not how, for I only had seen anger and fury, but somehow I had returned to the village. Somehow, I had reached my father's hut and had entered inside. I gathered my cloak and my father's dagger and walked across the village. I walked past the roasting pigs and the wet rags hanging to dry. I walked past the embers still burning in fire pits, the strewn bodies that took a morning nap in the scorching sun.

I walked past it all until I walked into her hut. I walked into her hell and saw the man who did what he did standing hunched over on his chair. His pants still at his ankles, breathing heavily, blood coming down his legs.

"You bitch!" he screamed when he heard me enter. "I will kill you!"

He turned to me in a vengeful wrath and grabbed my shoulders, almost tumbling over me so roughly that I dropped the dagger in my hand. Yet, for his violent nature, I had not expected his reaction when he saw me. Instead, he looked into my eyes and said something that I was not prepared to hear.

"Help me!" he screamed, "I beg you, please!"

Then, he crumpled onto the floor without me having taken any action. I did not understand the reasoning of the words that he spoke, words that had caught me off-guard and halted my actions. Instead, I stared at him, moaning and groaning in pain, as I tried to decipher what had happened. And between those rolls, I saw his hands, clenched between his legs, grabbing where his genitals used to be.

"God help me!" he cried in pain as he rolled back and forth.

It was then that I became angered beyond what I thought was even possible. Not because I had my wrath denounced while he was already in pain. Not because the vengeance I was about to give had already been committed. No, his words were what angered me. His words and his prayer to be granted favor by God. What angered me was the thought that God would stand in this man's sight and offer him aid while allowing the torture he committed daily to continue.

O, I was angry indeed. The fury burned within me like a phoenix rising from the ashes, and burned as intensely and viciously as the desert sun on a scorching day. It was then that I had made in my mind a picture, and I saw the clear path that was in front of me. I crept up to him and looked him in the eyes.

"Wait here. I shall get help. We must stop the bleeding."

I made my way outside and to the fire pits of the villagers. I had seen that image so clear, and I grabbed one of the empty pikes that pigs had recently roasted on, still sitting on the fire. I could feel my flesh burning, as it should from the scorching wood that heated it. Yet I did not care, for I had a purpose beyond that of physical pain. I had the purpose of righteousness. I quickly moved back into the hut and whispered in his ears.

"This will hurt a bit."

He shook his head in agreement as he stared into the eyes of his savior, for right then and there, I, in fact, was.

I grabbed a wooden spoon off the table for him to bite down on and told him to be ready as he bit. I then held the burning end of the pike to the stump where his genitals were.

His eyes darted open and he bit down and cringed as the pain overwhelmed him. I could smell the burning of flesh, the sizzling of the meat singing as I held the pike at his wound, searing the wound closed, and burning the blood to a clot so he no longer bled.

Then out of all his pain, all his torment, there was a moment of relief, he looked at me with gratitude in his eyes. Finally, he mustered a sigh of relief. It was the appreciation that I had been waiting for. It was what I had expected from a person in terrible need after receiving a heavenly hand of aid when in pain. I smiled back at him with a simple nod and then I did what needed to be done.

I moved the stick down away from his genitals and stuck the end of that pike through his anus, all the way through until it pierced its way through every intestine, every organ, every body part that was in the way and came out of his mouth and skewered him like the pig he was.

It was only after he could not move anymore, that he could not squeal anymore, that he realized he had not grabbed a hand brought down from the heavens but one brought up from the bounds of Hell, that I finally had my peace.

After I took in the sight of his mangled insides spewing out from his mouth and arse, I walked outside to the witness of all the villagers who had heard the screaming, the thrashing, the dying, yet dared not enter inside to stop it. They did not enter, just like all the other days they had not dared stop what he did to his child who screamed, and on that day nor did they dare to stop his screams.

I walked in front of all their faces so they could see my blood covered hands, scarlet hands that they did not have the courage to take on themselves. I walked past them as they gasped and shunned me with begrudged eyes, but they did not utter a single word towards me out of sheer terror.

I walked and walked to my little hut and sat inside for the judgment that was sure to come. But now I was a stranger to this hut, for I was no longer the boy or young man I had been. I was something different to them now, with all their fears and stories about me confirmed. I was even born with a new name, for Bastard would no longer suit a devil like me. No, now I had another name, a name that would follow me for the rest of eternity, attached to me in one way or another. The Impaler.

CHAPTER 4
Reckoning

I REMEMBER BEING ON A WOODEN WAGON CART riddled with pieces of quarried stone, bound, being taken on a scenic route to my death.

How clearly I remember that day, the warm breeze, the majestic rays of the sun, the smell of the grass, and the sound of dirt and pebbles as they were crushed underneath the round wooden wheels of the wagon that I was held as a prisoner on, but it was strange that I did not feel the way a prisoner should. My hands were tied, my body wrapped in coiled rope so tightly that I could not move, but even in that bound imprisoned state, I felt freedom for the first time.

Freedom, because I had at last embraced who I was. Freedom, because I no longer let the fear of myself hold me at bay. And freedom, because I had been and was a monster and now I proudly lived it and I felt no shame of it. I saw with my new eyes, eyes of a man who did not hide his inner self, his true self. What those eyes saw was quite different from what they had seen before. For they were no longer fear-filled eyes, that felt discomfort and unease at anything and all things that stirred in front of them. Instead, those eyes now had power in them and saw things of nature and land that I could not fathom before. It was if the world had been hidden to me behind a dark cloak all my life and I ran unseeing of my direction, blind wherever I went. Yet, the instant I embraced myself, I finally pulled the veil off and saw my darkness in the light and I was not ashamed.

It was a peculiar situation to be in, both in mind as well as body since the villagers had positioned me in such a way that I was seated on the edge of the cart. Perhaps it was to signify being on the edge of one's life. Or, more likely, that they did not see any value of me whatsoever and I was only an unwanted passenger on an important delivery and they fit me where they could. Yet they tied me well, for I could not fall or escape, even if I wanted to. Judgment was to be at hand, a judgment I would gladly accept.

I was a dreamer of sorts, and I liked to believe I was positioned that way to witness what was being taken away, taken from those that were around, those that were to live in glorious happiness and would never live near a monster such as me again. I believe they presumed I was to know all of this and think of it as my time came to be. However, that did not bother me in the slightest. No, I relished the judgment and the death that was to come.

There was one thought that lingered in the depths of my mind. It was an affliction that I could not get rid of and it plagued me deeply. It was the thought of seeing my father come after me as I was taken away. The thought of watching him run after the wagon to stop them.

No, not to stop them from burning me alive, but instead to stop them, to say that he was right. To say that he was disgusted, that I did not deserve his love, unloading onto me all his vulgar words so that he may rest easy. And afterwards, when he was done barraging me with all his built up hate, loathing, aggression, and detest, then he would wish me on my merry way to burn on a pillar of fire, like an unwanted ember being snuffed out under a dirty boot. That was what tormented my mind most.

To give him that pleasure would have given me great delight. To truly let him know that I was the center of his great plight, that my actions should've and would've been justified for his hate and his scorn. That I truly was the disease that he had warned others of. That I was the blight on the land, spreading and infecting others like the forsaken parasite that I had been upon him.

How I wished I could give him that happiness, for it would be the only happiness that I could offer him in the misery of a life that I lived. Yet he did not come, not even to say that or to scorn. He was not there to spit on my grave, to mock me when I burned, to throw a log into the flames to attain his redemption and needful revenge for my mother's murder. No, he was not there. He was not anywhere, and that is what made me sad.

It was not long until I reached my destination. I was taken to a circle on the edge of a river near a path that led onwards to a kingdom I would never visit, at least not in this life. It was the site where the witches were burned, where the adulteresses were stoned, and where men were crucified for all manner of unmerited reasons. And it was the site where I would plant my tender feet for the last time as they pulled me from the wagon and walked me to the stone circle of death.

A large, formidable wooden beam stood in the center of the circle. It had been charred black many times over, yet was thick enough to weather all of the heat it withstood. Such endurance was needed for a beam used for this unholy sanctimonious practice, for I was not the circle's first victim and surely not its last.

Like the others who burned before me, the witches, the sorcerers, the blasphemers, the unholy, I too was to have my judgment be a trial by fire. For I was believed to be the devil's son, the dragon's heir, and if I was to burn then they would be rid of the evil incarnate I was. Yet, if I was not to burn, as some feared, then they would know of my evil heritage and be justified in their actions, for it would mean that I indeed was the abomination of a monster that they thought I was. Regardless, in all outcomes, the cruel judgment of death was to be certain, for that was the law, and to them that law was just.

It was a just act because it was the only action they could lawfully take that allowed them to hide the injustice they allowed. O, what a foolish thought, to find it just to condemn a man who committed an unjust act. Yet, the hypocritical buffoons now did the same and committed the same crime they would punish me for. How foolish was man.

Then again, what action could be abhorrent enough to make it just to murder one for the sake of another? The answer is there is none. It is an action that is truly sinful in all its ways, from the very conception to the conclusion of the evil act. Yet, to allow another sinful action to take place without stopping it is also sin. So, to commit sin to stop sin is still sin. There will always be sin, but the true question was which sin to allow?

It matters not, for either choice condemns a man to hell, and if a man has no different outcome from his choices, then the reality is that there is no choice at all. All actions lead to wickedry, and all paths lead to sin. In doing so, all souls are damned to hell. I see now that humanity is just a funeral pyre waiting to be lit, in either this life or the next, but the fact is that we will burn. That is for certain. How brightly and how long we burn is the only choice we truly have. My slow burn was just about to begin.

I remember the smell of that day. It was a wonderful smell, with a clarity and freshness that I had not smelt before. It might have been the river taking away the debris from the circle, or it could have been fresh air from a delayed winter. It was pleasant and natural and something that I will never forget. When you are close to death, every sense becomes more vibrant, becomes richer. Every sense becomes so renowned, so full of mystique that it is scandalous to experience it.

I took in air that day, letting it travel deep and fill my lungs. It filled me with relief. A cleansing of some sorts, as if a burden had been removed. My shoulders, born heavy, now felt light. I felt as if my time was complete. I was a child that had been brought forward by death to right another life with more death, and now I stood to face my own death. Death was at my core and in my being and now I had served the purpose I had been given and the heinous calling was met, the contract was over. I had answered the call with unwavering action, or at least I thought that I had.

By that time, they had mounted me against the tree trunk of a beam and wrapped a rope that coiled around me like a serpent seizing its prey. The man who was to be my executioner spat on my face as if I was nothing more than filth brought onto his land, which was true for the most part, but it was nothing more than I had felt all my life.

"Do you have any words, boy?" the executioner squawked. "Any regrets?"

I had no regrets, that thought did not ever enter my mind. How could I have such thoughts? I had no tears for anything, no tears of joy, nor sorrow. I had done what everyone else was too afraid to do. I did what was right, what was just, even if it was an unjust act and for that, I was guilty. That was true and for that truth, I was to be punished. Set to face a sour end to a bitter existence but I had accepted that fate long before my action even took place.

In fact, this passing was predestined long before I took my path of blood. It was set in motion from birth, from my father's unsaid words, from the contempt and mockery the villagers pushed towards me. It was nigh time for the world to realize the atrocity I was and the atrocity I should no longer be. That day was now, my end would come, and I would happily accept it without any regrets.

"Very well! Be silent," the executioner decreed, motioning for a torch to be brought forward.

"Your words would do you little good anyway." He grabbed the torch and brought it towards me. "You will make an excellent flame," the executioner boasted as he held the flames so close that they singed my hair. "All the evil inside you shall burn brightly."

The foolish man continued to spout words as if he thought to instill fear within me. But fear I did not have that day. Fear was not a part of my thoughts. Instead, it was how beautiful a day it was to die. How great a feeling it was to end this life on a valorous act. O, how I was to be such a glorious roast, a wondrous feast to the beasts of flames that would take me. It was that ecstasy of death that had enveloped me and I could not wait. O how excellent I would smell, I wondered, as the scent would travel through the air and fill the nostrils of all those around, and cause hunger in the carnivorous wild beasts that I'm sure loomed abound. I would roast like meat, tenderized to the very core. How tasty of a morsel to the serpent of the flame I would become. How filling I would be as it would bite its stinging fangs into me and eventually engulf me in its cavernous belly. How delicious a treat I would be to that flame. O how delighted the gods and the devil would be with my scorched corpse. These were my thoughts, far from the thoughts that the executioner believed that he put in my head from his rambling. Without a word, I patiently awaited my end.

The man drew the flame through the air, showing me that he held the power of life and death in his hands, which in this moment he did. He smiled a wicked smile me as he saw my eyes were trained on the torch as he moved it about. He then, as if to incite concern, held the flames to the circle that was to be lit, and to that action, I smiled back to his shock.

My action almost caused the man to stagger; it was something that he did not expect. Surely, he must have thought I was indeed the devil, and any uncertainty he had before was quickly dissipated by that act. The only action he had left was to find out if he was right, but it caused him tremendous fear and concern for his own well-being and that made me smile even wider. I knew what the outcome would eventually be and I thought of how wonderful it would feel to show him that he was wrong when I would turn to ash, that would first cause a relief then a doubt, for every death carried the sentence of a tortured memory. I would have one last victory amongst the people, a victory of death, and for that, I smiled once again.

The superstitious, simple-minded man had no choice, for now he feared that he faced the devil himself and his life as much mine was in his hands. It was with those very hands that the man held the torch to the circle and lit the flame.

CHAPTER 5

A Demon of Fire

INSTANTLY, THE RED GLOWING FLAME leaped from the torch and sparked the circle to life. The fiery demon started to snake its way around the circle, leaving a trail of flaming footsteps wherever it traveled. The demonic serpent had been given life and now it had the freedom to roam and travel wherever it pleased. So long it had waited, stuck on the end of that torch, lusting, hungering for its great meal and now that it was freed it would feast on my flesh.

Soon, I knew the pain would be all-encompassing. Pain, like the life I lived every day. Pain, like the burning desire in my heart. Pain that I knew all too well and pain that would be my end. I knew how incredibly powerful pain was, and no matter how strong I was or thought myself to be, my senses would eventually be blinded, my resolve broken, and all I would be able to do would be to scream.

O how I wondered how I would scream. Would I sing as beautifully as the songbirds do in the morning, or howl deviously like an owl at night? Would my voice rise and travel beyond the hills, the mountains, and enter the kingdoms beyond, like the wolves who crouched at a full moon, or would I whimper like a rat, squeaking away 'til my flesh was no more, like the vermin that ran through the village seeking shelter when rain fell from the sky? I knew that it was a mere matter of time before I would find out, before the unknown became known as I watched as the fiery serpent make its route. It circled around me like an eagle does to its prey right before it swoops in for the kill, rising and lowering itself as if taking in breaths of anticipation as great as the anticipation that was in mine, waiting for the fire demon to take a bite out of its main course.

Yet, the serpent made quite a display before tending to me, as if wanted to toy with its food, to break it down before it even came to touch it. First, the fiery serpent whispered, and then hissed, then soon bellowed like a flame should, but before long it roared like a lion does when establishing dominance over its territory to trespassers such as I. But it did not come for me, not right away.

First, it let loose its minions of smoke into the air, blocking some of the sight I had beyond the flames. All the while, the villagers waited for my impending despair. The serpent stalked me from all sides as it circled and swelled. Then, the fire demon grew right before my eyes and blanketed the world from me with fiery brightness and smoky darkened skies.

I nervously waited for it to come, knowing not which way the pain was to come. I sensed its intentions from the corner of my eyes, felt its warm breath brushing against my side. It would soon be encircling me fully around, and all at once. And then finally, it took a step forward, just so I could feel its tremendous touch.

O what great power was in its touch, for even when it did not grab my skin, I felt its mere fingertips. I felt its strength, as the smell of my flesh started to sear and the burning sense overcame me, as I had feared. I could have sworn I was covered in sweat but that too was heated away and the cool instant relief was replaced with heat instead. As I had imagined, all my senses were quickly blinded, snuffed out. Every shake, every movement, everything I did was in vain. My strength was being sapped away as quickly as it came, and I did what I had thought I would—I screamed.

I do not know how I screamed, for I could not hear my own voice, just the hissing of the fire and the roaring of the flames, but I know that I did sing that burning song of dread and doom that so many before me must have sang on this pyre of death. That poisoned sword of dismay cut into the souls of those in its grasp. Yet, this was only the begging to my torment, for the demon had only licked my arms and then legs, and with that simple touch, the skin turned to an instant red. I knew it to be grinning for I could feel its delight at my agony, happiness at my anguish, cheering at my misery, but I was wrong for what I thought was pain was only the beginning, for I knew not what fire could truly do.

It was then, at the moment of my breath, my moment of hope that I could finally adjust enough, that I felt its true power. It was then that the fiery demon finally grasped my arm and in an instant, the skin on my arms expanded, sending a knife–like chill through it as if touching each nerve one by one. Then my arm boiled, like water on fire, as the skin on it raised and lowered, filling my arm with pressure. My arm swelled as if it were going to explode as the pus piled within, making it heavy and excruciating as it spread on the inside, ripping the flesh from the bone. And finally, when I could bear no more, those boils erupted. The skin parted with a slight pop and a hiss of its own for they belonged to the fire and not within me, yet it let out a surprising sense of cool as it touched the air, a quick moment of relief before being completely transformed full circle and back into unavoidable searing pain. This all occurred within an instant, an instant of pain, an instant of relief, and instant of agony, and an instant of nothing. A moment later, the skin disappeared, for it no longer looked like what it was. No, it turned ghostly white before simply sliding off as if it were being scraped off by a dull icy knife, leaving the skinless, red tendons visible below. The tendons started to bake in the heat as meat does in a pan.

But the anguish was far from over. Next, the demon touched my feet and did the same, striking the soles that were at first protected for they were pushed against the ground, but demon bit so harshly that the nails fell off and forced me to raise them. Then it traveled up to my shins with the same wretched, excruciating touch that it wielded so well.

I must tell you that being burned alive is different than one would expect, for people think only of the fear of fire and unending pain but that is far from the truth. Burning is different. It has its moments, its pauses, its bits of relief to remind you that there is normality of life, that there is life without pain, but it reminds you just enough so that you could compare it to the complete and utter pain that it likes to give. Yet, even with that, the strikingly strange and mesmeric thing about being burned alive is that it is cool. Not like the cold that one feels on a winter's day, but a bite of teeth made with jagged ice, that keeps biting as a rat does to a wound. It is like being feasted on by a swarm of those carnivorous icy bites everywhere, only stopping from its assault to swallow as you feel a bite somewhere else. That is what being burned alive feels like, that is what I felt. A feeling of being eaten alive while I watched, feeling every moment.

How much more misery I could endure, I did not know. The moment of my death had started, and the fire demon was to have its cavernous gaping belly filled, bite after bite, that was assured. O how it sent ravenous waves of flames to take what it wanted, which was always more. But before I could bear another agonizing touch and sing the end of my song of pain, and before the serpent could complete the malicious deed, a voice boomed from the heavens and the fire demon quickly became undone.

CHAPTER 6
The Grey Haired Rider

"HOLD!" A VOICE BOOMED over the horizon and almost shook the very ground from its immense power.

By then, the great demon of fire had blurred my sight with his steaming red hands and even thrusted its smoky legs into my mouth, choking my lungs and making me delirious from the act. My ears were on fire from a different type—they were burning with the sound of thundering footsteps as they came towards us.

By great fortune, a fierce wind caught hold of the demon, and for a few seconds pushed it aside, moving the blanket of darkness that covered my eyes. It allowed me to catch a glimpse of the wonder that I saw.

I do not know whether it was the lack of air, or perhaps the daze of pain and confusion that had come over me, or even if it were the blistering haze coming from the circle of flaming heat, but I saw a vision of silver light piercing through that steamy, dark blur. Sunlight shone brightly at its core and moved towards me as a wisp. That wisp of light moved up and down across the hills, a wisp of light that came from a cavalry of silver armored men, riding on their steeds, holding a banner of red that I could not decipher.

They held spears and swords and jutted forward, riding towards me as if they were the waves of an ocean sent to quench the thirst of the fire demon. They rode the ground like a tidal wave of grace, a mighty glimmer of light as the earth moved in place.

The flames of the demon gathered again, quickly blinding my vision once more. It was as if it knew that its feast was about to be taken away. After it recovered from the assault of the wind, and the intrusion of the galloping men, it quickly turned its malevolent attention back to me. It roared and reared on its legs of fire, high into the air, and came down to take another great big bite, ready to gorge itself upon my flesh. Yet, once again, it was stopped by the boom of the man's voice.

"I said hold!" the man called out, with such authority in his voice that the villagers quickly acted. Even the executioner himself hastily fought the fire down with large heavy cloaks.

Yet the fire demon was a ravaging beast consumed by a voracious hunger. It fought violently, shrieking and flailing, trying to grab and consume the men around it with all its different flaming hands of wrath. But in the end, it was to no avail. Outmatched, the demon eventually submitted, retreating its chance to fill its endless hunger, leaving only puffs of smoky minions that marched away in the sky, and dying ember children that went from bright red to darkened grey, as it hissed to a silent whimper forgotten to the world.

Yet, I had not forgotten it. I had been touched by that devious scarlet spirit and it left me with a constant reminder of our rendezvous. My legs were charred, darkened with black spots and a skinless red. My arms would never be the same, for they were filled with bits of white and grey that tingled in spots and felt as if they were being chewed on by a thousand rats. The top of my feet were skinless and in complete and utter pain from every movement of air or breeze that swept across it. All parts of my body burned, leaving only the feeling of being stung by a thousand wasps.

Even in that utmost misery that I had suffered from the villager's wrath, I was still fortunate for their fear was my ally. The villagers were so afraid that they had tied me so tightly to the stake that the roped regions had unwittingly protected me from the flames. The fire had not touched my torso, and to my most feared plight, not yet engulfed my face.

I remained looking like a man and even had all my hair, but my arms from the elbows down and legs from the thighs below would never look human again, and would spend their time as grotesque a vision as if I was wearing hideous gauntlets and boots that I could not remove. This was the mark of the demon of fire, the mark of the beast that all would be able to see, revealing the monstrosity that I was.

Soon after, my vision cleared, and my mind followed suit. My senses, that were so easily taken away, were returned to me. For the first time since the fire started, I felt alive.

Wretched as the pain was in those parts that burned, those scorned limbs, I was delighted to still feel, and fortunate to feel anything at all. My limbs were destined to be no more, yet there they were. Those limbs that were brought back from hell because they were put through hell, now there to carry on deeds that I had not dared dream, and take me to places I could not believe. Those limbs that were to commit atrocious acts in times that was before and times that were yet to come, and now appeared as those acts, as much from the outside as much as in. They bore their marks on the exterior and appeared like they should, like sin.

I had been saved by the grace of a man who spoke as thunder does in a storm. I had been offered a moment of peace from a raging hell for a reason that I did not know. If it were not for him, for his call, for his voice, I would have been in moments no more man, no more monster, but instead dust—saved thanks to one of those men that rode.

Those riders came, and there were many, but of them, I only noticed one. For it was to him that I owed my benediction. It was him that I owed my grace, and it was him I owed my sight and no other. That rider rode tall, saddled on a powerful horse and appearing as the oncoming storm. Calling the rider's mount a mere horse would not do it justice. It was a beast of majestic nature, as white and as pure as snow with a grey mane that flowed like the current of the sea. It moved with grace, agility, and such elegance that it seemed to float on the very ground, and running was an obligation and not a necessity. Still, that powerful grand beast with all its magnificence paled in comparison to the rider himself, who was very much it's equal in every regard, if not surpassed it a hundredfold.

The rider was brilliant man that I could not truly describe in just pure sight, for he brought with him an aura of power that was deafening to the soul. If a thousand war drums blared, one after the other, it would still not compare the beat of the heart that this man brought. He had the same flowing grey hair as the beast did, as if they were made from the same mold, the same wondrous out worldly godly nature that the beast held, if not more, the same elegance and wonder that beast provoked, if not more, and provoked the same awe-inspiring sight, if not more. No. No. In fact, it was much, much more.

No matter his attributes, his wondrous nature, his utter radiance, he still appeared as a man. That was evident by apparel that he wore, which was a silver armor that gleamed with the beautiful light I saw from the dark cloudy hell I was within. And on it, a golden lion emblazoned on his chest. He wore a tunic that hung from underneath and floated in the wind like ripples in a lake. His armor was covered with intricate and delicate markings, half made from intent, and the other half from weathering sword blows. Alongside those distinctive marks, a mighty spawn of rivets and mendings covered the entire visible area of the armor, and the plates moved in such a way that it seemed as much part of his armor as his own skin. Long battle chausses made of chain and plate stretched down his legs and seemed perfectly adjusted to allow maximum movement for battle. The lower legs bared shining silver greaves that protected his shins, and heavy armored sabaton footwear that looked well fit and of remarkable quality. And then there were the most significant parts, parts that showed his experience, parts that were covered with a blood-stained darkness that would never leave. A sign that he was a veteran and victorious warrior, for the fact that he walked with those stains confirmed that they were not his.

With all the glory of the armor and the mighty beast he rode on, he wore no helm. I could only presume it was so men could see his face. His sharp features, jutted chin, deep-set steel-like blue eyes, and long grey hair that flowed in the wind commanded respect and admiration. He must have appeared very much as a ghost of death brought into light, a specter moving and whisking away one prey to the next in the battlefield.

All those thoughts I had envisioned before they even occurred. All those visions I had seen before I even knew of this man. All those apparitions sprang forth at the sight of him. He commanded an eternal legacy that led forth before he even took a step. Such was the awe-inspiring presence of this man, the grey-haired rider.

And now this man had come to this place. He had come to the site of my execution to bid me an offering that would change my world, change my life, and change the very purpose of my existence—not just for now, but for all of eternity.

CHAPTER 7

Gideon

"

I know now that hope is misguided. That hope is an expectation of failure just waiting to be met. That hope is, in its all, a rude prank from the heavens that is held in front of us to follow such as a carrot to a donkey. And as mindless beasts, we follow with that utter hope to guide us, not knowing where it is taking us, even if it is taking us to the butcher.

"

THROUGH THE AFTERMATH OF SMOKE that had riddled the area, through the nightmare that I was waiting to be taken back to any moment, and through my dreadful existence in life and in death, the grey-haired rider arrived on his horse, parting through the crowds to make his way to the altar of fire I was staked on. When he arrived, he spoke not a word until he took in the full sight of me while still perched on his horse, watching my every motion. Only after he was satisfied with what he saw did he finally speak again.

"Is this the man I have heard about?" he asked.

"He is not a man," the executioner hastily replied "He is death, sire." He still held the flaming torch, ready to bring the fire back to life at a moment's notice.

The grey-haired rider did not seem concerned by the executioner's warning. Instead, he smiled at the man. "Good! I could use death on my side." The rider turned his steely eyes to me, an expressionless gaze that left me unsure of his intentions. "Is it true what they say? Did you take a man twice your size and run a spike through his arse until it came out of his mouth, leaving him stuck to the ground?"

I looked away, unsure of the right answer, but also unaware that by doing so, I had already given my answer.

The rider turned his horse away from me, and his attention towards the crowd. "This man is no demon. He is a mere man. In fact, possibly a weak man, for he cannot even answer my question without turning his head."

I glared back the rider, fuming at his words. He glanced over his shoulder as if he knew my response before giving it.

"Good to see you still have fire within you," he grinned, then turned back to the crowd and then continued his speech. "But he is a man," he said. "A man more than any of you." At this, the rider pointed to the crowd.

Before the crowd could even respond with insults at the rider's insolence, he hushed them with more of his loud words. "Yes! You, who sit back and watch injustice." He trotted through the crowd on horseback with calm and ease. "You, who let villainy continue and even hide its presence by punishing others. You, who do not have the strength to fight. You, who do not have the strength to do what must be done."

The rider stopped and leaned forward on his horse. "And unlike you, this man," he pointed at me with a smile, "this man picked up the first thing he could find and put it to good use."

He looked at the crowd once more. "I say you men are cowards."

Within an instant, the crowd was enraged.

"You should be more careful of your words, sire, for your own good," the executioner said, clenching his fist. "I do not know who you think you are to talk to us in such manner. If it is a fight you seek, you will have it."

"No, a fight is not what I seek." The rider smirked at the executioner, approaching him on his horse with the calmest of demeanor. As he neared the executioner he stared him straight in the eyes. "Because if a fight was what I was looking for, then I could use none of you."

In the most unexpected manner, the grey-haired rider turned his horse around to face the crowd, leaving his horse's arse in the executioner's face, infuriating the simple-minded man even more.

"Yet, if I were to war," the grey-haired rider bellowed to the crowd, "then this man I could use. I could use his strength. I could use his courage. And as determined by his actions, I could surely use his rage." He leaned forward on his horse. "What good is he to you?"

"I beg of you, let him burn," a villager from the crowd screamed. "He is not worthy of being a soldier."

The rider's face quickly changed, emotionless and silent. That same treacherous silence took over the entire area as the grey-haired rider trotted to the man without speaking a single word, not even a sound from the horse's footsteps. Then in a flash as quick as lightning, fast enough that I did not even see him reach down, he held the villager by his throat, lifting him off his feet, and stared straight into the man's eyes. "He took the life of the greatest warrior in your village, and you ask me to kill him. You fool!" The rider threw the villager back into the pile of waste of men that he had come from.

The invitation was enough for the executioner, who reached for the axe that lay nearby for beheadings. "You should show some respect!" he screamed, holding it tightly in his hands.

With that action, the whole the place was in turmoil. The village guards, in turn, pulled their blades from their sheaths, and in response to that, horsemen accompanying the grey-haired rider reached for their blades as well. The unarmed villagers retreated, ready to witness a different sort of death and bloodshed that they had come to see.

Yet, in an instant, the rider's men were quickly halted with just a slight raise from the grey-haired rider's hand. Those left of the armed guards moved ahead, standing next to the executioner who was fuming from the rider's impudent behavior.

It was then that the grey-haired rider finally unmounted his horse and jumped onto the ground. His feet struck below with a clang as his entire armor adjusted to the new terrain, much like cloth undoing its wrinkles until it fitted itself back into the pristine condition it seemed to be in.

The grey-haired rider flung his flowing hair over his shoulder and leisurely walked up to the executioner who still had his axe in hand, ready to cleave off the rider's head and mouthing off insults.

"You arrogant, errant degenerate! Do you believe you could just walk in here and start to insult us? Such disrespect shall not go unpunished! Who do you think you are?"

The grey-haired rider paid no heed, and moved close enough to the executioner for him to take a strike. "If you knew who I was, then I am sure you would know the mistake you're about to make." To add insult, he then turned around to look at the crowd. This exposed his back to the executioner who immediately raised his axe, ready to strike.

The executioner never got the chance to take his swing, to take the life of my savior who had come out of nowhere and broke all Hell loose on this small patch of dirt. The grey-haired rider spoke once more.

"My name," he said calmly as the executioner raised his axe to strike and the mounted horsemen watched in concern, "...is Gideon."

In an instant, everything stopped.

O I had never seen such a reaction in my life. It was not only men's actions that stopped, but as if the world had actually froze. For the crowd did not move, unsure of their actions, although that could be considered normal. What was strange was that could I not hear any voices, nor birds, nor insects. Even the river that ran behind me had calmed, and the wind hushed at the sound of this man's name, a name that I had never heard before.

Finally, I heard a sound, which was the clang of the axe as the executioner dropped it onto the ground, trembling in place.

The grey-haired rider glanced over his shoulder to the executioner with a smile. "Good. I'm glad that you've heard of me."

With that, he spun so quickly around that it seemed that it was incomprehensible to time. The grey-haired rider no longer had that cheery, calm nature that he had come into this place with. Instead, he fixed a steely, emotionless stare on the executioner, who crouched down and cowered in trembling fear.

"You ask me how I could show such disrespect," Gideon said. "I give my respect to the just, and not to fools of false pride and spineless courage such as you."

Then, Gideon turned his hawk like eyes towards the armed guards who immediately sheathed their weapons and retreated. "Well, since the introductions are out of the way, let's get some things in order."

Gideon proceeded to move through the crowd once again, this time on foot. "Foremost, as you know, I am a knight under the King's honor. And as a knight, I have a right in these lands as judge, jury, and executioner, all to take action in needs for the kingdom's well-being. And by that right," he said, "I say for the sake of the kingdom, that this man is not to die here today. If this man is to die, then it is of my choosing when, where, and how. Not yours."

Again the villagers remained wordless, only exchanging looks of silent wonder. Gideon let out a deep and disappointed sigh.

"Now, I am not a man who practices the law in such an un-fashioned manner, or to even meddle in village affairs," he said. "But it seems that you are all a witless sort that blindly follow rules that have been set out as guidelines, not knowing which one to take and which one to pass. So for that very fact, I practice one such ruling on to you and I state that this man will only die today, if he," he pointed to me, "chooses to."

The villagers muttered conversations at the strange edict. Then, Gideon turned his attention to me. He walked towards me until he stepped into the stone circle. He paused, and without looking raised his foot and smudged the last remaining of ember on the ground that had been slowly creeping on the ground unnoticed by the others, and wiped the fire demon's existence from beneath his boot.

Gideon raised his eyes to meet mine and his glare pierced me through to my very soul. He walked closer and closer, maintaining that resounding stare that felt as if I was gazing into the sun, yet I could still see. He walked on the scorched ground and through the circle of death that I was confined in, and up to the mantle of guilt I was bound to. All the while, I felt was that I was being crushed in his presence as if he held some vice around me that was tightening by a turn with each step he took. And when it was as tight as the vice could be without crushing my insides, leaving me with the inability to move out of sheer pressure, even the slightest motion, the slightest shift, he was standing in front of me, eye to eye, face to face, close enough that I could make out every detail, every line, every mark, and every thought in his head, which at this point was just one. And with that one thought, he stared straight into my eyes and spoke words as compassionate, strong, and direct as anyone could or ever had.

"Do you wish to live, boy?"

It was a simple question, but I had no answer for him. I was not sure whether to continue living in misery or whether taking the sweet embrace of a peaceful death was my choice.

O how I thought about it deeply and passionately, about the quietness that would soon follow the abrupt miserable moments of biting pain. The absolute eternal peace and pure serenity that I would attain in exchange for a few moments of excruciating agony. How much easier life would be, if I were snuffed out of existence such as a candle that burnt too low in its own wax. But what did death really have to offer? I was not certain. What wonders the afterlife brought, pleasant or destructive, was a mystery. Was I foolish to think of an end, sure and absolute, or was it, in fact, a continuous unending punishment? For that I was unaware and that made me, for the first time, afraid.

It was at that sight of my last thought that Gideon bore a smile on his face and continued his offer, for he had his answer.

"I shall be your ruler, boy. I will be your king. You follow my words and only my words and you will live. For I will give you a chance to attain all the wonders that you are capable of, that I know you are capable of. Otherwise," he said, and turned so quickly that I could make out nothing but a blur in between, "I leave you to the flames that they so desperately want on you."

He stared out at the villagers as I pondered my thoughts and they wondered theirs. Then he turned to me again, but this time, the pressure was gone as he moved to my ear and whispered words that traveled deep.

"It would be a pity to see your rage die out like a flicker, when I can show you how to rage like a storm." He stared straight into my eyes, but removed all of his barriers so that I could see his soul as well, and see him for who he truly was and what he was, which was a symbol of truth, a symbol of love and compassion in a time of need.

"I can show you an existence outside of this miserable world," he calmly spoke. "You are a prisoner of your own dungeon and I could show you how to open those caged doors and how to be free. I can even show you what is just, for you are just, whether your actions may or may not be. You have courage, my boy. Allow me to show you how to use it."

As I stared back into those strong, blue eyes, seeing a warmth that had not been there previously, I realized that those eyes could only belong to a man who absolutely meant what he said, a man that had seen and knew pain and torture and had come through it. Perhaps that's what he saw in my eyes as well. Or perhaps he saw a child ready to be molded, ready to be built into a creature of war. Or perhaps he just wished to save me from myself. Nonetheless, he meant what he said and that was all I needed to know.

Satisfied that he had made his point, Gideon turned and walked to his horse, who knelt in response in front of him as if he himself was king. He mounted his majestic steed and looked at me once more.

"You will die, that I am assured of, but the choice of when and how is yours," he said. "Die miserably now, or die valiantly later. That, I leave to you," and then he looked at the executioner to give him a set of simple instructions.

"Let him burn if that is what he wishes." With that, Gideon rode off, his men following behind.

The executioner looked unsure of what to do next, his mind toiled with contemplations. Maybe he had thoughts of continuing the plans he had set before Gideon's appearance. Maybe he had thoughts to complete his task and to lie if he was ever questioned, saying it was due to my bidding.

But even the executioner, the God of Death that he had so arrogantly pretended to be, was too frightened to disobey Gideon's simple instruction. Instead, he turned to look at me, at my command.

O how the simple-minded executioner wished I would make it easy for his conscience. How he wished for me to choose death over life. Yet that made my choice easier, for I would not give him the satisfaction, nor the villagers who started to chant, "death, death, death," with zealous anticipation for my response. No, if I were to choose death then that would give the villagers the redemption they sought, and retribution for a sick man's perversions on his own daughter. That was something I could not have done, no matter how much death was what I wanted.

There was another reason why I chose what I did, for I had lived a life turmoiled by being the victim of superstitions and beliefs. One such said that if I was to survive being burned at the stake, however that may be, then I was evil indeed, possessed by the devil, a monster of nature. And in fact, I had indeed survived. No matter how damaged my limbs were from the assault, I had confirmed that unfounded belief.

By doing so, that word would one day reach my father, who I knew not the whereabouts of. But it would surely reach him, and in doing so, his beliefs of me would be justified, he would have confirmation that I was the sinful creature that he had always known. That perhaps, I was not his son. That I was the devil's son, the dragon's heir, an evil that could not be extinguished by the fires of hell, for I was hellfire itself. And so that is what made my decision, for I would grant that final peace to my father's life, that I had so unintentionally brought such cruelness and misery to, and I would no longer be his son for from that day on. I would live to be that fire, and with that fire, I would burn the world.

CHAPTER 8

Sin

"

We walk a path of lightness and decay. Our soul may shine

bright but our flesh burns with putrid decay. We are tainted

souls, clean no more. Covered in a painted robe of flesh and

bones. Our innards daunted and untouched by the purity

of light, for we fail when we try to do what is right. All that

escapes our prison of flesh is sin. Sin to fall upon, sin to lead

forward, sin to sin, sin...sin...sin.

"

I WAS YOUNG BACK THEN. Sturdy and weathered through life's misery but still, rather young. Not just in age, in which I was just mere fraction away from being a man, but young in spirit also. If I were known as a monster now, and before that, as a wolf, then at that time I was neither. At that point of my existence, during that ordeal, I was merely a cub. I had my teeth ready to draw and bite, but I knew not how to use them. I was brash, untrained, and ignorant, all amassed into one being, unaware of what life truly had in store for me. With those childish thoughts, I had little of anything but simple desires, so I did all that I could to fulfill them.

That was the time before my journey even began. A time when I had just left the village on my own for what could be said was my first time. Yet, in a way, I was always on my own and never truly a resident of that infernal place. I had simply gained the freedom to realize it, instead of the burden of chains that I thought had confined me there.

I must tell you, it felt glorious to walk free on the land and know that those wretched souls who mocked my existence, who waited for my death, who wished for my misery, had not had their wish granted. Stranger it was, for the fact that the villagers had always wanted to rid me of their lands, but they hoped that my departure would be to leave this existence, and not to walk the lands outside. And now it drove them even more mad, for I was to bring wrath to the wicked and unjust as I did in that very village when they opposed it. Wrath to those who deserved such action, and every one of those actions I would take, I would feel right for that assault, the same assault that the villagers felt so wrong about. And I would feel only just for those acts because justice itself had come to see me. It had come to save me. It had raised its sword and pointed towards the path, and that path was named Gideon.

I left that day with farewells sent to me by way of looks of distaste, goodbyes sent to me with scowled angered faces and departing words by gritted silent teeth.

I had originally believed I went back to pack my belongings of which I had none, but it was evident that I wanted to look at those faces that mocked me daily, those looks that I had always seen but never understood. Now I saw them once more and an epiphany came upon me. A realization that I walked no different a path than I had walked before, but instead of the bitter darkened sorrow that I used to stroll through, I now walked towards a lighted day that I would gladly run to. There was nothing left to miss, well, almost nothing. There were still yearnings of two things that I desired; the sight of my discerning father, and the sight of my beloved, the one thing that I had ever loved in the world, Illyana.

For both of those sights, I attained neither. No mention or word was sprinkled in the air that taught me what had happened, or what had occurred to either of those wants. Nothing was said, nothing was mentioned, even behind closed doors or whispers in ears; I had become adept at discerning both. There was nothing left for me, if there ever was, and it made my life all too clear. The life I lived before was over, the suffering was done. The path I was on before was now gone, and the new path I walked, the journey of the Impaler, had just begun.

It was a journey that had little hope or direction. Yet the faith that Gideon had placed in me was strong, and that faith of my freedom was a promise that I had to keep. Because what Gideon gave to me was the same act that I performed for Illyana, an act of justice in an unjust cruel world. That kind act had to have meaning; for me, it was love, for Gideon I did not know. It was that meaning that set a debt on my soul, and that debt had to be repaid. So, I set out on my exodus to find the grey-haired rider and his men. To join in the likes and satisfy that debt with my fury, with my hate, with my vengeance.

A talent that I would use to become fire that acts as a sword, and to be that storm that he asked me for.

I had no horse, no boots, no wagon, nor a cart, but the soles of my feet were hardened with a tough life's sentence, and fortified with a determination that was built from angst and pain, with straps made of cold steel that were a need, a need to fulfill my purpose, my purpose of fury, the purpose of Gideon.

Even though my feet were skinless, in pain and still charred from the hate of mankind, it would not stop. It was on that vessel of will that I walked. I walked an endless path with little direction but the lure of a long road, a long journey that would lead me anywhere but where I was, and that was the only sense I needed. It was the only direction I needed to follow, and so I did.

I was set on a path that was covered with rocky gorges, unforgiving terrain, steep mountains on either side. I knew not why I went that way, but I did. I did for the mere feeling of my spirit launching me ahead and dragging me through with each footstep, knowing that every step brought me to a new life and away from the one I left behind.

Each footstep was filled with agony, hunger, and thirst, but I still walked. It was a journey that spanned endless days, and endless nights. I caught no sight of another man, or another being, animal, or quarry—just dust and trails, trees and dirt. A road that was marked harshly ahead, and at times, a road that disappeared. Other times, it was not straight nor crooked but waved through the land, as if drawn in the sands of time. Even then I walked that path, unwavering of my thoughts, unrelenting with my desire, and unknowing of what was to come. Still, I walked.

Yet with all roads and all paths, there comes a time when all is too dire, torturous, and the spirit falls. And during that time, when all hope had fallen, when my mouth quivered with the longing of water, my lips dry and tearing from the thirst, and the soles of my feet reddened even more than before, leaving a trail of bloody footsteps, and finally, when my eyes became glazed with despair—it was then that he came. But he had not come to me, for I had come to him.

It was a man that I had never seen but who had a presence that still felt familiar. He stood short and stocky, at a height of a mere four feet, draped in ragged clothes that dripped down his sides like the wings of a raven, his hand clenched around a wooden orbed mantle that sprouted a tree-like branch below, which functioned as a cane but seemed like another leg.

He walked on his three legs, near the edge of the wicked trees whose branches crept like wretched claws. He had not raised his head, and I did I not know if I was an intrusion to his journey or he to mine, but I was glad to see him. He was the first familiar sight in an unfamiliar terrain, in an unfamiliar world, and a known unknown in a path I had never walked before.

"Have you seen a rider with grey hair as rich as salt?" I called to the man with the little strength that I had.

The man did not speak, did not venture a raise of his head. He paused and raised up his free hand and pointed ahead to the straight and narrow road. Through the midst of the trees, and past the horrors of the mountains and the rising of a hill that seemed like the world stopped at the top. Yet that was to be my path and so my spirit was set on it as well. No matter the cost, I would walk. But I was famished from my long trek, days that numbered more than forty, and on a stone that I had not seen on the ground, I tripped.

To my surprise, the old man put out his cane and stopped my fall. What odd strength the man had I could not fathom. Or perhaps through my deliriousness it was something I imagined, but it happened. I was lifted in midair and resting on his cane that rose from his hand and the end did not even touch the ground, such was the strange ungodly strength of this little man.

Without even a glance to me he had put out his hands, sharp claw-like hands that had nails that curved from their length, and scorched marks that traveled below his ragged clothes that resembled mine. I would have been intrigued to ask him more but I had not the strength, so I reached for his hand to help me up. Even though I towered over him when I was to stand, he pulled me up with such ease, as if I was light as a feather even with my heavy burden on my shoulders. He then walked me to a flat rock and took out a satchel of the darkest cloth. From within it he pulled out bread and put it on a flattened stone that I had not noticed before, and offered it to me with a wave of his hand.

I took the piece, for I had not remembered the last time I had eaten. Maybe once, maybe never, but I did so at that time. I took what he presented me and I ate 'til I had my fill. It felt as I had eaten a thousand feasts all at once and my belly was quickly filled.

Then he presented me with a flask, with a liquid inside that was not water. Yet the thirst I had was great and I needed it dearly. So I drank from that flask, that I could only presume was wine, but it was the sweetest drink I had ever drank, such that no fruit had come close. It was the richest, freshest taste that traveled through into my nostrils as much as my mouth and reinvigorated me as if I had slept a restful thousand nights on a thousand beds of silk of which I had not even slept on in my dreams before.

I ate the bread that he offered, drank the wine he gave, and rested on the seat he had made; I had back my strength, and even more. Then, the strange three-legged man gathered his belongings and looked at me with his black eyes, crow-like eyes that I had never seen on a man. Eyes that were filled with emptiness and the unknown, but stared at me deeply as if I would not see them again.

Then, for the first time, he showcased a wicked, crooked-toothed smile. He pointed one last time to the distance, to the rise of the hill up ahead, that same hill that ended rather abruptly and seemed to drop off of the face of the earth. And even if my journey was to begin by falling, then so be it, for I owed this man's aid to continue for the strength he gave me. I gave the man a bow for coin I did not have, and I did not know if he was mute or possibly even deaf, for he had not said a word to me in our engagement.

Then the strange, ragged man with his bread, and his dark wine and darker eyes went off on his path on his three legs, clanking his way down the road that I came, with no more than a mere turn of the head, only looking to what was ahead.

I turned my gaze to where I needed to go, looking forward to the path that laid out, the path that he had showed me, a dark abyss-like path held only by a harness of leafless trees on every side. Trees that stood with twisted branches like claws frozen in time. Trees that appeared as if in wretched pain, calling my name.

And it was to be—that would be the life I would live if I took that path. Up the morrow of the woods and into the dawn of blood and steel. That would be what the warrior's path would give to me if I traveled that course. But an iron stomach I had, and a strong will, and I would do my bidding until I had my fill, just like the feast I ate of bread and wine.

So I gathered my strength, of which I had plenty, and I walked up the steep terrain and onto the top of the road. It was then a chill ran through my spine, and I turned around to look—only to see no sight of the three-legged man. The road behind me was empty, yet what I saw was also strange. I saw what I felt, as if my past life lay behind, entangled and twisted, staring from the trees watching me, in darkness only lighted by the unblinking moon, that I knew was there but did not dare show itself.

Yet, even though it was darkness that I left behind, I did not feel it so at that moment. For I felt that it was a darkness that was strangely close, a darkness I felt that was coming towards me no matter how much I moved away from it.

I continued my journey up the hill as the wind picked up its words, and the trees' shadows twisted their shapes as I walked along my moonlit path. Yet always, darkness followed behind. a darkness that would always follow, from now on and forever more.

CHAPTER 9

Dogs of Hell

"

In the darkest of times, there is the hope of light, but in the brightest of lights there is no place to hide. So I tell you now, my friends, that you should not fear the darkness, for it is your ally in life. But what you should truly fear is the light, for it shows all, even your darkest hidden parts.

"

IT WAS NOT LONG AFTER I TRAVELED the road the strange three-legged man had pointed towards that I found what I was looking for. I found the camp. I found the armored men. I found Gideon. And not much after that, I entered my first battle.

Most men would have quivered in their boots and worried their heads, but I was not like most men, for the love of blood was what I craved and searched for, and I had arrived at a most opportune time. What was to come was the promised retribution Gideon had so plainly laid out to me. He had so plainly said to me on my perch of death that I had no distress, only a lust for blood.

I was surrounded by men who sought the same thing, who had the same compulsion as mine. And now they laced up their boots, some armored, some not. Some stood practicing, waving their swords, axes, and thrusting their spears, as if to fine-tune their attacks so they would not die so soon, or so abruptly. And then there were those who enjoyed the last moments of the sun before the war raged as if they were at peace as a child, already in acceptance of their demise. And then, there were the others.

Others knelt on knees and said their silent prayers. Prayers to a god who did not wish to listen. Prayers to a being who had no mercy. Prayers to a creature who watched others fall into dismay and pain; this is the god that they sent their hopes and wishes to, in hopes and dreams that a mighty being or grand savior would come down and whisk them away before their doom.

How foolish I thought those men were to send their empty promises to an empty sky, all in the name of hope, when they could just as easily turn and walk away. But they did not, and at that time I did not know why.

Out of place from all those men, there was myself. I was unlike any other, for I did none of what they did, or were doing, or had done. Instead, I waited. I waited with what little I had, just a rusty sword handed to me at the eve of battle, one that I did not even know how to use. I sat bootless, just the worn out meat on my feet to stand with me. I sat armor-less, just the clothes that I wore on my back to offer a layer of protection from the sun.

Unprotected, unwanted, like the way I was at the moment of my birth. I stood there in my flesh, burnt arms and legs, a constant reminder of hate, hate that raged within me with such fury that I fumed to take on more action of sin, for that was what I was made for. That was my purpose. That was my goal and that was my hate, to destroy this beautiful world that God had so meticulously created. I would unleash a wrath unfathomable by nature, an umbrage of devastation to the lands, a rapture of dismay that would engulf the world. And when the world would beg for mercy, which it would, I would give them what the merciless being above gave to me, had always shown me, what it bestowed on me—nothing.

I sat waiting, watching, wanting, yearning. The moments that were before me were not peaceful like for some, but full of thought, full of hate, full of vengeance. That's what I waited for.

I waited for what I wanted, for what was to come. I waited for the raging war, for that was my peace, a moment of blanked thought, instead of the blinding of the misery I felt each day. Killing was the one thing that would make my mind rest, my soul ease, my hunger abate. It was the one thing I craved more than anything since I walked from the pyre of death, and I knew I would get it that day. The serenity of battle was to come, and it would come soon.

The sun gleamed bright, washing over the fields. The wind swept the lands, setting the fields ready to be trampled on, and the trees on the outskirts rustled at the unease. The horsemen sat on their mounts. The infantry readied their blades and gathered their footing. Soon, the first scout came running frantically over the hill, a look of terror, a look of worry, and we knew that the battle was near.

Yet with all our anticipation and lust, the army grew restless as we saw signs of the blackened troops, carpeting the hills one by one. Like a swarm of insects, they painted a line of black on the horizon and made the men quiver in fear. Then suddenly a hush spread, a silent strength sprouted from the lines.

Men rustled and parted as a lone knight from our ranks rode out, and even before I even saw who it was, I knew it was Gideon.

He sat mounted on his great steed; his armor adorned him as elegant as the finest attire, the sun glistening off it gave it an angelic feel. If I had worry in the slightest, then with the sight of him, I had none. How could we lose with such a man on our side, I wondered. Even in silence, he commanded a presence that deafened the world around him.

His horse went ahead of our army and stood valiantly. Gideon watched the horizon, watched the ever growing presence of death, but he did not waver. He did not worry. Instead, he smiled and smelled the air as the wind feathered through his hair. Then, he turned to us and said words that would change the tune of the battle, words that struck every man to his soul.

"Men! Do you fear death?" Gideon asked as he moved his horse in front of the army, standing there as if they were going to answer.

No words came, and that was answer enough.

"Do you fear loneliness?"

Again, no words sprouted from the ranks.

"What is it that you fear?" he asked leaning forward on his horse, listening with a sincere heart, waiting for an answer, but still none came. "Is it the memory of being lost in life or the memory of being lost to someone else?"

I know not why I felt those words set at me, for I was just a new soldier with no one else—if I were to fall, then there would be no one to mourn over me. Yet it struck a chord with me, as if he had tuned into my heart, and played the string that made my blood boil.

Then Gideon turned his horse to the side and pointed to the opposing army approaching over the hills, never looking away from his beloved troops.

"This is what mortals think of when they think of fear, oncoming death. But today, we can change that. For today, we have a choice to make. A choice to act without worry, without conscience, but with action and intent. We have a purpose beyond that of life, beyond time," he said.

A rustling was heard from the troops as they start to bicker among themselves, but Gideon did not let it disturb him. Instead, he moved his horse again to face the troops, turning his back towards the enemy, with not a worry in sight of a stray arrow.

"Yes, I say beyond time. For today, I give you a chance to be immortal in life. Immortal in death. To stand against the raging tyrants who threaten our kingdom, who fight for what is selfish and of no use to the greater good. Today, you have the chance to make a choice. It is a choice to rise above the tides of darkness, and sail on winds of glory to a brighter tomorrow. A tomorrow that has no fear, that has no misery, and that has no pain. For today, you will be greater than fear. Greater than all of what those men can put in your minds, because today you will lead and act, not with your mind, but your heart. And today, your heart will burn like a raging firestorm. It will rage like an inferno that bellows from the pits of the unknown, and destroys the darkness within, destroys the darkness that lurks at our footsteps and travels from the bottoms of the earth and on that hill."

Gideon's words hit the men hard and they started to gather courage. They listened and stood tall as he preached.

"So I ask you now, shut all eyes that lurk at the monsters that creep in the dens of your heart and the depths of your mind. For it is they who stand to witness your thoughts and concerns. They who will face the dread, and the onslaught that we will bring as we strengthen our arms. It is they who will feel our fiery rage burn and destroy the darkness that they bring. For on this day, it is they who will fall far from their hopes and dreams, and not us. For we will walk through misery like a dog through hell, and snap our jaws as we run towards our glory. We fight for a christening of a new tomorrow, and you will fight that you will live, and your enemy dead. For on this day, when we fight we will rage like a storm engulfing all those who stand, and only leave the dead in our wake."

O, what strength those words filled me with.

"That is what I promise you, men, that is what I see in the future of that line of metal and flesh that approaches us. I do not see death, I see kindling to our fire, wood to our stone, and fear to our wrath. Go forth and claim your glory, and let no man take it from you, for it is your right, bestowed upon you from heavens and the kingdoms beyond. It is your right to stand when they fall. It is your right, to make them scream and run. It is your right, to be standing gloriously tall in victory amongst your brothers, amongst your sisters, your fathers and mothers, and amongst your fellow dogs of hell.

"For when they come, and they will, they will not know what hit them. For we will open our jaws, and let loose from our chains, and tear them to shreds until they run from whence they came! So I say now, ready your arms and set steady your feet, for it is time for us to bite, and bite we shall until we tear their flesh and reach into their bones. Today, we fight. Today, we roar like victorious lions from the dens of Hell!"

O, how well Gideon preached those words. Words that I had not heard the likes of before. O how well he sang a song that I had never heard played before, and hummed a hymn that I had not the wits to decipher before. But the reality was, no song was actually played, no verse was truly hummed, and the words he spoke were ungodly and not those that should be preached, for they held no words of salvation, but only words of doom and glory, and that was all that I wanted to hear.

And so I heard. I listened to it as music to my ears. It played its soundless tune. It sang its song-less song. It hummed its hum-less hum, and I took it into my soul. And before I knew it, the men too roared in anticipation.

O how glorious—they lusted what I lusted; the words filled their minds as much as mine. O, how I heard it over and over, repeating in my head as if Gideon had set the melody of a song I could not forget. I heard it just as clearly as our army marched across the fields, our footsteps thundering on the ground. I could hear it clearly over the thumping and the roaring of the drums, as the opposing herd of men approached with clanging weapons and adorned metal armor. I could hear it clearly as they moved closer and closer, moving towards their death, towards my blade. And soon, my desire and the deed was to be done, the war would rage, and the battle begun.

CHAPTER 10
A Taste of Blood

"

I feel it foolish for men to fear death when it is an inevitability

to mankind. There is no escape from its clutches; one either

succumbs to it or becomes a tool of it, it is certain. That is the

true nature of such power, such force, one that beckons our souls

and works its way into our minds. On that day, it was proven.

"

O THE ANTICIPATION WAS OF AN EERIE NATURE, incomparable to a regular man. There was energy, fear, and darkness all at once. An energy that crept over the body as both armies stood staring at each other across the field. If death was a figure that traveled and found its victims, then it was certain that it was near. It was certain that it walked amongst us, watching what was about to take place. Yet even though I could not see the figure or imagine what it would look like, I knew it was there and I knew it was most pleased, for I too shared that opinion. I shared that vision, and I shared that craving that death must have had. I wanted to fight. I wanted to kill. And as much as death wanted it, I too wanted war.

O how I despised the world and what it brought. For it was evil and decrepit—frail flesh destined to rot. I would break it into pieces of a carrion feast for esurient vultures to devour. This majestic vision of the mighty would end its long hauled out plan, so carefully constructed with all its pieces in place. I would not only clear the board, but I would break it. I would bring unending misery with the edge of my sword, take life and bring forth the greatest evil the world had seen, rip every tissue, tear every muscle and break every soul from the seam, and usher forth annihilation to begin the defilement of humanity. That was my meaning now, that was the destiny that I had created. Heaven and Hell should watch in shame, for I was the pitiful creature that was going to bring the world to an end, an end full of pain.

O the other army must have felt what I had felt, the coldness, the harshness, the anxiety, the tension, all at once. O it was overwhelming, so dreadfully beautiful. It was that dark compulsion that must have launched the opposing army into a running craze. They roared and rode and ran towards us, an endless wave of silver and black, blanketing the once green grass as they swept towards us in their enraged attack.

O what a sight I saw. The first wave of soldiers crashed upon us in a vicious frenzy, raining the skies in red, crisp, violent blood. The blood bath had only just begun; the words of Gideon had put the men in such a state that they did not fear their inevitable, dismal death. No. Instead, they fought back with such resounding conviction, such glorious might, such brutal harshness that the frenzied wave was calmed to that of howls of dying men. It was a choir of shrills, and wails, and blood-curdling screams of death, and it was so, so beautiful.

I, too, had little intention of holding anything back. I, too, wished for certain unescapable death, a death that I was denied before, that was taken from me once before, and a death that would be taken from me once again but I chased it anyway. Instead of that death capturing me, it guided me. It crept into my hands and struck forth from my blade and with each swing. I saw that death once more, at my fingertips, at my blades end, so close that I could taste it. I set on my path of releasing men's souls into the air with each strike, as if I were scissors to threads of life. I cut and cut until the floor was covered with strands of men that could not be stitched back together again.

The meat I took, I chopped, I minced, I ground, I diced, I hacked, and I slashed until they no longer thrashed. I took every action that was known to man to kill, for that was what I craved, that was my disgusting dark thrill, and I would walk onto this field devouring everything until I had enough until I had my fill, soiling the lands with the tainted souls of men being defiled by my merciless blade. Unleashing the impurity of evil that I knew I had within my limbs, within my heart, within my soul, I took and took until I could not take anymore.

I do not know how many I had killed. I must say that the first and second murders in my life were for the sake of necessity. One for my life, and one for my heart. But the third, now, this was for the sake of pleasure. The sake of a desire to unleash all my pain on my enemy, to unleash all my built up relentless vengeance, unrelieved unfairness, unremitted cruelty, and unforgiving misery unto others on the tip of my blade, and this murder was unlike the others for it was grand and I enjoyed every moment of it, and I was not alone.

Those men that surrounded me were the same. For the first time in my life, I felt as if I was part of a family. We were all murderers there, all men that were born to take the blood of others and we had embraced it. We were the dogs of Hell that Gideon had promised, and we had won.

I stood on that battlefield, wearing with my ragged clothes that were darkened with dried blood crusting, as if it were bark on my skin. It felt as natural to me as it does for a tree, watching the broken bodies of countless warriors laying decrepit on the defaced field, starving for a gasp of dissolving life. They looked like wretched shattered souls, mangled and twisted as the darkness I felt inside of me raged. I let out the darkness out for the world to see, and how carnivorously I craved more.

How I craved that taste of blood, now that I had felt its sweet, wonderful presence upon my skin. In front of my eyes I saw it shed, covering the ground like a carpet of red hiding the filth that lay below. The wonder of it all, the beauty, nature. How sweet, pure and divine, and how quickly it becomes corrupt from the effects of time. That life-giving, vibrant red of the blood spoils and turns dark so easily the moment leaves the sacred home it was sanctified within. What a marvel it is to see that metamorphoses, to see death firsthand, by my hand. First, the warm blood turns a cool, dry, cracked black, the flesh pale white, and the eyes, once vibrant and full of hope, quickly become cold and full of sorrow, as sorrowful as mine were every day of my life.

How I wish to see that look, the effect unleashed on those who stand against me when I embark on my quest for vengeance, on my quest for redemption, on my quest to show my world of chains. Those who hold steadfast to their life, those who live a life without worry or concern, those who love and play, wishing for good things to come their way when there is nothing to gain.

How I wished to show them the truth and make them pay, for the world has no love and deserves no love, and I would make certain of it. I would end the blissful ignorance of it all. Because it was through my blade that I would share my thoughts, and my words. Through my blade I would share my misery and sight, and through my blade I would share my truth, my pain.

I knew then that the world was diseased. It is set to die, and I would be the inescapable cure of the appalling affliction that had taken hold and spoiled the land in a drought of blissful hope. I would fill that need with pristine waters made from tears. How sublime it would be when I would make them cry when they saw the unavoidable truth. Because truth is what they needed to see, not the ill-judged lie that they lived.

And now that I had tasted the revitalizing blood, the feel of ameliorating war, and the touch of glorious, irreproachable death, my rage was roused, and the world would feel my wrath, feel my despair. That was what I vowed.

"

Now, it might surprise some that I would speak so openly and truthful about this matter, a matter so distasteful. It might even fill the delicate with writhing disgust, and I would harbor them no ill will for those thoughts. In fact, I believe many would call me vile, wretched, blasphemous, evil, and deviously spiteful. Still, that is far from the truth.

For the truth is that they should not fear me, nor the dark and forbidden words that I tell you. For I tell you how I felt, and how I feel. That is the truth, and that is nothing to fear. No, the truth is that they should fear the constant lies we hold within ourselves. The darkest fears that we carry are also within ourselves. What we can think of. What we can create. What we are capable of doing and how truly inhuman humans can be. That is the scariest truth of them all, the one that we all know but continuously lie to ourselves about. That is what I unleashed that day, no more hindered and holstered by those incessant lies, but just pure, raw truth, my inner truth, and it roared violently.

"

CHAPTER 11

A New Name

"

How terrible of a man I truly am is not unknown, and that

is evident in the memories of time. The viciousness that I have

within me shines through from time to time, but I am just

a mere vessel that has been built in the image of the divine,

and molded by the hands of man. It is the actions of man that

created what they sowed, and now it is time for the sickle to slice

its way through the world. I am not just a creation of man; I

am the aftermath of what man had wrought.

"

WE HAD WON THE BRUTAL AND BLOODY BATTLE. The day had gone away as quickly as it came, for the world felt slower and not able to catch up with the excitement of the invigorating clash of war. It was now long past that day of the dead. The bodies were gathered for us to ensure that they were dead; the loot stripped, taken by those who desired it or had none, such as I.

New boots I wore, probably from a man who had just bought them, or even a gift from a loved one. New clothes I adorned, still stained with blood from the skirmish and even torn, but still, they were in far better condition than the ones I wore previously. There was no place for my once rusty sword, which I had broken in the heat of battle; countless more scattered the ground for my picking. I picked up one after the other to finish the act, until one resided in my hands through it all. A sword that might've been a family heirloom or bestowed for a divine act to rid the evil from the land, and now it laid in my hands. How bizarre it was that it laid at my cursed side now, ready to corrupt, mangle and dissect all those who stood in my path. Not meant for any holy deed, but instead the unholy acts of death that are carried out in the false name of light. That is what we would do then, that is what we all did, and that is what we will continue to do.

Yet, all this had happened earlier and now, far in the past. For it was a different time, one that had all recent happenings finishing and the tension to be undone. It was time for the wrath to be gone, the fire to be quenched, the darkness to hide in light of a new day, which became a new night. It was a time for relaxation, to unknot all the tangled concerns of pain and worries of death. It was a time to rest in glory and sit in serene refuge, but I did not feel that way. No, I felt something else.

I still craved more. I felt the blood rush, the veins swell, and the ecstasy of the battle fill my soul. Even staring into the campfire in the dark night, I felt its intoxicating glory. I felt its euphoric rush. And I felt its beckoning inescapable call. I sat wishing for the next battle to begin again and to never end. I could not wait for that next fight, for that next skirmish, for that next war, for that next death to be in my hands again.

"I felt the same after my first battle."

Those words had broken me out of my stupor and I turned to see Gideon walk out of the darkness of the night and into the light of the campfire. The fire showed Gideon in a new light, one that I had not seen before.

It was the first time I saw him as a mere man and not as a soldier, a warrior of untold brilliance, or a majestic being. He wore no armor, just a simple white shirt, a well-fit vest, and white woven leggings. He had not even his weapon at his side. And from what I could see, he had no wounds, not even a scratch. He appeared as plainly as any man you would meet in the village. If it were not that he still commanded the presence that he carried, a presence that made even the fire quiver as he walked, I would have not known it was him at first glance.

"Is it always like this?" I asked.

"No, never again," Gideon said with a sigh, filled with almost as much disappointment as I was.

"Sadly," he continued, "death is something that you get used to quite easily, and quickly. To end another's soul and purge their life from existence becomes all too common in the way of the sword. In the way of our world."

I looked at the fire in front of me. It must've been true what he said, maybe what I had felt was that calling, the way of the sword. I felt it calling from the moment I took my first life, and I felt it grab hold of me even more. I felt its need, a nefarious compulsion that I could not and cannot explain.

"I do not know how I can go on with this feeling always lurking near."

"You will get used to it. They call it bloodlust, a warrior's bloodlust. It's a taste of war that you will never forget, and one that you will always thirst for, but never achieve again." Gideon sat down next to me and continued. "That's the beauty of death. It calls to you once you've had a feel of it, like a mother looking for a lost child." Gideon gave me a strange smile and drank from his wine pouch. "Unfortunately, you are now a child of death, and it embraces you. And one day it will take you, as it will take me as well."

"I was born a child of death, and before it takes me I will take as many of them as I can."

Gideon took another swig from his pouch. "Yes, I saw you fight. You did well for your first battle."

"I wish for more."

"That will come in time. There is no rush in running towards death."

"I'm not afraid to die."

Gideon laughed. "That is no good," he said, opening a leather sack he carried next to him. "Everyone should be afraid to die." He pulled out a leg of lamb that must have been freshly killed for its blood was still dripping.

"Why?"

"Fear is necessary." He got up to put the lamb on the fire to roast.

"Fear makes you weak."

Gideon sat back down with a sigh. "No. No it does not, Vlad."

I looked at him, taken aback by the strange name that he called me. He met my gaze, but gave me no answers.

"Fear makes you strong. It makes you smart." He tapped his head. "You see, people are mistaken about the concept of fear. Fear is normal. In fact, it is natural. It is there because we are an intelligent being, one that knows what death is, what pain is, and the fact that it is a certainty. But what people mistake is that fear is not cowardice; fear is intelligence. It is knowing what is at stake, and what can be lost. Fear is the sight to see what can occur without having it transpire. It is to see the future, a possible outcome, and then know what is at risk. Once that is understood the entire concept of fear becomes quite easy, and you are no longer controlled by fear, such as a coward. Instead, you become brave. For one cannot be brave without fear. One cannot have courage without fear. One cannot attain anything without knowing what is at stake. With knowing that fear, every action you take becomes worth the risk that your fear had shown you, and then your action becomes far greater and far more direct. That, my friend, is the beauty of fear."

"I have never thought of it like that."

"We all fear," he paused to examine me then said that strange name once again, "...Vlad. Even you, even I. We are born of dust, and one day will return to dust. I, like yourself, will perish one day, for that I am assured. In the meantime, how I do it is up to me, as it is up to you as well."

There was a long silence before I finally asked, "Vlad?"

Gideon looked at me with a smile, examining the heat of the flame with his hands and not saying a single word.

"Why do you call me that?" I asked again.

"Because the name has much meaning," he said, pausing as he picked up a log for the flame, "and because you have much meaning in this world, and in mine." He threw the log into the fire. "It is a name that has more meaning than that spiteful name your father bestowed upon you."

I stared at the new piece of wood that was so quickly enraptured by the fire. It burned brightly, with a crackling of screams roasting the sizzling piece of meat that sat above.

"You think too highly of me."

Gideon let out a sigh. "I do not think highly of you. It is you who thinks little of yourself." He poked the lamb with a stick, testing its tenderness.

I sat silent. I had not heard any man, being, creature, or soul talk of me in such regard. Not even my closest family, which was my father, had said a single word of goodness in my presence. Now I heard it, and how odd it was that it came from a stranger.

"There is greatness in you, Vlad," Gideon said again, patting his hands clean on his sides. "I can see it as clear as the sun on a cloudless day. I saw it on the battlefield, shining bright, and also on that day when we first met, in the darkened gloom of that pyre that you were staked on. I even felt it when I first heard the story of what you had done. It is something that you were born with. Now, it is just a matter of time before you embrace it."

"You believe I have greatness within me?"

"I believe many things, Vlad, and many things I believed have come true." Gideon stared straight into my eyes as if reading my soul, then he returned to looking at the dancing flames, making sure the spotted lamb was cooked thoroughly. "In fact, I believe that you shall rule one day, have a kingdom of your own," he looked over at me as painted the image with his hands. "Perhaps, even one besides mine," he smirked, grabbed the roasted lamb off the spit of fire and continued his fairy tale.

"Now then, Vlad is a good name. And a man needs a name if he is to be anything. Vlad is a far better name suited for a ruler, don't you think?" he said, getting up.

I wondered what this man talked about. Kingdoms? Status? For commoners like I, I was even lower than low. I was a bastard, even lower, truly an orphan of life, for I was motherless, fatherless, and abandoned. What place did the world have for a being such as I except to frown upon and mock its existence?

"It's fine, if it's your wish," I finally said, smelling the intoxicating aroma of the lamb that had simmered to a perfect finish.

"Good. Vlad it is then," Gideon smiled and took a bite from the lamb. "Delicious! Good enough for a king," and he handed me the roast with a beaming grin.

I took the offering from his hand. Then, he started walking towards the army of men that awaited him to rejoice in the victory, but before long, he stopped and turned to look at me, perplexed. "Although..." he paused.

I looked up at him with a mouthful of meat stuffed in my cheeks.

"I rather like the other name that the villagers called you," he said, "What was that?" he thought as he rubbed his temples.

"Ah!" He beamed a vibrant smile. "The Impaler! Yes, that was it. We will keep that part!" He spread his hands across the air as if my name was writ on a sign, "Vlad, the Impaler," and looked over to me with a brilliant, enthusiastic smile. "That's good! I like that." With that, he walked off into the darkness from whence he came.

I was left on my own that night to wonder the words and thoughts he had planted in my mind, which quickly grew as branches on a tree and stretched their way to the corners of my dreaming mind.

Within three months, from the start of the day I met him when my world was about to end, to the now. I had gotten everything he promised me, and something else that I had not expected—a new name, for I was a new man. And it was on that day, that I bore that third name. A name given to me by a man I would never forget, and one that I would carry for the remainder of my mortal life. Vlad, the Impaler.

CHAPTER 12
A Life Unknown

"

It is a wonder to think of where we belong in the scope of reality, for reality itself is a dream. All we have created as man, we have made out of our visions, out of our desires, formed from the very essence of dreams to live beyond mere vitality. For it is that we are no more than flesh and bones, only living a life to procreate and survive. That is the point of our existence, no more. It is our dreams that take us to any point beyond.

The civility, the laws, the religion, we have all made within society to live by rules generated by man's dreams. In specific, dreams to rules others, rules to govern our own existence, to follow in trends with the masses, so they have little thought, so they may not dream and create their own rules to surpass our own. Yet all these thoughts were but once a dream, a dream to live, a dream to survive, a dream to create, and once we take them away from others, we can only achieve our dream by destroying the dreams of others. So it is sane to say that the man that dreams the most is the most destructive man, for his dreams, if large enough, will devour all others in its way.

"

THE NEXT DAY CAME, BUT IT WAS LIKE MY FIRST. I did not know what to expect, for on that day I was different than I had been the day before. I awoke with a sense of belonging and camaraderie, which I had not ever felt before. Yet it was also a feeling I did not want, for I did not know what it was. I was born an outcast, neglected, shunned, and disapproved, and the fact of the matter is that I had gotten quite fond of it.

It is such a strange thing to say but it is the truth. I preferred the company of misery and not of friends, because misery has no friends, has no brothers. It is self-inflicted, self-doubted, self-imposed, and self-involved—nothing else. For when a man has nothing to lose then he is at a gain, for no outcome but the worst can occur, and no wager can be made for him to lose what he has, if what he has is nothing. But when a man is given something, he is at risk to have it taken away, at risk to lose what he values, cherishes and holds dear. I was given hope, and I wanted none of it.

Maybe that was what Gideon had spoken of, that the risk of losing something is the fear. Maybe that day was the first day that I actually felt fear, for I was at a loss of my old life, and attained a new one, a new identity. A new life that I did not know how to live.

It was a fear that I did not and had not felt on the battlefield, even when my life was at stake. It was a fear that I did not and had not felt when I was sentenced to death on a pit of fire. And it was a fear that I did not and had not felt when I was living as an unwanted curse at the village I grew up in.

I dare not call that place a home, for home was not what had been given to me. Home is a peaceful place, a place of serenity and rest, and not once had I felt that on those wicked grounds of despair and hate. No, my true home was one that I had just recently found, which was the battlefield.

The battlefield that I felt so much ease and comfort when I stepped onto. The battlefield that I felt was part of me since I was born, that fulfilled my deepest desires and darkest thoughts. The battlefield that was calling to me when I stepped away. That was my true home.

And now that the battle was over, I had that fear come over me. A fear of uncertainty for I knew not when I would return home again, when I would step on those fields of war, and let my rage fill my heart. And now, even more, I had been given hope. Hope of a new life, this life, and it made me afraid.

I was afraid every moment I walked it, that I would be sent away from it. I was afraid to be discovered for the horrid creature that I truly was, what the villagers had always known, what they had always said. I was afraid that the army would soon realize it as well and I would be cast out once again, away, never to find my feet planted on the soil of my home, in the gardens where I felt at peace, where I felt serene, where I rested, on those pristine fields of war.

These worries, I wondered about during that day, as a band of men came towards me disturbing my thoughts. They were familiar ones, ones I had seen on the fields of my new home, tested like myself in battle. I had fought alongside them, without my intention, during the war.

"Good day fellow warrior," one of them said.

"I hear your name is Vlad," another said.

The last simply waved his hand, accompanied with a smile.

I was surprised that my new name had already traveled across the camp. Nonetheless, I had no concern to associate myself with these men on the grounds of friendship, only that of war patron. So I sat silently, unwavered by their introductions. In fact, I could not even recall their names as they sounded off one after the other, telling me who they were and where they were from.

On and on they went, one by one, telling me stories of such things as if I found them entertaining, but I did not. I did not want to hear their beginnings, their tales, because it only made me angrier, more vengeful, for each of their lives that they stated were difficult, hard, and harsh.

I scoffed at such diminutive remarks. I had gone through what each man had gone through, all compiled into one and vastly more, and there I stood unbroken. Unlike them, who whined about their meager pitiful existence. These men were weak in my eyes. They ran because they could not handle the menace, the cruelty of their so-called hard lives. They ran for a trivial matter and not one of intent. I, on the other hand, had been recruited, and I was found and brought to the battlefield with a promise, and a debt that needed to be paid, so I came.

Through their endless stories and their whining history, something did catch my ear. They had seen me on the battlefield and told me I was a talented warrior, yet a bit wild, a bit reckless, and that if I refined my unstudied techniques I would become a true force to be reckoned with.

So after a bit more trivial talk, where they spoke and I sat and listened with half an ear, they eventually came to the point. These were the men that practiced on the morrows of battles before the war and sunny mornings that came in between. They were trainers and they taught and aided the untrained troops in the ways of war.

This interested me most for they spoke directly to my carnal need. For the lure to kill better, to invoke my wrath further, to shed more blood beyond what I knew. This would feed into my monstrous ways, and I would go on being who I still was, unchanged by friendship and companionship, but instead a more ruthless, more vicious, and more efficient killer.

With a simple yes, I had made the promise to join them the next day in the open fields to do what I desired most, to feel at home once again, and to become even closer to the monster I knew I was on the inside—a better fighter, a better killer, a better murderer.

CHAPTER 13

The Practice

"

In the span of the world, we exist as a flash of light. It is up to

us how brightly we burn, to show how much light we share.

In the brightest lights, exist the darkest shadows that cover

the earth, and still we shine, brighter, in the glimpse of time.

But in the end, we do brim to a fade, a distant memory, to a

luminescent glade, but our shadow remains, only growing in

strength, into the darkest of the darkest shades.

"

THAT MORNING WAS A USUAL ONE. The sun was out, the clouds were about, some troops were still in bed burying their heads into their sacks that they used as pillows. Others were just welcoming the new day, smelling the warm, breezy air, and stretching their weary muscles.

It was all rather typical for the troops as they awakened to a new tomorrow. After what seemed an eternity, the men who approached me the other day awakened. One by one, they came out of their individual tents. They grabbed their meals, ate their rations, gargled and drank water, all in a needless ritual to welcome the new day. I saw it all, for I had not slept, not even a blink of the eye.

The excitement of the bloody battle, the simple notion of it had filled my body with energy. I longed to take my sword once again in my hands and to strike it on anyone, whether it be friend or foe. How I lusted for the battle, craved it, thirsted for it. How I relished those moments and could not forget.

Those moments on the field where my sword drove down, cutting my foes one by one and making them no more. The power, the strength, the gratification, it all came rushing back at me, as I saw it over and over as if it were the now.

Perhaps this was how the army was able to keep their lust for the battlefield at bay. They donned armor and lifted swords, and waved them at each other in pretense to get a taste of the battle back in them again.

I could not wait for my chance, and I held the sword tightly and did not loosen my grip of it all night as men slept, and all morning long while men awakened. It was to be part of me now, as much as my own hands, and where I traveled so it would also. It lay by my side as if it were my fingertips, and as I reached for others, it would also, and touch them with all the sharpness and coldness that I felt in my heart.

Finally, the men gathered, and after their pointless morning squabblings, started warming up for practice. More and more men joined as I watched. That is when a strange feeling came over me, as if someone was watching me as I watched the men, and that feeling made me turn.

Even stranger was that I found myself staring at Gideon's tent. It was odd, for he was nowhere in sight, nor had I seen him the entire morning. Still, I felt his eyes on me. Those cold, steely eyes, even as I looked at that tent were staring back at me somehow. But I could not figure out from where. After a moment, I went back to my original intention, which was to quench my hunger, end my thirst, and swing my sword so that I could stop thinking once more, that I could get that moment of serenity I desperately craved from my everyday madness.

Once enough men had gathered, I walked towards the practice. There were a good number by then, for that, I made sure. I would not want to go in first, or even when there were just a few. I spent a well thought out time in anticipation; no matter the desire, I had to wait.

* * *

I waited so I did not have to spent time talking and exchanging useless information until we were all ready to actually fight. I waited so I did not have to hear stories of their families, of the joy that they would feel when they returned. If they returned. More than anything, I waited so that they would ask why I did not feel those things, have those things, or even want those things. The explanation was simple enough and the same. No matter how many times I would have said it, no one would accept it. The explanation was very simple and to the point. I was a monster.

The first lesson was simple and straightforward. It was also very basic knowledge, common to any man who has fought or even picked up a sword, and even still, I found that I was doing it wrong.

I found out that I did not grab the hilt the way I should, so that it would make it easier to parry a blow, or to re-swing after taking a swing. All I thought was about hacking, and I had done it well with no skill whatsoever. Lesson learnt.

The second lesson was how to recover from a parry and best use our footing so we did not trip, so we did not fall from an attack. This was also something I did not know. It was in the midst of battle that I fell many times, lucky each time to have the body of the dead to block my fall, or protect me from another's blade, all which I used without any know how, just instinct. It was an instinct that I could have avoided using, for the simplicity of how to place my feet to keep my balance. Simple moves, simple knowledge, that should not have been called into play, and it made me a better, more efficient warrior, another lesson learnt.

It seemed the men were far too kind when they said that my skills were merely unrefined. These simple lessons had shown me that it was a wonder how I survived that last battle at all. There were a few more quick lessons, all of which I needed to learn. I was eager to do so as my blood rushed through my veins, for each one of those skills brought me closer to my goal of being a more proficient murderer. After it all, it finally came for the time for us to practice.

In the dirt circle they had made for us, two men walked inside and practiced while others awaited outside for their turn. Those two men inside would swing, parry, thrust, parry, step side to side, and watch each other's actions. All the while, being in control, in slowed actions like that of a child's, so that the other had time to react. For practice swords, we did not have. Unlike the rich, prosperous and bustling war academies that had coin and need for such things, we had only our blades that we carried into battle. They were to be our teachers and the marks they would leave would be permanent. And because of it, we had to rightfully allow each other time to learn using those blades, hence the slowed motions. This was clear and we began.

I followed the lead, a swing, a parry, a thrust, step side to side. Well done and again, I went. I swung, I parried, thrusted, stepped side to side. Once done, I stepped out and watched the others go in a gauntlet-like circle, over and over again. It was a practice made to fatigue as much as build our blows. When it was my turn again, I went into the middle of the dirt circle, but this time, something was different, yet the same.

I felt the sense of those strange eyes watching me again. That presence was all around, and as I turned to look, I saw Gideon in the distance. He was standing motionless, watching like an eagle. Even though I could not see his eyes, I felt them as if they were right on me, as if they were right in front of me like the very first day I met him.

This shook me to my nerves and I did not want to disappoint. So I did my bout once again; I swung, I parried, I thrusted, and stepped sided to side, and repeated until it was a turn for another. I took my leave and went and waited again, always aware of my watcher, until once more, it was time for me to go again. So I walked to my new opponent, one of the more senior fighters, and did my bout as told, I swung, I parried, I thrusted, and stepped side to side. Again, they called so I did.

I could hear one blade clanging off the other, louder and louder it chimed, like a music of orchestrated of metal played its tune so finely and beautifully, and I wanted to hear more.

O how glorious it was to practice, so again, I swung, I parried, I thrusted, he stepped side to side, and again, I swung, he parried, I thrust, he stepped to the side, I swung, he parried I thrust, he stepped to the side, and then I swung, he parried, and swung, he parried, and I swung, and swung, and swung.

O how the sound of metal clanging grew louder and louder, as beautiful as it can get, muffling the cries all around. So beautiful that I heard nothing but that magnificent sound, over and over, more wondrous with each blow.

O how I hacked and hacked, letting the parrying sound riddle the air. I played that sound until I finally felt another arm around me, trying to pull me to the ground, in an attempt to stop me from finishing the symphony of metal that I was creating.

How dare he do such a thing? I threw him off and felt another and then another and another until my head was no longer clouded with the lustrous sound of the blade but instead, deafening calls to stop as I hacked away at the poor man. He was riddled with gashes and blocking with all his life, but my blade still continued to swing rapidly down, over and over again.

Four men it took to subdue me from my rampage, and another four to knock me senseless so that I would stop and come out of my rage. After that, they did enough to make me unconscious for even then, I know not why, but I fought. And eventually when they did, my eyes went black and I saw nothing but red, the instant red that normally fills the sight and then quickly turns black, but this time, that red stayed and I saw it until I awoke again.

CHAPTER 14

Shame

"

The path I walk is a dreadful one. One of loneliness, despair, fear, and sorrow. Yet, I walk with a light foot, as a feather does falling from the sky, never too immersed in one location before I reach another. I travel on the road to this oblivion and obliviousness, in hope of that light, in hope of that dream. In hope of a hope, to lighten my burden. To take me away from a solemn existence and breach forth into new found glory. I travel on a web of dreams, pulling away from each one until I find my own. No words, no prayers, only a head full of screams. I travel and travel, with my footsteps, with only my thoughts for company, and always alone, for every move I make is a sin that I atone.

"

MY EYES FINALLY UNCLOUDED and then I could see again. However, it was some time before I came out of my stupor and realized my surroundings. Although blurry, I could make out the inside of the tent in which I was being cared for.

Surprising to me, I was not abandoned and left on the side of the road as I had deserved to be for my actions. But there I was, being treated with compassion. I felt the wet cloth on my head, as well as the tender bruises, slight bumps as I moved my fingers over them. This brought my attention to my arms, which were wrapped in bandages that were cool and had some sort of ointment inside. Although I knew it would never remove the marks I received from the burns, it did soothe the stinging pain that I had gotten so quickly used to and felt as if I actually had skin on them again instead of festering scabs. A bandage was wrapped around my ribs and traveled all the way up to my shoulders and past my neck and around again. I do not know what injury I had suffered there, but I presume it must have come from the men tackling me for it pained to breathe. This complete care from a chaos that I had created I found quite strange, for common sense would dictate to be rid of me, and in part, that is what I wanted. Was it not that just moments ago, from my recollection, I had tried to kill a man? Why they took pity on me only left me befuddled with more questions than answers and only increased the pain in my head.

Soon, my eyes cleared even further and I could make out the rest of the tent, a tent that had tears and was mended together back many times and housed many of the injured that went through it, some survivors, some not. Blood-soaked areas were constant reminders of what war and the way of the sword brought, which was death, as well as the makeshift bed that smelled of ale but of the strongest purest kind, that stung the nose with each breeze that traveled through the opening of the two folds that lay open like canyons cut through rock. And there, to my shock, I saw Gideon. He stared at me, not saying a word.

It was a blank stare that showed not a hint of expression on his face, as if he were examining me, trying to solve a problem. He had every right to dislike me for the upheaval that I had caused, every reason to detest me for hurting his men, every reason to hate me for my murderous nature. Yet I felt no judgment from him, just a curiosity that seemed more of a challenge than a nuisance.

Still, somehow, for some reason, I felt guilty inside. I felt ashamed to have him see me this way, have him see what I harbored inside that now showed outside. It was always my hope that he would not find my secret, that I remain hidden from no man more than him. The secret that I knew would come out one day.

The secret was that I was a monster. A secret that I would have shared with any man so easily and openly, but with Gideon I felt I had to hide it. For what he saw in me was far different from what I felt, and I did not want to let him know that what he believed in was a lie.

The truth was stark and real, and very void of hope, a hope that he believed so dearly and shared so carefree with me. I could not bear to share the truth with him. A truth that I accepted a long time ago, that I was not worth being a human, that I could not be called human for I was inhuman, and of a most devious kind. I was the monstrosity that everyone believed me to be, and I had no quarrels with that sentence.

It was only in the presence of Gideon that I felt this shame for who I was. All before, I never questioned my actions, the inaccuracy of my thoughts, the fault in how wrong my motives were since they were all simple and straightforward, but for some strange reason, I wanted to do differently in front of this man. And even though I craved the blood and fury, and the warring of ways, which he had so freely accepted me for and even related, I felt ashamed.

I, at the very least, felt I owed him more than what I gave. For he had tremendous hopes and dreams that he spoke of to me, and through it all, through his effort and kind words, in the end I was a disappointment to him, just as I was to my father.

Even stranger was that I did not feel remorse for my actions on his fellow men, I did not care or show a hint of regret. That is not what I felt wounded about. What hurt me the most, more than my wounds, more than my pain, was my conscience, for I did something that was not out of my character, but instead uncharacteristic for this great man. I made him a liar.

For every word that he spoke to me and I had heard from him was truth, powered by his belief, and set in motion from his actions. And all he had said, revealing himself openly to me about his dreams, his feelings, his wants, and his desires to see me succeed and become a great man was all in vain. Not only did he give me trust for the first time in my life, of which I had received none before, but he had also given me hope and meaning. In return for that gift that he bestowed on me, I gave him a broken promise.

A promise that I would be a great soldier for him one day, that I would become a firestorm to rage and follow his dreams, a shining light of example and fortitude, and instead I was, as he said, a flicker on the field. In fact, all I had given him was one mere battle that I fought. I may have succeeded, but now I knew that I had not even succeeded all that well.

For no difference would it have made if I had fallen on that field of battle like so many others that came and fought on that day. No difference would it have made had I been forgotten into the lands, never to be seen again. No difference would it have been if he hadn't said those words to me like he did the night after, which he had the choice not to do, but he did anyways. No difference did I make for this man and his dream that he so gallantly followed. That is what I felt guilty for most, not my actions but the lack of my ability to make his dreams come true. For that I was sorry, nothing else.

With that last thought, my eyes went red once again, but this time they slowly turned black. I saw nothing else that night, just eerie blackness. Not a single dream entered my mind, but time passed. Even though I was asleep, my mind was awake thinking of my actions, of myself, my worth and my guilt, and I knew that I had made a grave error in my decision.

I had harmed the one thing that had any faith in me, the one thing that showed any care in my entire life, even above my own supposed father, my own blood. It was this man that took me in as family and offered me a place to sit at his table, and in return, I threw away his invitation and spat in his face. That is what I had done in response to this man's kindness, and even then, he had not said a discerning remark towards me. Instead, he waited patiently, for something. For what I did not know, and that is what kept me awake.

CHAPTER 15
Honorable

"

How strange it is that we always get pulled back to what frightens us most, because all that we know is fear. Familiarity becomes security, and security becomes livability, even if living that life is hell.

"

SOME TIME HAD PASSED since my frenzied assault in training, and this day was like any other after that event. I traveled with Gideon and the army of men. They marched forward and with them, so did I. When the army stopped and rested, so did I. When the army took commands, so did I.

This was the same as before but it seemed my dark hidden fears had come to light, for they no longer saw me as one of their own. I was a creature of war like them, but not part of their pack. I was something else, a vagabond amongst vagabonds, a rogue amongst rogues, an outcast amongst outcasts. I was a brother-in-arms but not a brother at all, for my darkness had tainted that bond and it could not be repaired.

And it was so, that they did not attempt to talk to me, consort or socialize with me. They did not even bother to tell me of their pitiful lives and absurd stories of family. No, I was shunned once again, just like from the day I was born and all my days after. This was natural, comfortable for me. It was what I wanted deep down, to be unattached, unworried, unburdened with friendship, just a lone self. It is what I wished for, or so I thought.

And yet even though the army disliked me, did not trust me or my actions, and were wary of my every move, I still walked beside them. It was in the misery of myself where I felt most at home, yet I did not feel so anymore.

And as much as it would have pleased the troops that I would disband and leave on my merry way, I did not, and they did not make me. It was Gideon and Gideon alone that made the choice to remove a member or not, and no one else. But oddly, Gideon had not said one word to me about my misdoing, about my rampage, or the storm that raged within. He had not acknowledged my act of heresy during the friendly training. He had not even said one word to another man about whether my discipline would take place. In fact, he sent no words towards my direction whatsoever. No words since that night by the campfire where he gave me my new name. Where he exalted me with praise before I muddied his words with dirt.

Yet, I did not know how to feel, for he did not shun me like the others, either. He never showed an unkind glance, and unlike my father, he acknowledged my presence and always had a pleasant demeanor, even sending a smile or two in my direction when he saw me. He was a mystery in all his actions, so much that he had me mesmerized with his moves.

Even when I inspected him with my eyes for more truth, I received not a hint of a clue. It was the same smile, the same look, the same glances that I had known him since I first met him. So cordial, so proper and real that I wondered if this was a façade, or maybe I was living a dream.

I knew that he was a master tactician, a great leader, and well versed in the scheme of politics. He knew when to smile and nod, when to object, when to say things that sounded true but were false. Maybe this was one of those times, to show one thing but actually mean another. This was most intriguing to me and I spent a lot of time observing him for that very reason, to find the fault in his perfect image, but with all my efforts, the only thing I had found was that he had none.

The rest of my findings were trivial at best. I saw that he spent little time in his tent, and most days walked around the field gathering his thoughts, or formulating a plan, at least I assumed that he had such thoughts. Yet from time to time I had no sight of him, as if he vanished into thin air, but then he would appear again, rejuvenated as if he had just awoken from a long nap. It was strange, as if he knew I was watching him during those times, and as if he turned the tables on me and watched me instead, for I felt those same unseen eyes when I could not see him.

During those times, when I could not see him, could not hear him, and had no knowledge of his presence, I could still feel his presence. I would use my time wisely nevertheless. I would sneak around the camp, out of sight, but in earshot of what people said. It was the only way to get information because they would not share a word with me since my assault, out of disgust. I was fortunate that during my childhood I had become very adept at not being seen. I used that to my advantage and learned a great deal about our leader and his character.

To my surprise, none of his men thought anything less of him than holy. I had learnt he was valiant, a warrior, and a great leader, as I had originally thought, but even beyond that of what I expected from a knight's chivalrous acts. I found out that Gideon talked to the men as if they were his brothers. He talked to the harmed as if they were his children. He talked to the elders as if they were the gods themselves.

Not one man in his troop had any ill thought or word of misfortune towards him, something that I was not accustomed to. In fact, the only thing that wasn't completely positive that came from their mouths were his dealings with me, where he took no action to punish me, which befuddled the men as much as it did myself. Even then, it was more of amusement and intrigue instead of malicious talk, as if they knew he had a plan since he always had a plan. Still, they did not understand how or why he kept a nuisance such as me around, and were eager to find out when that plan would come to fruition.

It was strange to know that a man like Gideon actually existed in the world, and I believe any man who walked on the earth such as this must have been watched by a mighty figure, for he had much to give the world, and in return, the world had much to give him.

I wondered these thoughts often, for Gideon was in my mind often. I had never met a man worthy of praise before, or admiration, but if any man was worthy of it, then this man was worthy many times over. In fact, his lack of rejection towards me like the others in the troop earned him my respect. His words to me by the campfire earned him my heart, and his trust in me earned him my faith.

I did not want to diminish the trust and faith he had put in me any further than the damage I had already caused. Even then, I did not know how to react to such faith, since no faith was ever put on me before. What was a man to do when all a man knew was how to hurt, to kill, to murder, maim, and ruin? What was a man to do who had not a friend before, an ally, a comrade in arms? Who had not even been given trust before? What was a man to do to gain respect when he had none of his own? All those I would soon find out, and the path I would have to walk to get there was one that I would never expect.

CHAPTER 16
The Immortal Army

THERE IS MUCH MORE TO TELL, but before we continue, I must first tell you a little about the lands we inhabited, the King's land and the role of the King, as well as Gideon's role and who he truly was within those lands.

The King was a mighty King that ruled the entire realm that was inhabited with civil life, all the way from the edge of the seas to the edge of the mountains where no affable man roamed. Beyond that lay the deserts where ruthless barbarians and primitive desert folk stayed, those that were savages and not considered of civil nature.

I might have felt very much at home if I was born there in the outskirts and forsaken lands, but I was not. Instead, I was born in a green fertile paradise, as a vile poisonous fruit that no one wanted to touch because they would get sick or their hands soiled.

Gideon, on the other hand, was the furthest thing from who I was. In fact, he was the pristine example of a prestige and prominence. He was an honorable soldier, a knight, and the most gallant of all Generals under the King's command, and respected throughout the realm. He was also unlike any other knight in the kingdom, unlike any general in or outside the lands. Gideon was unique.

In those times, when armies were employed by the kingdom, the King would reward them for their victories, supply them with weapons, armor, rations, even gifts. Those who stood would be rewarded and those who fell, their wages were taken to reward the victors even further. But those were the men that were employed under the King, and Gideon's men were not.

No, Gideon's men were unique, just like him. They were not formally trained in the schools and war academies of the kingdom. No, these men were self-made, vagabonds, scoundrels, thieves, and brigands. They were the type of men that were seen as shame and the King would not recognize them and did not pay them because it would be poor politics to do so.

Instead, Gideon supplied them from his own wages, riches, and spoils of war. For every victory, Gideon's army would survive to fight another fight, because they could afford any losses. That is what made Gideon and his army so unique and unlike all the others under the King's command. But it was not always that way.

When Gideon was a young knight, he was given a small, trained battalion to control. He was shortly put to the test to wage a battle under the King's order. There was little hope for survival, for it was an impossible mission. Yet Gideon took this order and followed it with his heart, for if it were important to the kingdom, then it would be important to Gideon. And so he set forth.

Under Gideon's guidance and his supreme tactics, his troops raged and fought like a force of nature, crushing those that stood in their path in such a way it was an unimaginable victory. In doing so, the King was very pleased and tested him again, and then again, and soon to wage all his wars, and in doing so became the victor of all his battles. In the process, Gideon traveled great distances, conquering the lands to every horizon in the King's name. But since Gideon traveled so far, distances which took more than months, and at times even years, to reach, he had no support from the King, and when his troops fell, no more came.

That was accepted, for the cost of war was great, the lands were already taxed, and the able men assigned to other troops. Even if there were men available, no more could reach him in the necessary time, for the enemy would seek Gideon's reduced numbers as an advantage, and assault him at his weakest.

Yet Gideon, being the commander he was, became savvy and prepared, and with the King's blessing, built his own army from all sorts of men, recruiting members and warriors from all walks of life. From the villages he strolled through, to the towns he visited, Gideon started replenishing his numbers from the places he traveled, recruiting his men. Those very men I talked about, those men like myself, unworthy in the King's eye, but worthy to Gideon.

As his victories grew, so did the stories of him. Once the stories spread, it recruited more and more men, and even led to those that traveled to find him to be part of his glory, to be part of his being. In doing so, every place Gideon walked, every field he stood on, his numbers were increased, and had not withered away. They started calling his men the people's army, and eventually, the immortal army, for the numbers never diminished.

However, that was false. The immortal army was just men, men like I, that joined him for a different cause than being policed on salary of the King. Men that joined for the honor to fight alongside a man such as Gideon. Men that fought for glory, fought for passion and followed Gideon's every whim, not for money, not for riches, but for the love of such a man as Gideon. Such a righteous man who existed in an unrighteous world.

Even though we were not worthy of such a man, even though we were not skilled in the formal art of war, he took us in. Because the truth was that we were untrained, unguided, and unknown to the scheme of war, and a burden on any army, but Gideon saw things differently. He knew there was a great advantage at play, for his varied troops had a wide variety of styles unique to the fighting warfront.

There were so many different styles that the enemy had not seen nor could even prepare for, since many of the fighting styles were unique to each man. Some fought recklessly, some fought strategically, but every man fought with his full heart. No fight for the enemy was alike, for no man he faced was alike. They could not wish to prepare for the mass of men, for preparation was not versatile enough and even when they fought the occasional skilled man, who knew how to fight, how to battle effectively and efficiently, they were taken by surprise for they knew not which man it was, and when it would come. That was the advantage, for how can you prepare for the unknown?

Yet we were not all buffoons wielding swords, there were those in his armies that were extremely skilled men also. These skilled men were usually the vagabonds, bandits, and scoundrels that Gideon recruited, which held another type of advantage. The advantage was that unlike most of the King's army, many of these men had actually fought before—in real fights.

No, not the nurtured and practiced kind, in the safe sanctimonious halls of the King's academy, but in real hellish life. A reality where they lived rough lives, survived tough battles and had to do anything to win, from dirty tricks, to dishonorable warfare. These men knew the way of the sword in true war, and not those stipulated and romanticized in castles' stories for the privileged to hear. No, these methods were true and those felt by the scorned. They knew the truth, they knew the taste of blood, the stench of the field, the feel of the soil on their feet, the rush of the anticipation before the battle even started, the emptiness in the pits of the stomach before that, and they knew how to survive. They knew this, and they knew it well, and after the taste of my first battle, so did I.

It was once I learned all of this that I realized I was more than just myself, that I belonged to a greater cause, a cause that was led by one man that I can now humbly accept as the absolute in my world. A man who was greater than any man I knew or heard of before, for he offered kindness and justice when there were none. That man was Gideon and I would vow to serve him until my end. I would become a link in his chain of success, a link built with blood and forged in the heat of war. Yet how truly strong a chain he had forged, I would not find out until much later.

CHAPTER 17

The Beggar

"

Desperate is he who walks on a path of redemption for no being can pay for the sins that he has committed. The mark on his skin is as deep as the one on his soul; no man or force can remove it, whether it be holy or unholy alike. It is a scar that goes to the heart and beyond—to lose sense of it is to lose sense of what put it there. For the act of removal only begs for the action to repeat the sin again and again, over and over, until we are marked for eternity.

"

IN SHORT TIME, I HAD BECOME OBSESSED WITH GIDEON, or more so obsessed with the idea of being back in his good graces, even though he made no motions to show that I was not in them already. Yet, I felt I needed to earn that trust to the degree he first gave me, the faith that he first put on me during our talks. He, in such a short span of time, already meant more to me than anything that existed in my life, more than the acceptance of my father who I had already forgotten, and as great as the love I had for the heart of all hearts, my lovely Illyana.

I had spent my entire life thinking and believing the lies that the villagers talked about, that I was a baneful existence, unneeded, unwanted, and that I served no purpose, but that was no longer true, for now I did.

My purpose was to serve, to serve by using my wrath, my skills, my vengeful nature, and all my dark abilities that the villagers feared. I would use them in service to the light that Gideon shined, and I would do that obediently and full heartedly and I would let no man stand in its way.

We walked on our journey through the forests, past some villages where Gideon made his appearance. He met the villagers and the admiring children who cheered us as we walked past; they ran behind in our wake. He was a heroic figure to the lands, in ways always known to the unknown.

Yet this also had me concerned, for how easy it would be to ambush a man like Gideon, who put his trust and heart before his security. Any one of those villagers, those polite gestures, could have hidden malicious intent. It would be what I would do. For unlike Gideon and the men that followed, I knew what true evil lurked in the hearts of villagers and what agony they could inflict on those undeserving of it.

Still, we walked past the villages with relative safety and approached the forest line. But it was that concern that made me sneak into the front ranks to watch Gideon closely, for I was worried about his well-being. And as we neared the trees, my fear came to the forefront and something did threaten his life.

I did not know where the poor man came from but he appeared quite suddenly from the forest line and was near Gideon faster than I would have enjoyed. He carried something in his hand I could not quite make out but it launched me immediately into an angered, violent frenzy.

Who would dare to intrude on an extraordinary man such as Gideon, such a divine leader? Who would dare to try to end him from reaching his goal, his dream? Within in an instant, in my mind I saw a vision that filled me with absolute terror. I saw in my mind, as real as a dream could be, the only light of my life being snuffed out. I would have none of it.

It must have been instinct, or perhaps pure bloodlust, but I had already grabbed my blade, unsheathed it, raised it as high above as thunder, and moved forward as quick as lightning, with such speed, such vigor that I could have sliced four men in half at once, and the others could not see me but a flash.

The poor man barely saw my blade, and did not even have the chance to scream, frozen in front of me as a deer staring at the face of death. My vision went dark and I all I could see was murder, all I could see was blood, the prey to feed my blade, to feed my hunger of blood, and fill my body with murder's ecstasy.

Yet for some reason, my blade did not travel down. It did not touch the man whatsoever. Instead, it stood in place a mere hair length from a man's head, silent and unmoving. I had not had the strength to bring the blade down any further.

It had halted and I did not know why until finally my senses cleared and the rage subsided. I witnessed Gideon standing in front of the poor man with not even a hand or weapon raised to parry the blade. No, he stood in front in trust of my blade not coming down. And although my blade did not touch his flesh, I could not have believed what just conspired, for even in my frenzy I had been stopped, frozen before my strike. There was great danger to Gideon, who risked his life for another without concern, who stopped my sturdy steel by his trust alone, his trust in me.

He had risked all his plans, his entire legacy, all his victories, his very survival in countless wars for a mere man such as this beggar against a lunatic such as myself, with no defenses placed but pure faith that I would stop.

What was this power that this man wielded that I respected even in my blind rage, that made me see light in the purest of darkness?

Of course, in reaction, Gideon's army of men had their weapons in hand ready to end my life, which I would have happily welcomed. It is, in fact, what I deserved for my careless action and the risk to Gideon's health. It was true that I was the only threat to his life.

I was the greatest danger to my revered light, and not the men who surrounded us, not the villagers, not even the enemy who fought us, and surely not the poor, decrepit beggar who stood there mortified at what was taking place. What I feared most was about to take place because I was about to commit it. Because I indeed was a monster, a beast that could not be tamed, that should not be tamed. Instead, only put down by the swords of others.

And so I waited. Even though his men were armed and poised ready to strike, Gideon's men did not attack. They did not turn on the rabid dog that I was. They stood waiting for Gideon's command to unleash their wrath, all sure that he would eventually give the word. For why would he not? This was another infraction and there would not be a third, there could not be a third.

Yet Gideon befuddled me furthermore, for there was no hate in him for my action. There was no shock. There was no fear, or any retaliation whatsoever. Instead, he wore a smile and said the first words to me since that one night by the campfire.

"Easy, my friend," and then he placed a hand on my shoulder, the same hand that had offered me a roasted leg of lamb before, the same hand that he had waved at me before, the same hand that guided his followers and had eased my pain and taken away my rage.

"Trust first, attack later." He looked at the man armed with only an empty mug standing on his peg leg. "Because sometimes a beggar is just a beggar."

Gideon reached into his pouch and gave a gold coin to the man who wielded his mug in thanks, bowed to the deserved savior and waddled back on his peg leg into the forest from where he came.

Gideon motioned for his men to move on. Yet again I had witnessed a marvel, and it witnessed back. He once again saved me from the brink of death, piercing through the darkness, my darkness, with his absolute light. He saw something in me that I did not think I possessed; he saw good in me. I did not understand.

I stood there frozen in my thoughts, still holding my sword in hand, unable to move because of the clouded thoughts in my head. What could have happened because of my blind action? What could have happened because I leapt before I thought? What could have happened if I allowed myself to be myself?

Although Gideon had no recourse for my actions, his men did not share his sense. They snorted and sneered as they passed me on the road, ready for one wrong move. Yet I did not have the strength or mindset to battle any longer. I was still in awe at what just occurred. I had not ever seen a man stand in the face of death, not with fear, nor with hate or rage such as mine, but instead, belief.

I needed to find this belief, this peace, this tranquility, this purpose to live the way that Gideon did. To be at peace in the face of death was serene and something that I would have never imagined possible.

I had always thought death brought fear to man, that it brought their worst nightmares to life, that it brought their greatest darkness to light. I was mistaken, and that is what I relished to see. Death was something more, more than the end of one's life; death had meaning. I just needed to know what for.

CHAPTER 18

The Garden of Fire

"

Discard your ideals of good and evil, for they are far different than you can imagine. The making of the darkened man does not begin with a single shred of evil, or even malice, but that of a single drop of light.

"

THAT NIGHT, WHEN WE REACHED CAMP, a sleep took over me. A sleep that was more than a sleep, it was an experience. My body was left behind, and my spirit had traveled to another land, left by time, left by rules of the common folks, and had whisked me away where all made sense and also nothing at all.

I saw a garden when I arrived, beauteous and lush in nature. It was planted with every assortment of fruit, every assortment of tree, every assortment of what the mind can decipher. It was there. It was a plentiful garden, green, blue, and red, vibrant in all its ways of color as if a rainbow had been planted into the soil and had sprouted wings to reach all corners.

I was on the edge of the garden, yet I know not how I knew that, for the garden stretched all around and there was little to discern one's location from another. But I had a feeling and a sense of my center in the world, and it was if it told me where I was and where I was to travel. I walked within the garden, moving what I sensed to be forward, moving through the thick of the soft grass, barefoot, naked, and unashamed.

The feel of the cool dirt and the warmth of the grass tingled with my every step, and made me rejuvenated with its every touch. The sky above yawned and stretched, and waved in patterns as if it were water, as if it were oceanic waves of clouds passing through and opening up light between. The light shined a crystal clear beam that sanctified whatever it touched, making the whole landscape sparkle in brilliance.

I walked for what seemed miles, what seemed days, what seemed eternity, but it crossed in a blink of an eye, and the distance I traveled seemed nothing more than a long stride. No matter how long I looked, I had only glimpsed the beauteous, abundant nature that surrounded me on my path, for there was too much beauty, too many senses to be able to be witnessed by one soul alone.

There were many trees, two of every kind I would presume. There stood three large mountains stretched out in one corner, pointed and sharp like a three-headed crown as they towered. And in the garden, four streams grew in size as they parted to the borders in different directions. In the center of it all stood a single tree, but not like any other tree I had seen in reality before. Not even like the trees that I had seen walking through the garden, but a tree that seemed as if all the other trees had combined into it as one.

The trunk was of a mighty oak, the bark of birch, branches that twined like that of an octopus in the form of what is now known as a Banyan tree. The leaves were shaped like those of maples trees, and the flowers that sprouted similar to almond trees, and other parts that I did not know from whence they came. Fruits of all varieties hung on the branches, from pomegranates to oranges, and apples to almonds. The mind would be at a loss to grasp at what to pluck.

Yet I was not one to shy away from a feast, and I thought little with my mind anyways. I leapt and grabbed at the first fruit I saw, plucked it off the branch. With little more than a thought, I was alarmed to discover that I had already climbed the tree trunk, and had plucked another and then another.

Like locusts to crops, I pulled and pulled, stripping the tree of its fruits. If it were that a fruit was out of reach, and I had to break a branch of the sacred tree in the process to possess it, I did so and I did not care. I did what I wanted. I made my way to my desire in any way possible, pulling, yanking, breaking branches and raping the tree of its goods to an exorbitant amount, more than any man could eat, more than any man could want, more than any man deserved. All the while, throwing them all in a large, unforgotten pile underneath, as soon as my hands possessed them.

My desire was infinite, and my resolution even more, and the action to achieve it, relentless. It would have continued unending if it were not the glimpse of a figure I saw below.

I saw the wisp of a red cloth, like a shawl, flying across the ground, accompanied by a beautiful white dress, and the alluring, gentle smell of fresh jasmine. It was the vision of pure beauty and elegance, innocence, a fabulous presence; it was the sight of my one and true beloved, my lovely Illyana.

"

O how I see you now, still as beauteous, virtuous, untainted,

unspoiled as the way you were that day. All the ideals and

traits that I no longer possess. I wish to keep this memory of you

forever. This is the way that you should be to the world. The

way it was in my mind, I wanted it stay that way forever, and

still want that to this day. All that came after should have not

mattered, and if I had the power to stop time and see a moment

forever, this would be that moment. This would be that time,

that vision I would burn into my eyes, and fall asleep to s

eeing over and over again, hoping to never wake, but alas it

was a dream.

"

It was at her sight that I stopped my ruthless assault on the great giving tree. I climbed my way down to meet her, only to find her vanished and no longer in my reach. I turned and saw her once more, just beyond the tree, in the gardens past. She was smiling at me, holding her arms out, reaching to embrace me.

How I longed for it, and still long for it now. I quickly ran towards her, passing the tree, only to trip and fall on the pile of fruit that had rolled in front of me. I stared at the pile, which was now covered with spoil and decay, deteriorating by the second.

I got unto my feet and looked ahead to Illyana just to see that she was no more. I turned to look behind me, but no sight did I find of her. I was only accompanied by the squirming worms, wriggling maggots, and soiled dirt that riddled the ground and infested the once great fruit that I had brought down with my own deadly hands.

No vision did I see of my love. O how I lusted for her to be in my arms, near my soul. I lusted a deep lust, one of longing, one of need, companionship, and love. I cried out in frustration, screamed in fury, roared in envy, and howled in furious bitterness.

My disrupting shriek changed the land that I stood on, and the green garden turned to darkened grey, the skies became a bitter orange, and the luminous milky clouds a dying crimson.

O how I wished to see my Illyana, how I longed for her vision, and I would stop at nothing to see her once more. World be damned, and whatever would stand in my way would burn to ash, singe to dust, for my deep yearning was unstoppable and my destructive wrath unsurpassed.

And so the garden responded to my whim and turned, mutated, and reshaped with my ever-growing desire. It lost its luster, and all the vibrant colors that it once held. It was stripped of them all. My feet dug into the lifeless twigs and mud that was once grass and dirt; the skies turned to brimstone. The smell of charcoal filled the once pristine air, and the wholesome garden, what was once beautiful and a giver of life, started to burn, and ash floated into the air.

It burned with my desire, flames shooting from the branches of each tree, each bush, each shrub and twig, until it bellowed like a demonic beast, raging and scorching. Nonetheless, my heart burned even more, it raged and pulsed with even more fury than the greatest inferno.

My eyes were red and my skin darkened; my mind empty. I was only kept alive with murderous desire. For it was time that my fury was to be unleashed. It had come time for the fingertips of my sweltering desire to reach the infinite horizon. I would stop at nothing to have my Illyana. I would let no distance stand in my path. No obstacle or wall, no man, nor demon, no dream or reality, no destiny would dare to stop me.

Then a voice boomed through the garden. It boomed through the heavens, and the three crowned mountains rose higher and higher and overwhelmed the sky. It stared down at me and opened its eyes, breaking my vision, breaking my dream, breaking my desire, and it awakened me.

I opened my eyes to see Gideon standing at the tent entrance, the moon at his back.

There was a thought that crossed my mind, the memory of the day before, the memory of my foolish rage, and my closeness to insanity and darkness, which was apparent even in my dreams. Gideon was my savior during that day, maybe he was my savior that night, from my deranged dream.

Or maybe he was there for what needed to be done. Maybe he was there to extinguish the flame that so desperately burned out of control, such as in my dream. A flame that would burn all that came near it, and a flame that needed to be put out.

All those thoughts crossed my mind in a moment and then Gideon spoke.

"I want you to come with me."

"Where to?"

"To hunt."

"In the night?"

Gideon flashed a wicked smile towards me. "There is no better time."

CHAPTER 19

Night Hunters

"

It is the smallest journeys that can change a man's life. To allow him to face a judgement as he has judged others. One who makes judgments must always realize that his actions are being judged by others as well.

"

THE TERRAIN WE WALKED was rough and jagged, full of foliage, branches, and trees. My eyes had taken some time to adjust to the darkened light. The night was darker than usual, with scattered clouds barely allowing us to have sight of what was in front of us. If it were not for the half-lit moon shining through at moments of passing clouds, then we would be blind as the worms that lay in the dirt. It also did not help that the very air was condensed, and heavy with fog, which made breathing burdensome. The air was riddled with a chill of the mist that touched the skin and made the hair stand on edge. O, it was a dreadfully beautiful night.

We walked into the forest, Gideon and I. I followed his steps, watching his every move. For even now I did not know if we were truly hunting as he said, or if this was a ploy of Gideon to eradicate my nuisance without the knowledge of his men.

I did not know. I did not care. For if that be his will, then it was his right. I was told by him when we first met that he would choose when it was time for me to die, and it was a sacrifice I was prepared to make, a deal I would honor. All I wished to have was the knowledge that I was right, that every man had his demon, and every man a monster to slay, and a monster I was.

Gideon held nothing more than a sword on this so-called hunt. It brandished a cool blue glow on its blade from the reflection of the moon, as it sat on his belt. It must have been sharpened recently, for even the light was cut at its edges, and glanced off of it as it swayed near his side. He must have caught my eye staring at his blade because he started to speak.

"Have you ever hunted, Vlad?"

I nodded my head yes, for I had.

Often, I was unable to find food, since my father did little to feed me. The times where I could not thieve myself a piece of bread, or a morsel from the garden, I would take a dagger and hunt in the wild. I would capture myself a prey, something usually small, something slow, enough to consume. But still, I was not a good hunter, and many times I found myself digging the dirt for grubs to feast upon. Gideon must have also thought this as he continued.

"Yes, many men say they hunt. The real question is, have you ever hunted a boar before?"

I shook my head no, for I had not, but I had heard it had become a rather popular sport.

Was he truly out here to hunt a boar with me, in the midst of darkness? Or was this another way to distract my attention from the blade that he wielded? I wondered deeply as he continued.

"It is quite exhilarating actually."

Gideon crouched his way through the vines, bushes, and trees, careful to make sure that not even a lone branch was broken with each of his steps, since there were many.

"There is excitement that is not unfamiliar," Gideon continued.

It was an eerie site up ahead. Odd, for all the trees branches reached for the sky as if gasping for air. There were so many that it made the path look like a row of bars in a cage, all trying to escape the ground from where they had been given birth.

"It is the same as with battle. When man faces the harshness of nature, or man faces an animal, man faces another man, or even when he faces himself," he looked at me. "That is true excitement indeed, Vlad"

"But why in the dark?" I asked, curiosity overcoming me.

Gideon took a pause and stood still, no longer moving, no longer shifting in the slightest. His back was towards me. His sword readied, held tightly in his hand. Strange how I had not even seen him draw it. My neck tensed and was ready for him to swing around and strike his blow.

"The greatest hunters hunt in the dark," he replied, "owls, bats, even snakes." He turned to look at me. "And I have even heard some tigers hunt in the dark."

I stood silent as he watched me with his eagle-like eyes.

"There is nothing wrong with darkness, Vlad," Gideon continued. "You see, fear overcomes many in the dark because they do not understand how to use their senses in the dark. They rely too much on sight alone when there is so much more."

Gideon closed his eyes and smelled the air. "When you take sight away, then men are truly in danger. When there is no sight, then the other senses are all you have. You are forced to rely on the very things you do not value. And if we learn only to rely on sight than we devalue those things we were born to have. Values we are supposed to have, Vlad."

Gideon took another deep breath and opened his eyes once again, staring at the night sky before moving his sight back unto me.

"And that is why the greatest hunters hunt in the dark. For all prey, from the smallest to the largest, eventually lose sight of their other senses when they are not needed. They become stale and superfluous, and that gives us quite an advantage."

With that, he turned and started moving forward again, aware of everything that was around, guiding his hand as if he was touching the very fabric of the air around him.

Maybe this was a final lesson, or maybe it was as he said, and we were simply hunting a boar. But then again, there was much that did not make sense, if that was all we were to do.

"I have heard that boar hunters use spears," I questioned further.

"Yes, they do." He started to circle the tip of his blade in the air, as if he was prodding the air ahead. "Do you know why?" he asked.

I shook my head no, and even though he did not see me, he knew my response.

"They use spears to keep the boar at length, praying for safety, which is quite cautious, and to the common man, a very intelligent move."

Gideon stopped his actions, and turned quickly to look at me. Those same piercing eyes I saw at the site of my would-be execution, the eyes that made the executioner tremble.

"But nature has a way of surprising the common man," he said and came close to me at a remarkable speed.

"You see, those men have never felt the presence of a maddened beast. One that impales itself, trying to reach its killer."

His eyes widened like an owl, and his glare became stronger. "An angry boar, if mad enough, would lunge forward and forward, regardless of pain, regardless of the outcome, and move and move itself as the spear pierced its body, regardless of the damage it would cause to itself, just trying to gain vengeance, even at the sure cost of its own life."

His eyes filled with maniacal tension that I had not seen before, as if he was thrilled, excited, and angry all at once. "You see, a boar has no thought, but death. No fear of pain, only anger, furious, unimaginable anger, anger that does not stop until redemption is at its hand. That is what's so exhilarating about a boar, Vlad. A beast that is pure vengeance when angered, and has unimaginable strength that even death holds no bounds to it."

He turned his sharp eyes back ahead of him and went back to moving through the terrain as I let out a sigh of relief. "That's why I prefer a sword, Vlad. You could fend off the boar's attacks, and with a powerful enough thrust, through the neck, sever the arteries, and let it bleed to death."

"A boar can be that fearsome?"

"A boar is the very essence of anger, Vlad," Gideon replied. "An anger that needs to be quenched."

Then he stopped, as the air rapidly changed and became thin and utterly dark.

"It is time." His hand tightened on the hilt of his blade.

He looked over his shoulder at me, and with one giant leap lunged toward me, with his blade thrust forward.

I did not move. I stood still and waited for the end, embracing the cold comfort of death that I so rightfully deserved as I felt the hit.

Yet, the strike came before what I thought it would have, and not from where I would have expected. I felt a fierce slice on my back, accompanied with a loud grunt that was so powerful that it sent me tumbling forward towards Gideon's blade, which was still ahead. It must have been one of Gideon's other men who had snuck upon me while Gideon distracted me with his stories.

I flew forward, moving closer to Gideon's readied blade. It crept closer and closer to my neck, so close that it was just a few inches away, but he expertly moved his blade.

Then, as I hunched over, Gideon leapt from the ground and stepped on my back, and before I knew it had leapt into the air, soaring like a bird of prey coming down for the kill behind me.

I crashed onto the ground and spun around to see Gideon coming down with his blade, but not at me like I had imagined. Like I wanted. Instead, he came down where I stood, striking at a mighty boar. The very boar that we had come to hunt.

CHAPTER 20

An Angry Boar

"

It is the act of killing that makes us feel alive more than

anything else. It is as if we steal the energy from the very thing

that we snuff out and in doing so, it strengthens us. The more

we take action against our prey, we become the prey. We become

a prey to that call and its powers that beckon us to take those

actions, only realizing when it is too late that we can only

become alive by taking the lives of others.

"

O WHAT A MONSTER OF BEAST IT WAS, more than a man high and twice a man wide, with four glistening white tusks that could be called swords, two that sprang upwards, two that sprang downwards. Thick spike-like hair riddled every inch of its body and head, and a tufted short but powerful tail on its behind. In front, it held a long but crumpled snout and its skin was as thick as any leather armor I had seen. How devilish it looked with its head saddled with two large bat-like ears that sprang outwards to hear all prey and housed two beady, dark, merciless black eyes. Its four legs bulged with striated muscles that the thick skin barely could maintain as they tensed and eased with power as it reared its hoofed footing, unmoving from Gideon's unforgiving assault.

If this was the creature Gideon was hunting, then I see why he spoke of it as such. For I knew then, what it would take. Death was certainly in the air, and it was not directed at just myself. No, it spilled into the air to both of us and it would take all of our might to not be taken by it.

The monstrous boar grunted a malicious grunt and rapidly thrashed his heavy head in such a way, in such a furious assault, that it riddled the air with strikes from his tusks in blinding quickness.

Gideon was a far better swordsman than I had even thought, or ever could have imagined. He deflected the blows with such precision, such swiftness, that I could barely see his blade move, and it only left behind only flashes from where the light of the moon hit off of his blade. His strikes were so pronounced, so impressively quick, that it seemed as if he were wielding the power of the moon itself.

It was a sight to be seen, unlike any that one can imagine. It was no longer an animal versus a man, a beast versus human. No, it was much, much more. It was as if watching two gods of battle waging war, strength versus grace, fury versus control, savagery versus wisdom, and it was O so beautiful.

"What are you waiting for, Vlad?" Gideon yelled at me.

I had not even thought to take part for I did not know what help I could give, but if Gideon wished it, then I should follow.

I quickly gathered myself; my mindset, my arms and feet ready. Then, I reached for my sword, only to realize I had not brought it with me, for I was sure Gideon would take my life on this night, and I was not going to resist him in any way.

"Here, use this!" Gideon realized my predicament and threw his only sword towards me, leaving himself defenseless and unarmed before the ferocious beast.

It was shocking to witness his trust in my hand once again. Just like before, he put his full faith in my ability, of which I had none.

I grabbed the sword and made my way to the monstrous beast. As I feared, it thrashed and trounced any advance I could make and I found myself being knocked back by the boar's raging head. It was certain that I was nowhere near the swordsman Gideon was.

"Is this not the excitement that you've been craving for, Vlad?" Gideon yelled as he started laughing, gracefully leaping side to side, in hopes of avoiding being impaled by the massive boar.

I quickly got up again, the exhilaration taking over me as well. I beamed, rushing toward the massive boar once again.

Gideon's laughter became even more apparent and frenzied, as if he truly enjoyed defending the assault of the monstrous beast, like a child playing with his favorite toy. He agilely moved from place to place, his feet barely touching the ground, as if he floated on top of it.

I raised the blade and I struck the beast's side, but the blow was futile for it just glanced off of its thick, hardened skin as if I was hitting stone. Even though it left not even a mark, it was enough to get the beast's attention. It quickly stopped its attack on Gideon and turned its enormous tusked head towards me, locking eyes with my own.

O how angry it was; I cannot tell you, for such was the fury that it was if I could see the rage burn around the boar in a dark sinuous aura. It thrust its snout towards me, all four of its sword-like tusks launched in my direction at once.

I could do nothing but hold the sword in front of me, as sturdy as I could be. I doubted that I could block any one tusk by itself, for surely it would impale me wherever it touched. To my fortune, I had blocked the blow, but the beast's power was so immense, so drastically overwhelming, that as soon as it collided with my blade it sent the sword hurtling from my hand. With it, my entire body launched back into a trunk of a tree.

O how magnificently powerful this beast was, and it was very impressive to take on a foe such as this. It indeed brought those feelings back, those feelings of war, those feelings of lust and blood. It filled the entire body and pulsed through my veins. This was indeed exhilarating and I wanted more.

I quickly braced myself, only to see the beast stamping its feet, ready to charge as I lay defenseless. Before it could manage its final assault and gore me to death, Gideon raised his hands and wildly jumped on its back, grabbing it by those demonic ears. He held on, gaining its attention once again and sending the boar in a frenzy of thrashing motions as if it was a bull.

"Isn't this fun, Vlad?" Gideon roared with a maniacal laugh as the boar lunged forward and back, trying to throw him off.

Yet no matter how hard the beast thrashed, Gideon held on. His arms locked onto the beast with an un-giving grip as his body flew left and right, riding the air. Instead of screaming or worrying, he roared with hearty laughter.

I could do nothing but watch in shock as the boar hastened his bucks and kicks, and soon started smashing its side repeatedly into a tree, trying to catch Gideon's body in between.

So great was the force that there were crackling sounds as the tree started to bend, certain death indeed if the beast did manage to catch Gideon with it, but Gideon kept dodging by kicking his legs off to the other side, each time just mere fingertips from being crushed.

"You...might...want...to...hurry," Gideon shouted between leaps, catching his breath each time as he bounced side to side. "I...can't...be...doing...this... all night...you know."

I quickly came out of awe-struck stupor and got my footing back. I ran towards the sword, which lay some distance away.

I grabbed the blade and made my way back to the boar as Gideon's face was finally showing some concern. It seemed his grip was fading, but not because he had not the— he was slowly ripping the boar's ear off its head.

"Finish it!" Gideon screamed as the boar's ear finally ripped clean off.

With an immensely powerful buck, the boar sent Gideon hurtling into the sky, far enough and high enough that he crashed into the thick of a tree, caught on the twines of a tree high above.

If there was any time, then this was it. It was the final moment, because the beast would not allow another chance.

I took the blade as the boar was focused on Gideon, who was perched upside down in the tree. I took that opportune moment, and lunged at it with all my might, with all my power, with all my exhilaration, fury, and strength and I plunged the sword deep into the beast's neck.

The sharp blade pierced through the leather-like hide, sliding in as a knife through butter and plunged so deep that only the hilt of the blade still showed. The raging beast instantly stopped moving and I in turn leapt backwards to watch it fall, in glorious anticipation for our victory.

Yet our victory did not come, for the beast did not fall. It stood there staring ahead blankly, as its colossal body took in deep breaths as if taking in the last moments of life. I had seen this before many times on the field. I had relished in it, the slowing of the breath, the moment where the body accepts death and for that mighty beast to come crashing down as it took its final one. But to my surprise, it did not. The breaths did not weaken at all. Instead, they intensified, not withered away.

No, the breaths grew and grew, became deeper and deeper, until finally, it fumed with so much rage and its muscles were so tense that it quickly snapped its head towards my direction and, to my shock, broke the hilt clearly off the blade and dropping it on the ground.

The boar stared at me with those demonic beady eyes, flaring nostrils, and a crumpled mouth that seemed to be sneered as if it were grinding its teeth. I could see no sight of my blade which was still embedded inside its body, which must have been causing it great pain, great anguish, but the boar did not care whatsoever, for it was angry. It was vengeful, and it wanted revenge.

"Now what?" I yelled to Gideon, unsure of what next to do. I quickly glanced at him, still hanging upside from the tree that the boar had launched him into, and to my surprise he seemed as perplexed as I.

"Huh?" he asked with astonished amusement.

"Huh?" I retorted, awaiting my commands. "What do you mean 'huh'?"

The boar started to stamp its feet once again and held its head down towards the ground. Its sword-like tusks pointed towards me, readied to take a murderous assault. Its eyes were focused on nothing but my presence as if the world had gone black and it and I were the only things in the universe, and I was the beast's only goal.

"Gideon?" I yelled, staring at beast, waiting for my next set of life-saving instructions, but no answer came.

I could only see Gideon from the corner of my eye, for I did not want to lose sight of the boar, not even for an instant. But he was still dangling upside down, busy trying to undo himself from being entwined in the tree's grasp.

"Gideon?" I screamed again.

Finally I saw him put his arms down, and give up on the twining rope-like branches and leaves that firmly held him in place so high above.

"I guess..." he said, calmly kicking his legs against the trunk of tree that made him sway back and forth as if he was on a swinging upside down on a swing.

"What, Gideon?" I frantically called as the beast's motions became fiercer.

"I guess..." he paused and then said with an uncertain voice, "I guess... run."

Then, as I feared, the boar charged at me with full might, full speed, and full vengeance. But, I did what I was told. I ran. My God, how I ran.

CHAPTER 21

A Good Day

THE NEXT DAY WAS VERY MUCH A DIFFERENT DAY from the night before. Clouds had moved out, revealing a warm sun. The fields of grass stretched around our camp and spread over the hills in the distance. Patches of green forests snuck in between, but mostly, it was empty and open to the sight of clear blue skies, warm sun, and yellow grass. A wonderful day.

Gideon and I sat together that day, side by side. We were still high from the euphoria of what had happened the night before, on our hunt. We sat and ate, filling our bellies of wine and boar meat, which roasted on a hearty campfire. The soldiers were gathered around, feasting off of the boar meat as well, for the beast was large, and the triumph was a benefit to all.

It was an interesting event for myself, being surrounded by those soldiers, warriors who not long ago, shunned me. Those same warriors were now all around; some stood, some sat, but all listened to our story of the hunt that had taken place the night before.

Yet in the midst of the crowd, in the center of all attention, Gideon and I felt, somehow, alone. It was as if it were just the two of us in that moment and the world had hidden away. The night of the hunt had bonded us as more than allies in combat, but now, as true friends.

"So tell me, Vlad," Gideon said, beaming with an amused smile befitting of a brother to another, "how many fields did you think you had to run through until that infernal boar finally died?"

The surrounding men toiled in laughter as they readied another large piece of boar meat for the flames.

"I lost count after seven," I laughed between sips of wine and meat. "How long did you take to undo yourself from that tree?"

"I say it was one of my most…fiercest of foes," Gideon laughed.

"Why would you bring a sword for such a creature like that?" I asked.

"Why would I bring a sword?" Gideon said, shocked. "Why would I..?" He stopped himself before continuing with bellowing laughter, "At least I brought something, lad!"

Then Gideon stood up, held his mug of wine into the air and announced.

"Leave it to this man, to not even bring a dagger along on a hunt!" and then he toasted me with a drink.

"I salute you, sir…for your bravery," he said as he took a large gulp of wine, "…or stupidity." He finished the mug, snickering. "I have not made up my mind of which."

The men roared in laughter at his prodding, all of them now drinking in my honor.

"Well, that whole thing about the spear, that only the common man hunted with a spear," I said as I too took part in the jollies, "well, I wish I had one."

Gideon looked over to me and spoke in a most sincere and concerned voice. "My good friend. To tell you the truth, once I saw how big that confounded thing actually was, I would have preferred a spear as well." He chuckled, and then proceeded to down another drink with chortles of laughter in between.

We continued our jests back and forth, laughing in joy, at ease with the troops for this event had changed us. The troops had quickly forgotten about my previous miss-happenings, and for the first time felt calmed in my presence.

Strangely, for the first time, I too was at ease. I had not the normal worries that afflicted me with such thoughts that I normally had. I enjoyed this moment in its entirety for I had never felt this joy before. Maybe it was the bonding, the brotherhood of being around men in arms sharing in the festivities, or simply the euphoria from the wine, drink, and even the laughter, all mixed together once. I could not recall this feeling, this moment of bliss, to have ever occurred in my past, and up to this point, this was indeed the happiest day of my life.

Later that day, Gideon and I took a walk. We made our way on top of a hill, staring out over the plains that traveled all around us.

We had done nothing but eat and drink that day and we would have had it no other way. Suddenly, Gideon took a step forward but found himself collapsing onto the dirt from the effects of all the wine. In an attempt to stop his fall, I fell myself, not having the faintest clue that I too had been wobbling as I walked.

Gideon laughed a hearty laugh and rolled onto his back. After a few moments, where we both streamed tears from our eyes at our lack of senses, Gideon finally propped himself up on his elbows so that he would not topple again.

I soon joined him, sitting next to him, crouched forward. My hands wrapped around my knees as we stared at the scenery in front of us as children would, enjoying the sight we were granted that day of peace and serenity, away from all the darkness that had plagued our days before, and that had riddled our lives.

But my mind had a tendency to remove those pleasant moments from my life. I had always felt I was undeserving, uneased by calmness and joy, for I was not familiar with it. I preferred the company of darkness, the company of hate, the company of misery, for anything else was unnatural. I realize now, that it wasn't death, pain or sorrow that scared me, but instead, happiness.

"Why did you take me?" I asked.

"The hunt?" Gideon said as he chewed on a long strand of grass that he had plucked from the ground.

"Yes, the hunt." I looked out at the emptiness of the vast fields ahead. "There are far more experienced men in your army than I. Some are even actual hunters; I have no place by your side."

Gideon let out a deeply disappointed sigh and then sat up. "Vlad," he said, "you are so quick to dissolve your worth."

I had nothing to argue, for he spoke the truth.

"In the face of death, there is no equal to you, because you welcome it so freely. I have seen it when you battle. I have seen it in your eyes with the nearness of the flames. I had seen it even with the beggar. Quick to act, little to thought." He pointed the tip of his chewed straw at me as if it were a sword. "That is you, Vlad."

Again, I had no remarks to say, for he spoke the truth.

"I took you simply because..." Gideon said as he laid on his back, staring at the clear sky above, "...because I wanted you to see yourself, Vlad"

"Myself?" I asked, alarmed.

"Yes, Vlad. Yourself," he replied, "Because you remind me of a boar, Vlad."

He sat, staring at the sky.

"No fear of death. No fear of its own pain, only vengeance. Only to attack, move forward, destroy." He waved his chewed piece of grass in slashing motions. "Those are your goals, Vlad. No more."

It was true what he spoke. I had never thought of retreat until that night. I would have most surely welcomed death, and in fact, before that night ended, I had.

"I also brought you along so that you too could see it for yourself. See what you are to another man, to a hunter. One who understands that very nature, one who knows how to use it, and one who is willing to fight it."

"So the reason you took me was that you think I am some sort of animal?"

"Yes, in a matter of saying, that is true. But that is just one of the reasons. There is another."

"Which is?" I asked.

Gideon sat up, looking at me again. "You see, the reason I took you was so you could be a firsthand witness to the animal that you are, as well as witness the hunter that you should be, and could be."

Then Gideon put his hand on my shoulder as father does to a son, and with sparkling sincerity, kindness, and wisdom said: "The hunter that I know you truly are, inside."

I could tell that he believed what he said. He believed enough that I too, started to believe, but I knew not why.

Why did this man value my worth so much? Why did this man come to my rescue in my life? Why was he showing me mercy when I deserved none, showing me guidance and friendship, when friendship I had never imagined? Truth be told, I had little want of those things, or at least, so I thought. For before this, I saw no place of friendship in my life, but now I could not imagine a life without it.

CHAPTER 22

The Righteous Path

"

It is the will of man to be brought forth into a world as a

seed with nothing and be embedded in dirt and filth. It is

through time and patience that we become something different,

gathering strength from the very sources that we are disgusted by.

It is destiny to hate where you come from, only to realize that

hate is necessary to become something else than what you were

and blossom into something entirely different.

"

THE NIGHT THAT WE HUNTED TOGETHER, I had thought that Gideon was set to destroy me and rid the army of the nuisance of a raging beast. Yet as time went on and we traveled, I discovered that he had indeed done that. For I was changed, unlike anything that I could have imagined, anything that I could have hoped for.

It was a destruction that was necessary in order for my life to continue onward into a new direction, a destruction like so many others who tried to create. Unlike all those who failed, Gideon had succeeded. He did it not with a blade, nor negligence, scorn, or even fire, like so many others that tried before him. No, did it with something entirely different, that I had not expected. He did it with friendship, kindness, and love.

He offered me a hand when I was at my weakest, and showed me the light by showing me myself in the darkest of times. In those dark times I raged like a beast, moving forward and lunging frantically and aggressively only for vengeance and nothing more. Just as he said, I had been an animal, but an animal I was no more.

It was true. Then, my life was as menial as a beast's and consisted of only two things, receiving pain and giving pain. Pain was my only companion because I had kept it so close, so near, to the extent that anything else felt unnatural. But now, things were different. Pain had no place by my side, for Gideon stood in its place instead.

I was reborn on that day, on that night. The pestilence of the monstrous murderer that I was had been cleansed. Although, I was not rid of the beast entirely—it still lurked inside. It was caged like the animal it was, hidden in the deepest of dark parts in my heart and the most hidden corners of my mind. Locked away and the keys thrown for the first time, I stood free to be a man, and no longer the monster that I was born to be, like the boar.

That night left a vision, a picture embedded in my head, and I thought about it often as we traveled—the boar and the hunter.

Many times, I would pull myself away from the ongoings of war and travel to reflect on my thoughts. And in those times, I would have renewed faith in Gideon, renewed faith in my purpose, renewed faith in our friendship, and renewed faith that I was indeed, what he said, something more.

I had gained more than friendship from Gideon since I joined his army. I had gained a purpose that was even stronger than just a mere commitment. No, this was a grand purpose. A purpose to stand by his side, to serve as a warrior of caliber and worth. A purpose to be the shining example of what a man can become, and to follow in the lighted footsteps of my savior, Gideon himself. This I faithfully did and would do to my end.

During those times, as I walked that path of servitude, righteousness, and justice, years passed by. They came and went, as they always do, and when the first grey hair showed on my head, we had traveled great distances and reached the furthest outskirts of the King's lands.

By then we had been in countless battles, raged wars like no others, and gained a following of tales and stories to leave behind for generations to come. Even I, myself, had become respected within the army.

I had honed my craft, the art of the blade, and practiced many times in the company of myself, for I dared not risk the lives of others if my monstrous tendencies leaked out such as they had before.

No, I had learned on my own, and had become a rather skilled warrior, all from under the guidance of a watchful eye, and the harsh, unmerciful punishment of lessons in battle. Through it all, I had learnt a great deal about the art of death, which I had always wanted.

So much of a talent I had gained that my name became known from within the reaches of our travels. Unlike before, it was no longer scorned, disgusted, or mocked. In fact, even my past had changed in the stories that were told. The truth of being burned alive at a stake no longer haunted me. All the stories of the cursed being who walked the lands, a devil brought unto the world, were gone.

No, now the tales twisted, turned, and transformed from one weaver of words to another, creating a tapestry of fascination and a legacy of my own. They provided strange and fantastical explanations for my scarred limbs, that were, in truth, burnt and black from the pyre of judgment I was placed on. But that is not what the stories made others believe.

No, in those tales, those very limbs were, in fact, forged by a dragon's mouth to rid the world of evil, or so some said. Others even said I had those scars because I was the son of a dragon and could turn into one at will. All wondrous tales and fascinations of the mind that took away from the truth of who I was and had been at birth—a vile creature, not a mythical one.

There was so much exaggeration that, at times, I even forgot my own nature. But there was something always hidden deep below that hungered, that crept in the shadows, that clawed its way out, reminding me of who I truly was. A constant reminder that I was what I was. Although my actions had become noble and honorable, they were originally born from hate, born of dread, born from the fires of Hell, born from sin.

The monster was still alive inside, this I always knew. Although buried deep, hidden from the world, there would be one day that it would show its fangs again. The only question that remained was when.

CHAPTER 23
A Reflection

"

The fact that we cannot attain what we dream but strive for it with all our hearts is what makes us human. Man is a spectacle to watch in the midst of time, always trying to run faster than the time that is allotted for us to do so. We are those men that reach for glory that cannot be attained and climb a ladder that rises to infinity. With each peg, we get closer to our dreams, and we smile brighter and brighter, but we do not realize that the fall below grows with each of those very same steps, and the past grows darker and darker.

As we rise towards that light, the light of our dreams, looking forward to our future, the past becomes an abysmal creature, unseen by those oblivious to their surroundings. We are those men that wish not to see, and are ignorant because of our vainness and our vanity, focused only on what's ahead and not below. For to grace our dream is heaven and it overwhelms any fear or distress that it can cause, and we presume that is hell.

That is a lie. That is not truth, because we cower from the truth.
The truth is that the closer we travel to the light, the darker
our shadow becomes. No matter how much we lie to ourselves
that the hunger we feel inside of us is for our dream, and of our
dream, it is, in fact, not.

No, the truth is that it is the hunger of the abyss like a shadow
beneath our feet, gnashing its jaws full of razor sharp teeth. The
more we reach for our dream, the more it reaches for us, waiting
for our fall from grace, our fall from our own personal heaven,
to reach its depths and be swallowed up in its hell. It waits,
famished and ready to feast its fill of darkness and sorrow, as
much as we feed on the light, in hopes and glory. So the creature
waits and waits, and it hungers, calling our name.

99

IT WAS A STRANGE NIGHT, a very astonishing sequence of the mind that led me to see things I wish I had not seen. Even if the dream were not real, it bothered me as if I was sickened with a plague that infested from imagination to reality, for the dream worried my mind with thoughts and ideas that overflowed its capable boundaries. Yet still, I could not decipher even a drop of the dream's intents and I was left in more confused state than I had ever been before.

I had dreamt of a strange land, unlike any other that can be imagined in this day's times, or even those. It was a land filled with giants and demons alike. They walked with arms swinging, knuckles scraping on the ground like those of apes and not of men. They were large-limbed creatures, with heads on their chests and not on their shoulders, unlike those that we have known to exist, but it was not just any head.

It was a head made from bone and flesh, skinless red and the color of blood. Its eyes were utter blackness that filled the entire socket of the skull, as if they were holes in time that reached to grab any soul to fill its void, for it had no soul of its own. Those are the creatures I saw parading on the land, for there were so many that they walked on every speck of dirt that riddled the ground, on a graveyard of human bones and discarded clothing.

Even more gruesome was what they ate. They ate a flesh-like substance that they pulled and teared from ground as if they were pulling strips of cloth from a curtain. I could not make out what it was exactly but I assumed it was what I feared, for clues were left all around. The mangled bodies of corpses, deboned, and even odder some were still living. They were bodies discarded by war, discarded by lust of a victory, discarded by mankind, and discarded by those that would give them mercy.

These were the remaining products of war cast on the earth, those that had survived but lost their flesh to sin, murder, and death. They were meals for the walking abominations that now ate them. The beasts feasted well, all the while the flesh screamed but not with their mouths for they had lost the ability to do so long ago, but with their eyes. They screamed in silent anguish as their souls were harvested into these giants of crimson flesh that walked under the scorched red skies and ash-covered earth.

I was quite afraid, even though I knew that this was not reality, it could not be reality. Still, it stung me like a hornet's nest in my mind, and brought forth a feel of terror that I was not able to escape. I could not even force my mind to think of something else, and that brought forth a realization that even in this dream my life was at stake, as much as my soul.

Yet I was fortunate, for the flesh-eating behemoths had not set their empty eyes in my direction, and I would keep it that way or become a meal to their endless hunger. I did my best to cower and hide behind any objects that appeared in front of me, from piles of bones to a broken statue of unknown human origins.

I hid and moved without notice, watching the extinction of humanity in front of my very eyes. Even though I saw all this death, all this devastation, I was not filled with sorrow. I was not filled with remorse. No, I was content.

I had not paid any mind to the others that laid beneath my feet who had not yet been devoured, as my attention was on not being seen. That is, until one of those discarded beings grabbed my ankle. They stared with their sorrowful eyes and I could not meet their gaze, for if I did, then humanity might creep inside me and the beasts of war would look in my direction.

So I quickly moved my feet away, kicking him off, kicking them all off, one by one, only to have another grab me instead, and that too I kicked off. I quickly made my escape. Scurrying to another corner of the land, I found myself in an intriguing place that I did not know had survived, could have survived.

As I looked in front of me, I saw that strange sight of a land surviving the torment. I saw a city made of mortar and white stone, that of a marble-like appeal, but not of it. A straight light made into the ground as if a force had cut the scene of carnage outside from that of the prosperity inside, where square buildings of all sizes lived. The buildings were stacked one on top of each other, left and right, encircling the entire region as if space was the upmost important commodity. In a handful of places there were long, paved streets with thick stones; the roads were beaten from many feet traveling on them.

In the center of this region, of this sanctified land, rose a temple that towered above all else. Seven spires circled the temple's perimeter, all reaching out above as if hands joined in prayer. In the center of that temple, in the center of all its surroundings, stood a massive rounded dome made of gold, and it rose so high that it touched the very sky. That was where the strangeness of this place became unprecedented: the entire temple was reflected upside down in the sky, mirrored and connected at the spire's point, a perfect reflection inside a darkened cloud that spread, very much like a mirage, but, in fact, real, as if man and being could walk on both sides without a loss of connection to the earth.

This city of mortar, stone, and gold was not stark. Instead, it bustled with life, a life that I could not imagine of busy citizens. They saw not what went around them and not what happened beyond them. They lived in the sanctity of city and were unaffected in mind and body by the carnivorous demons that roamed around.

Yet I felt in this place a grave terror, a fiendish presence that scared me more so than the outskirts of the land with the body of graves, and a presence that I could not shake as it burrowed down to my inner being and beckoned me forward. So I walked into the city simply because I was being called to move forward.

I walked through the very streets that the people walked, and in them I saw people move about. Yet they looked more lifeless than the souls I saw outside, those in despair. For these so-called people moved about with no mind to guide them, but in an absence of any thought, of any free will. Each place they moved to was done as if they were an instrument playing notes to a dark piece of music. It served a purpose, I'm sure, but it only invoked the feeling of dread.

I walked and walked, down the paved streets, the stone corridors and past all the blocks and stones until I reached the temple and walked on a carpet of the most lustrous red, a red so radiant that I would not have known if it were a pool of blood. Yellow frills at the end gave it away as a carpet, frills that seemed as if golden hands were reaching out and grabbing the ground so that the carpet would not move on its own. I walked on that carpet, inside to the temple.

Then, I walked through a grand hall, with large curved ceilings that rose within the temple. The ceilings towered and were decorated with carvings of pictures and words that I could not make out for they were written in every language, in every dialect, in every form that were to exist and was to exist, and it was written to infinity.

Through the hall lay a room on each side, one that held a pedestal of water that I did not attend, and another a darkened corridor with a door, which I also did not attend. Instead, I continued to walk down the long hall, into another room, a room that was at the end of it all.

I stopped at the outskirts and stared into a small room, which had another door that lay open. Yet, I could not see beyond the fact that it was a door. Inside?

Darkness, and beyond that darkness, a voice, a voice that kept repeating and repeating, calling my name, "Vlad. Vlad. Vlad."

It was then that I quickly opened my eyes, and was not able to sleep again. I was too baffled with the meaning of my dream. Yet, I could not fathom, could not wonder, or even dare to understand what a dream such as that truly entailed. I decided to use what worked best for me to clear my mind, something that I practiced with little thought and more on instinct. That was to grab my blade and go in the night to swing my sword.

CHAPTER 24
Night Council

MY DREAM HAD LEFT ME IN A DAZE and I felt eerie myself. It was a rather unusual night as well. There was a heavy, thick fog, which had settled into the valley and decided to take residence there, exactly on the chosen boundaries of our campsite, and it would not leave. It was a pleasure for me to practice in such condition, for I never tired with the fog. It was rejuvenating to have it touch skin and mask sweat with cold refreshing beads of water. It was perfect to hide the intrusion of my swordplay to those who slept and the perfect disguise as a man suddenly came out of the fog and into my sight.

I had my sword already poised to strike but the man walked slow enough that there was no harm. As he came closer, I saw that he was a fellow soldier and not a beast or incarnation of my mind that had me in such an upheaval. Yet the soldier looked pale and worried, and not from my blade.

No, he had no fear of me or my sword, which many men were cautious around. Instead, he approached me almost unaware that I held it. He spoke quickly, said what he had to say, and vanished back into the fog, just as mysteriously as he had appeared. But what he told me stunned me, for I had never heard it before. He said that Gideon wished to see me in his tent, to join the council in progress.

I stood there a little dazzled at the thought, for only the most trusted of men attended the council. Although Gideon treated us all equally, only the most senior in command were invited to such a council, for it held many important decisions that needed to be made for the sake of the entire army. Often, direct words from the King were heard through a private messenger. It was truly an honor unbefitting of me.

I walked that night through that misty fog, still baffled at the amount of the trust that I had so quickly earned from Gideon. Even though it had been years that I fought in his service, the time flew as quickly as it came. Maybe it was due to the night we hunted, some time back. Maybe it was due to the talks that we shared on those rare occasions when we did, but every time we had one, I would remember it for the rest of my life. Maybe it was just because Gideon wished it, and if it were his wish, then I would not object to following it.

Finally, I saw Gideon's tent up ahead. Yet it was hard to make my way for the fog was very thick, the land also still new. We had recently changed our camp formations, just as practice to not allow enemies a chance to gain knowledge of how we set up our camps. This would cause further confusion to an enemy if he were to sneak in. I knew that it was Gideon's tent indeed, for I stared at it often enough that I knew the folds of every corner when it was put away. In fact, I knew of every wrinkle, every patch that mended it together. I had seen it from the outside on so many occasions that I could describe it, even without sight.

Gideon's tent stood that night, lit up with a few torches that were dimmed for the fog's dampness, which did not allow them to burn as brightly as on a clear night. Even so, with their dim light, they seemed to see all that came in front of it, like glowing monstrous eyes in the haze of the fog. I must say, even with all my knowledge of the tent, it almost seemed larger than I had remembered it. Then again, I was always so far away, never up this close. And as I came even closer, a dark figure opened the tent's entrance, allowing me to enter. Yet, even up so close, I could not make out which of the men it was, since the fog amplified the light closest to the source, and hid the face in a haze of mystified light.

Nonetheless, at last I entered Gideon's tent to see what I always wondered when I stood opposite of the camp staring in this direction, staring at the marvelous tent that held an even more marvelous person, a tent that I had only had dreamed of entering one day. Now I had entered it, and saw the inner chambers of Gideon's tent for the very first time.

Gideon stood hunched over a long, wooden table that rested on the ground. It had four elaborate but crooked, thick legs that looked like they could be undone at the top to be moved easily for travel. The table itself seemed rather sturdy but had many marks, scratches, nicks and notches, and scrapes on top of its surface. I presumed it functioned for whatever purpose it needed to, but tonight it was needed for something very important; a large stitched map of the King's lands was placed on top of it.

Gideon seemed more serious than usual, and some of the other men gathered around him debating something that I could not understand. They all stopped the moment I entered. At the sight of me, Gideon's face turned from serious demeanor to that of a light-hearted friend.

"Vlad!" he said with a bright smile. "I did not wish to disturb your night, but I am dire need of you. I am glad that you came."

I was shocked to see him speak of me like so openly like that. The other men must have felt the same shock, for he had not spoken to anyone in so jovial a manner, especially in the tension-filled atmosphere that they must have been working in.

"You looked surprised, my friend," he said as he rested a hand on my back and led me to the table. "Don't worry, we will catch you to speed." He parted his men, moving me to place near to him to view the map.

I was still taken back at the surprisingly bare tent. It was far different than I had expected. In fact, there was little difference between a tent like his and that of mine, except for the size.

He had his sword and armor set to one side, as well as his riding gear, since he liked to keep his horse Re unhindered at night so it felt free whenever it had the chance. On the other side, huddled out of the way, was bedding made of what seemed to be made of few sheets of blankets stitched together, more comfortable than the single sheet that most men used, but still, unfitting for a leader such as Gideon. On the edge of the tent, a simple wooden chair, and even that seemed like it could be easily dismantled. It was far from the sturdy throne I would have imagined him to have.

"I don't live the extravagant life that you probably imagined," Gideon laughed as he noticed my wandering eyes. "But that is a matter for another time. Let's get to what is at hand." Gideon shifted my focus to the table. "I need a trusted voice in this room."

Immediately after he spoke, one of the other men from our garrison resumed talking. "Yes, as I was saying, sir. The barbarians haven gotten rather bold. They have overrun the passage outpost and fortified themselves within it rather strongly. It is most likely that they are readying themselves for an all-out war against the King."

I remained rather quiet, still uneasy with the situation as the man continued.

"We have gotten reports that they have already sent out messengers and his generals with forces of their own recruiting across the lands. They are offering substantial amounts of coin to anyone that joins. If a large force like that continues to grow, it can pose quite a threat."

"Interesting. What do you think our choices are?" Gideon asked.

"I say we should go on the defense and retreat further inland. We are far out of the reach of any genuine support. It would be difficult to muster any real strength from here, even from the villages since there are so few laid about."

Gideon kept listening to the man, staring at the chart as if deep in thought.

"In the meantime, we should warn the King, and mount our forces and prepare for an attack against us in defensive position. The barbarians are vicious warriors and extremely strong. Their troops would take at least a few months to return, and that would give us enough time for the King to offer support, if need be."

Gideon thought about this for a while but he was busy with something else within his head, something he felt uneased about. This I could see very easily. What Gideon's commander said was very true, but I had not known

Gideon to ever retreat from a battle. It was surprising to hear that he would even consider such an action.

Suddenly Gideon turned his attention to me. "What do you say, Vlad?"

"I say that it is a good idea," I responded, not wanting to tread heavily where I did not belong.

"True, it is. In fact, it is a very good idea, and reasonable. But," Gideon paused and smiled at me, "what do you really think?"

I hesitated.

"Come on, Vlad," Gideon urged. "I invited you here to tell me what you thought, not what we wanted to hear. So tell me, what do you think?"

"It is unlike you," I said reluctantly.

"Exactly!" Gideon smiled, giving me a large pat on the back. "See, finally a man who understands me." Gideon took a few steps back and sat down in his wooden chair, his body relaxed to one side as if a burden had been eased off his shoulders. "And if you were me, Vlad, what would you do?"

I took my time before responding and examined the map. What stuck out to me was the distance of the figures from each other—that must have been what Gideon was thinking as well.

"Go on, Vlad," Gideon said with a smirk, knowing that I had come to the same conclusion.

"Well, you say that the barbarians sent out most of their generals with forces outwards. Then, he would be weaker at the center. If we waited, he would be able to recruit his forces, or bring them together to make him stronger. I would not wait for an assault. He is divided and that has weakened his numbers. That would give us the best advantage."

Everyone looked at me quietly.

"At least, that is my opinion," I said, worried that I spoke out of line.

Gideon started clapping. He stood up and smiled a giant smile. "You see, now that is more like something I would do," he said emphatically.

"But sir, we must inform the King before we take any action," the commander spoke in hesitation. "That is the nature of taking an action against another kingdom, even if it be in our lands."

Gideon sighed and went back to his chair. "Yes, we must."

"The castle is a long way. It would take some time, maybe a few weeks to reach at best," the commander continued.

"That it is." Gideon sighed again.

"It will be hard to convince the King to send forces this far out," the commander added.

Gideon said nothing but he thought about those words, for he did not wish to trouble the King.

"Sire, who will we send?"

And then, like always, Gideon said something quite unexpected. "I will send Vlad."

"Me?" I asked, as shocked as the men around me.

"Yes, you, Vlad. Do you not feel that you can accomplish such a task?" Gideon asked.

"No, I am just surprised that you would trust me in that regard, sir."

Gideon let out a deep sigh. He walked over to me, placed a hand on my shoulder, and looked me in the eye.

"Vlad, you have bled with me in battle, fought alongside my men, and saved many of them as well. Just now, you spoke as I would have. You are as capable as any of them, if not more. And since I must remain, I would trust no man to better speak for me, than you who understands me most."

"But I have not even seen a castle, yet alone entered one," I argued.

"And you had not picked up a sword before you fought on the battlefield, but you managed quite well," Gideon interjected. "So will you in this, I'm sure."

I stood, halted by his trust.

"Now, are there any more of my orders you wish to question, Vlad?" Gideon said with a playful smirk.

"No, of course not, sir. I am sorry."

With that, Gideon joined his hands together in a large clap. "It is settled then. Tomorrow morning, Vlad rides off. In the meantime, we make preparations."

Moments after that decision, Gideon showed the gathering of men out of his tent, leaving me alone with him. I was deeply conflicted about his decision and his full-hearted trust in me.

"What's the matter, Vlad?"

"There's something that I need to speak to you about."

"What troubles your mind, my good friend?" He eased back into his chair as he spoke.

"I am ashamed to say it."

Gideon quickly got up. Intrigued, he moved closer. "You can tell me, Vlad. There is trust between us and I will not let you down." He stood, listening intently.

"I do not know how to ride a horse," I finally said.

Gideon let out a hearty roar of laughter and patted me on the back. "You're right! I've never seen you on a horse, have I? You are always on foot or cart." He settled himself down into his chair as I stood embarrassed. "Don't worry, Vlad," he said. "I will give you the ablest horse we have. All you will have to do is sit and hang on," he smiled.

CHAPTER 25

Ride

WE RODE OVER THE GREEN HILLS, passed through the grey stony mountains, ran through the fields of yellow, dashed through the villages, and speeded through the forests. When we hit the open road, we sprinted and traveled great distances in gallops of pure brilliance. Time seemed dimmed to just a mere fraction of what it truly was.

I could never have imagined that I would be riding such a beast. Its muscled body trampled the ground below me as I sat on its back, and as Gideon said, I held on, held on for dear life as we set out for our destination, the castle of the King.

How easily we moved, as if we were not even touching the ground. For as soon as we did, we were already off of it. It filled my body with exhilaration, as if I was flying in the wind myself. I felt what the birds felt, as they flapped their wings and soared high through the lands, seeing all of life in an instance, just hoping to keep their eyes awake so they did not miss a second. I had never dreamt that one day I too would share that feeling of flight, but on that day I did.

It was then that I learnt why Gideon rode the way he rode. Why he traveled through the lands the way he did, and why he picked this horse of all great horses that must have come before him to be his own, as well as be his closest companion in battle. For this was a mystical creature that flew when it wanted, that shined in brilliance as blinding as the light, and set a standard that other horses wished to achieve. This was his horse, and its name was Re.

It was a perfected and precise creature and it used only what power was needed when it was necessary, even though it had it in spades. It was truly intelligent and thought through all its actions before they occurred, always in full control. In comparison, I was just a novice.

Not once did I feel its giant heartbeat become erratic, but instead, heard it steady as it held its rhythm, always exact with the hitting of its rear legs as it pushed off and moved forward. It knew what journey was ahead better than I. It knew the distance more than I did. It even knew the importance more than

I. And through it all, it planned accordingly. What a beautifully intelligent, marvelous beast.

I could see no other beast to be worthy of Gideon besides this, and I could not see any rider worthy of the beast besides Gideon. Yet, there I sat as a peasant in their kingdom of wonders, riding on the wings of their brilliance, getting a taste of what he told me that I could achieve one day. Now that I had that wondrous taste, I wanted more.

We rode through the unending days and nights, such long distances in a short time that I knew not how far we had come, or how long we traveled, but knew only that we were almost there.

And by now, I was sure that this beast was not earthly for it rode with a heart that was endless, and with energy beyond that of any creature on earth. It rode and rode; even before the beast could tire, I had to beckon it to stop so that I, myself, could rest. I had not slept a wink since we traveled, nor had I eaten, or even taken a sip of water. All I did was hold on as tightly to the reins as any man could, just as Gideon had told me to do so.

It was strange to be so exhausted when I all had done was sit while the horse ran, but it listened to my concerns and respected my wishes, as if it knew my words and spoke my language. Before I knew it, it trotted to a stop in a perfectly sized clearing, as if it knew of the place beforehand.

I jumped off the mighty beast and stretched my muscles and arms, which were sore from gripping Re's harness. Soon after, I set myself a camp and built a fire as we rested. I pulled out my rations and gave half to the horse and half to myself. The horse I fed first and the horse I gave water to first, for it was a faithful steed that worked hard for its master's command, which was not I.

Gideon had told me the name Re meant 'godly in nature', another name for a king. It seems that Gideon's steed was equal in name to my own, and I would treat him as such. Although, I found it quite funny. There we were, two kings who sat resting near a fire on a peaceful night on their way to see another King. So many kings in one simple land that there was bound to be turmoil at a moment's notice.

Re had stretched his front legs, sitting in front as if they were hands on a table, his rear legs shifted to one side. At moments, he waved his head, stretching out his powerful neck muscles before returning his gaze to the flame. Strange, but I did not feel alone with this horse. For truly, it was more than a mere horse, more human than most humans that I had known.

I admired Re for his strength and poise, for his obedience to something greater than himself—Gideon's cause. I could only hope to attain that same sort of brilliant devotion that he had, and for that I was both envious and thankful. I moved near him and ran my hand through his beautiful grey mane to show appreciation, as one does a pat on a back to a soldier, for Re was a soldier in our army, beast or not. He deserved it for all his hard work and devotion. He seemed to rather enjoy the gesture and rested his head on his front legs.

There we sat, together on that pure and brilliant night. How calm that moment was when we sat watching the fire sparkle, letting out embers that floated into the air before they vanished as if they were stars disappearing in the darkness of clouds. The place was at peace and we were truly alone. No town or village was in sight, and only trees in the distance gawked a dark, ominous eye.

It was then a chill ran over me, as I was reminded of my own journey searching for Gideon, walking through a forest such as the one I now saw. It also reminded me of the strange man that I could not picture in my mind, no matter how hard I tried. I know it was not the same forest, for I had even passed the very route I walked on. Nevertheless, this vision reminded me of the same and the darkness that came from within it. The same darkness in my dreams that sent a shiver down my spine.

I wondered why I dreamt of such things, strange dreams that left a bitter taste in my mouth and a stain on my soul, each time I dreamt of them, or even thought of them at moments like this. I wondered why I did not dream or think of pleasant things, pleasant places, pleasant people. Then in that moment of gloom, in that moment of worry, I thought of my Illyana.

Breathtakingly beautiful and delightfully familiar, how pristine of an image she left, even now. O my Illyana, even the thought of her brightened that very night and I no longer worried or thought about those gloomy trees. Instead, I stared at the heavenly stars above and saw her face within them. How well the stars reminded me of how the light shone in her eyes. Even when filled with sadness, which is the only image I had of her for I had never seen an un-sorrowful smile, thinking of her made me smile. There would be one day that I would see her again. That would be one of my dreams, alongside the many I had gotten in the time I spent with Gideon. That dream of Illyana though would be higher than any other on my ever-growing list of things to live for.

It was those thoughts that brought me fear and made me aware of my life, for the thought of living without seeing those dreams brought worry and concern. But those thoughts were not for the present, they were to be worried about in the future. For now, an important task was at hand, a task that Gideon had entrusted to me and me alone. A task that I needed to accomplish. By the week's end, I needed to reach the castle and speak with the King.

CHAPTER 26
The Power of a Name

WHEN I SAW THE SIGHT, I wanted to say what I felt was the majestic beauty of seeing man's creation taken to the extent of genius. I wanted to say that seeing the sturdy stone pillars, large brick mortared walls, and powerful iron gates were an achievement of the archaic times. I wanted to say that seeing the spectacle of a brilliant, lustrous, and grand castle that I had only dreamed of aspiring to see lived up to everything I had imagined, and in a way, it did. But I cannot say those things even though they were all true, for the feeling that one gets from those things differed greatly to the feeling I felt when I approached the gigantic walls of the castle's exterior that day.

Maybe it was the deed at hand, maybe it was the countless days of travel, maybe it was all those feelings that festered inside and made me uneasy to any notion of enjoyment, but it all took place, and its hold was overwhelming.

In front of me stood a massive iron gate that could withstand a giant's assault if it needed to, and a large stone wall with bricks that looked as if it took a hundred men to move just one, with iron locks and steel plating carpeting the walls as if they were as easy to acquire as dirt. All of that gave an eerie, mortifying nature to the already gloomy place, a place that was ridden with a stench and filth as if it had been left abandoned for centuries. However, abandoned, it was not.

My nerves stalled as I approached the outer gate, a gate that towered and felt as if shifted in the dense fog, like a titan awaiting its meal. Two torches that reminded me of the gloomy torchlight outside Gideon's tent shone through and guided me onto the bridge that hung over a low moat. The moat was too dark and murky to see how deep it went. As soon as I stepped onto the surface of the thick wooden bridge sitting on top of the moat, a man's voice boomed.

"Who goes there?"

My eyes traveled higher and higher until my neck was strained. I saw a number of guarded men peering over the wall, and on their sides, flickers of light glancing off steel points, which could only mean arrows sitting on drawn bows.

"I am Vlad," I yelled back. "I have come to see the King."

The response I had hoped for was for the gates to be raised and to be led inside, but I was only met with laughter, which only escalated my unease with the situation.

"Okay…Vlad," the guard responded, peering out enough so that I could finally see the smug, fat face of the soldier. "Vlad who? Vlad of where?" the fat-faced guard asked, arrogantly shaking his head.

I paused, for I did not know how to answer. I had not a last name, and the truth was I was at one time condemned to death, to be lit on a pyre, so I could not even say where I was from. I was as much as an orphan to the land as I was an intruder.

"I am Vlad," I said, as loud I could. "Vlad…the Impaler."

The guard looked at me strangely. "The…Imp—" and then burst into laughter before completing his sentence.

After settling himself down out of sight of me, the guard peered again over the top and spit into the moat next to me. Then he rested his forearms on the wall's ledge and responded.

"I say, you obviously have no rank, boy," he said in a most arrogant and condescending way, "You wear no seals or clothing of a knight, or even a messenger. You have only a name, and not even a last. Besides the marvelous steed that you rode in on, that I am sure you must have stolen, or taken from a richer man than yourself, what with you wearing that meager attire. You must be some sort of a peasant or prankster, or worse, a thief asking entry to the kingdom."

Then, the man looked at me rather sternly.

"What manner of ill-fated stupidity would allow a guard such as myself to offer you entrance into our glorious kingdom? One that you obviously do not belong to," he bolstered.

My previous self would have launched at this man, my sword drawn full of rage and hate, and sought vengeance for his insulting tone. No matter of height, no manner of walls, no amount of barriers would have held me at bay, as I would have stopped at nothing to behead him. No amount of arrows fired at me, or swords thrust into my breast would have stopped my vengeance. But on that day, I was not that man. I was no longer that monster. I was no longer that angry boar that I had hid inside. And no matter how much I wanted to be, especially after hearing his demeaning response, I was something else, something more. For I no longer represented myself, I represented something greater—the word of Gideon.

I had come this far, and Gideon's horse had made a travel that would have killed any other horse to accomplish in such short a time, all so that we could act in haste and civility. And for that I had to be wary of my actions, for any delay would suffer a heavy due to the entire army, but more importantly, a delay to Gideon. And as I thought through my dilemma, my patience was rewarded as I overheard the voice of another guard speaking.

"I know that horse, sire," he said to the arrogant guard who mocked my presence.

"Yes, what poor man's horse is this?" The guard smirked at me and sat his fat face on his forearms. "Tell me so that I may return his horse to him once I dispatch this fool."

"Sir, that horse cannot be mistaken," the man said with worry in his voice. "That is the horse of General Gideon, sir."

Following those words was a wicked silence, a display of concern so frightening that even I felt the tension from this distance. Although at relative safety, mounted high on that wall, and behind their impenetrable walled defense, they felt very much threatened and weak.

"Are you sure?" I heard him ask the guard in a whimpered and frightened voice.

"Absolute assurance, sir," the other guard responded, gulping down air himself.

The fat-faced guard proceeded to clear his throat. He peered over the wall and stared back at me, trying to hide the shock he had just acquired, but his widened eyes and the stuttering of his next words easily betrayed him.

"My humblest a...a...apologies to the...the General...and you, sir," he frantically said and then bowed a most humbling bow, trying to hide his ignorance in unwelcomed formality. "It... it was not my intention to insult you, or the... the General's honor." Before he could lower himself any lower, he pleaded. "Please! I...I beg you not tell him of my transgression."

"Or ours, sir," the man next to him shouted.

An instant later, the winches roared alive and the massive iron bars that had held the way shut raised to let me through.

I was fortunate, I thought, for if I had not met Gideon, no manner or number of words that I could have spoken would have opened those gates, but a mere thought of a man such as Gideon raised the jaws of prosperity open and allowed me to enter the King's protected domain. What power Gideon truly held over the kingdom I had no idea.

CHAPTER 27

King of Kings

ONCE INSIDE THE MAIN GATES OF THE KINGDOM, I made my way past the three massive stoned walls that separated three types of lands, each splitting up the giant regions into classes of people. The first must have been the lowest class, which lived in the outskirts of the town. They seemed to have little in terms of belongings, the buildings shabby and empty, and the area was mainly farmland. Past the second wall must have been the middle class; the houses were nicer and I could smell the baked goods in the air. The third seemed the noble's territory, the rich, those of proper upbringings far from the likes of mine. They were the closest to the castle and had nice lavish homes of the likes that I had never seen. Nevertheless, even they had a wall separating them and the castle itself. It seemed the King had his concerns of his own people as much as of the enemy. Yet each time I walked, a bridge dropped and the gate opened and let me through as I made my way.

I made my way onto the devil's bridge that was laid across a massive moat. Pointed spears stood submerged, seemingly waving as the ripples from the wind caused the reflection to shift. Beyond that, I made my way past the entrance of the castle, where heavily guarded men stood at every footstep and gripped their hilts tightly in their hands as I made my way near. Finally, after all of that safeguard, after all that protection, after all the nuisance of security, I entered the castle. A castle that I had only dreamed of seeing one day.

The atmosphere was nothing that I had expected from a castle. It wasn't full of joy and hope, warmth and beauty. No, it was stark and cold, and the tension inside was so thick that I could feel it heavy in the air, as much as I felt it at the gate. It made me wary of every movement I took, but I was not bothered. I walked inside freely and explored the castle, since no direction was given to me and the men stood in silence.

I felt as if I was nothing more than a ghost in the court of the King. I was watched with every motion of the eye, but I was undisturbed by all. I was allowed to travel where I pleased, but always felt a hint of fear from the soldiers, as if at any moment I was to make a rash action and assault them.

And if I were to, it seemed they would not know what to do, or how to react. And those times, when I went into those rooms where there was no one, and I was alone, I still felt eyes from the walls, eyes hidden from scent. The castle had constant eyes, watching my every move even when I made none.

I felt an unnatural discontent to be surrounded by so many men born of iron and perfected into weapons of war who still feared my actions, when I was clearly outmatched. It was a wonder that I could invoke this reaction, but the truth must have been that it was not I that caused such concern; it was Gideon who spoke through me, and made me a vessel of his power. He made me a vessel that could walk from room to room in the most prestigious and renowned chambers of the King's court. All the while unaffected, unbothered, unhindered by any man to stand in my way, or at least so I thought.

"That is as far as you go," a voice hailed from the hallway.

I had entered the courtroom, where all decisions of any importance were to be made. Yet no man sat on the glorious throne in front, which rested on a raised platform with two unnerved, full-plated guards standing at attention. Instead of the King, a strange man came from the edges of the room and made his way to the center.

He was a lanky, elderly man, with robes of the finest blue silk that draped so elegantly off his frame that they seemed to be waves of the ocean, and hovered over the ground as he walked. His eyes were dark and sunken into his head, but as round and large as an owl's. It felt as if they saw all that occurred throughout the lands. Maybe those eyes were the ones I felt watching me, but he made no motion to even look at me. His entire face had keen features that converged to sharp points, especially on his nose, as if he once had a beak. His hands were larger than normal and due to his thin frame they were unnatural and sharply pointed forward when he grasped them together. Although wrinkled with age, I felt as if those hands had enough power to strangle a large man.

This was the man that stopped in front of me, his body turned to the side, not acknowledging my presence in the slightest bit, as if I was standing not in the path I was, but on the other side. I did not want to object or be rude, so I did as the voice commanded and halted my exploration of the castle.

"I was sent here by Gideon himself," I said, hoping to invoke that same sense of terror and gain the man's attention. The same terror I had felt in all the others at the mere thought of Gideon.

However, that same feeling of terror did not come. Not from this man. In fact, he did not even move his head towards me, or raise an eye. He stood solid and unmoving, so much that I felt I was being a bother to his deep thoughts.

Could this be the King himself? I wondered, but this man had no guards accompanying him. He had no royal attire that I thought would befit a king.

He was a man, and dressed strangely, more so than I had seen anyone else in my times.

"I have important information and was sent here to speak to the King," I explained further.

Finally, the man introduced himself. "I am the messenger of the King. I shall listen to your wish and deliver your message."

Still, the strange man did not even turn his head to look in my direction.

"I will not speak to anyone else besides the King himself," I said, "for that is the importance of the message that I bring, and that was what I was commanded to do."

"I am the messenger of the King. I shall listen to your wish and deliver your message," the man repeated, again without turning to glance at me.

"I must..."

Before I could fully object, the man turned his full body so sharply and quickly that I felt the air in the room shift, as if he was a chess piece that was just moved into position ready to strike. This man was no pawn, but he was no king either; he was something far more powerful, as if he was the board himself. Finally, he looked at me, although then I wish he hadn't. For his gaze commanded much power, enough that the two men guarding the throne felt at ease and I in turn felt the way they must have before.

I had not seen this sense of strength from anyone besides Gideon, but this man had it in unnerving abundance, and I felt as if it drained me of my energy. I felt merely a puppet of masters who worked on levels beyond my own, pulling strings to work an act that I had no control over. Still, for the sake of Gideon, I needed to remain strong. With that thought, I mustered my strength back to speak again and hold my ground.

"I must speak to the King," I said, determined not to fail.

The strange man raised his head and studied me with a studious eye. Then he took a controlled deep breath, and spoke in the pauses between his breaths without any emotion, as if he was reciting from a book. "You are unborn of right, unborn of truth and unborn of any prestige. You will never see the King yourself. You have done well and have come far and that is as far as any man has come before you," he spoke with such conviction that I had no ability left but to listen.

"So I assure you, what task you were asked to do, you have committed, and your quest is to be marked complete."

Again he paused as I fully absorbed what he said, and as soon as I did, he continued once again.

"But I tell you now that you must not insist, for the quest you have come for will not venture any further from this spot," he looked at me sternly, "and will only harbor complete failure if you do not comply. So without any further due, tell me what message you wish to deliver, and I shall do as you were asked. I will take it to the King," he said calmly. "That I promise you, even though a promise I am at no liberty to even offer to one that was birthed as you."

Did this man truly know who I was, where I came from? I wondered. How? He had spoken to me with such certainty that I dared not question his words, but took them to heart. Although he mocked my birth and insulted me with his actions, which only would be met with my refusal, there was much at stake. I could not fail Gideon in this task.

So I took what I was offered by the strange man. I gave the message of the invading army of barbarians that came into the King's lands. I told of Gideon's wishes and requests as he had so carefully instructed me to do so. I told him the outcome of the projected turbulent future that Gideon proposed if no action was to be taken. I told him all the words that Gideon spoke to me, words that I had repeated over and over on my journey so that I had them fully memorized and would be certain to be completely accurate.

I told him all that was asked of me and then, I told him more. It was as if the words I had within had leaked out without my permission, coming out as blatantly and uncontrollably as anything I had ever done. All the while, the man listened intently to all I had to say, without any reaction or even the move of a wrinkle on his weathered face. He took in all I had to give and then straightened his posture and moved out of the room, in what I could only presume was to deliver the message.

Afterwards, I waited unmoving. I stood in that room, impatient and anxious but unmoving, for I no longer had the strength to do so. I waited for him to return, and he delivered a message of his own, a message I did not want to hear. A message that I had to take back to Gideon, who had put his trust and hope in me. A message that could only harbor disappointment, but still, a message I had to deliver without delay.

CHAPTER 28

Returned

THE RIDE BACK WAS A TREACHEROUS ONE. The road had become barbarous. The air had become blistering, and even seemed as strained as the heavy burden that I had on my shoulders. So much staleness and bitterness was in the air, that it felt as if it took twice as long to head back than it did forward. It was as if the life had been sucked out of me by the words of that strange man.

When I finally arrived at the camp it appeared as if all was well, but my presence seemed to dull that spirit. The glow that surrounded the place normally was converted into a sanctum of a bothered mind, imprisoned by my message. The rustling of the leaves sounded as the rattling of a collared chain. What were just shadows of trees on the green grass of the hills, seemed like a bars on a cage that trapped me in a destiny decided by another. Even the cloudy sky seemed as a ceiling about to cave in. Everything seemed to deject one's psyche and made the task even harder to carry out as I made the long slow march up the hill to Gideon's tent, weighted down by carrying the unwanted news.

As I entered I saw Gideon, standing eager for the news from the castle. He was just as eager to see me as well, as I was greeted with a vibrant smile.

"Good to see you, Vlad. I was wondering about your return. I hope that Re took good care of you."

His joyous nature did not make the chore any easier, for I had never wished to displease him, even if it were not my fault.

"Yes, Re was beyond anything I could imagine," I responded.

"I tell you, I have searched through all the lands, and he is one of a kind. A rare breed of horse that never tires and never strays, loyal to the core," Gideon said as he stood over his table, "but that is an amazing story in its own right. I will tell you someday. For now, we have much more pressing matters at hand. Tell me, Vlad, what of the King?"

He was right. Even though I spent the entire trip back agonizing over how I would deliver the message, I still had not found a way to do it properly, but

I could not delay. The time spent on the trip was long and soon our options would be even more limited, so I did as I was instructed by the lanky old man. I told Gideon what he had said, what he had allowed, and what he did not allow. I spoke the words as if the man spoke them himself from within me. I spoke as Gideon listened, silently and keenly.

After the long message was delivered, there was an even longer silence before Gideon spoke.

"It was as I thought," he finally said, rubbing his temples in concern.

There was a moment where Gideon looked deep in contemplation of something that I would not understand, like many of his thoughts. He was always in his mind, unravelling layers of some mystery, always seeing things without the confines of reality, as if he saw another world than we did.

"I'm sorry that I was not able to deliver the message to the King," I said.

Gideon waved off the apology, "No matter, the message was delivered." He moved to his single chair and settled himself down, afflicted with unsettling thoughts.

"The man you met is called Myrddin, the closest and most trusted advisor to the King. So well trusted that he commanded the kingdom himself. For no action is taken, no word is known, no path is set without the guidance from him, which the King follows with all his heart. He is a complexity that I cannot decipher, for no one has spoken to the King directly in recent times, and Myrddin has delivered all words to and from."

"Yes, he was very strange. I felt as if he was unnatural of man," I said, sitting on one of the sacks of rice that lay on the side of the tent.

"Yes, that he is. They say he is a seer of sorts. One that has a forecast of the future. The King puts far too much trust in him, I fear."

"If he can do what they say he can do, see the future. Then, does that not mean that his answers are always correct?"

"No, not necessarily. His visions are said to come in pieces and in no particular order. It is like reading a book where you know the ending but you do not know what or how you got there. His dreams are part of the larger puzzle that is life, pieces that are constantly changing. It would take a man's whole life to decipher just one vision, but Myrddin is adept and has done it a few times already. He has said and saw things that no man knew was coming and they ended up being true."

"And the times he was wrong?"

"Those times have ended in great tragedy. I fear this is one of those times," Gideon said, deeply concerned and conflicted. "He relies too much on his visions and not the truth at hand. It will harm the kingdom if no action is taken."

Gideon took a moment. "Nonetheless, it is a remarkable power. I must admit, I have often wondered what I would do with such ability if I had one at my disposal." Gideon took a long, unsettling pause before he recovered his thoughts. "But then again, that is not the here and the now."

"So what will we do now?"

Gideon got up rather abruptly and beamed. "What we have always done, my dear Vlad. Protect the kingdom."

"But the advisor said no action was to be taken against the barbarians. He said for us to wait for the King's men to arrive from their current mission's end so they can aid and guarantee a victory."

"Yes, and it would take months for them to gather, and even more to arrive. Vlad, if I did that," Gideon said, discontent by the advisor's warning, "then who would protect the kingdom from the barbarian's wrath while we waited, doing nothing? The people would suffer, Vlad. The barbarians have already invaded. There is no opposition to them and if they continue, they would overrun the lands. Where is the sense in that?"

Gideon shook his head in agitation. "The advisor is a fool if he thinks it so simple. A guarantee?" Gideon scoffed and turned to me with a most sincere, troubled stare.

"If I know one thing, Vlad, it is that in war, there is no guarantee of victory, just odds. But one must fight for what is right regardless of how difficult the odds are. That is the right thing to do."

Gideon walked over to his sword and shield that held his knightly crest, which were two golden trumpets over a roaring lion's head, with a red setting sun behind. He stared at the image deeply, for it meant much to him and everything he had put on the line for the King.

"I made a pledge to the King, Vlad. And that pledge was to do everything that I could to protect the kingdom and its lands. If I do not follow that now, then I would have to break that pledge. That is the most important pledge a knight can make, one not for one's self but one for the greater kingdom. I cannot allow that pledge to be broken, Vlad." Gideon held the hilt of his sword as if was reaffirming that vow and then turned to look over to me.

"We will protect the kingdom even if the kingdom does not wish to be protected, Vlad," he said, staring at his sword. "That is our duty. That is what makes us knights."

He had the same reassurance in his eyes as he always did when he made up his mind, a mind that was strong as steel and set in motion an enlightened spirit of all those around and set their minds at ease, mine as well. It was the look that I have gotten to know all too well and one that I cherish most.

Had I known that would be one of the last nights I would see that look on his face, I would have endeared it to my heart with much more detail and thought than I had done. For the decision we made that night set into motion a series of events that set us to our final path of our destiny, a path no man should ever take if he truly knew what lay in store, what sacrifices that were to be made. And just a few weeks later, we were in battle once again.

A Message from Vlad

"

War can be best described as chaos. It is a fire that cannot

be controlled. It rages, and consumes all those within it.

Although it lingers with light as its disguise, it is a light with

a most sinister and dark intent. Its purpose only revealed

by the escaping darkness of smoke that attempts to cover the

devastation it causes as it embarks on its most malicious deeds.

That is the same fundamental of war, to hide the true nature of

attack by covering it in a blanket of darkened shame. Yet, like

fire, it is unable to be controlled and affects all those within,

possessing them in agonizing torment. And if fire be the greatest

uncontrollable force that nature can possess, then war is the

greatest uncontrollable force that man can possess.

"

~Vlad

CHAPTER 29

A Game of Death

THE AIR FELT EMPTY, windless, colorless, tasteless. No smell, no odor was produced from it, leaving a sense of cleanliness that wiped away the long, harsh sweat of the soldiering march. The march led us to see valleys ahead sprawled out with evergreen. A green that was bare, but sprouted with the dream of life, bare and fertile, steady and wondrous, an open stretch of land that would be rich for farming, rich for men to flourish, rich for men to live, but that was not the destiny of this land.

No, this land was destined for death. Life would be the furthest thing from what this land would see today. All the plans of this site being a place of sustenance and a rich life set forth by the gods would be wiped clean from the table, and a new plan emerged, one built by man. A plan that would break not only the ground of the field, but the bodies of men to create it.

That was the plight that this land would face, one that even the clouds knew. They scurried away from the skies, leaving a stark, clear sky, clear enough for the Heavens to witness from above. And when they watched, they would see us standing on the field, gathered in numbers of thousands, waiting, ready to war.

Gideon's red banners were raised throughout the army, high above for all to see. It was the only sparkle of red in the mass of brown, black, and grey armored men that had gathered. Red filaments appeared like cuts on the dark body of the army, that would be soon accompanied by so many more. They waited so patiently, so ready to wage a war that would bring forth wondrous doom. Each man was ready to face his doom, for each man knew the outcome when they joined. They left their villages as Gideon walked through them. They ran away from their campsites as Gideon walked past them. They were freed from their enslavement when Gideon took up the sword to free them. Men gathered, from love, kindness, and the gentlest heart, to take part in the most un-gentlest path. They were willing, and they were ready.

When Gideon traveled, his legend followed him as much as his men, and those villagers left because they wished to be part of his dream. They knew that they would be immortal in his legacy that would surely reign one day, that would be told to children going to bed and fill their dreams at night. Those men now stood behind us. We prepared and waited, standing on a hill, looking towards the other side and waiting for death to show itself.

Gideon had eyed the battlefield all night, stood watch and had not slept a wink for he knew this day was to come. He wanted to be melded to his surroundings as much as the grass and the trees were to the field. I also had not slept, for I eyed Gideon the entire night, stood and watched as his protector, for I wanted to be melded into his world, as much as his dream that he brought into reality.

"Do you sense it, Vlad?" Gideon asked me, not turning his head, which was locked on the green hills and clear blue skies. "The flavor of the land."

"Nothing. Just the spring air," I said.

Gideon smiled. "Yes. The smell of nothing. The feel of nothing. It is a beautiful thing to be so pure, so clean and unspoiled."

Gideon leaned back, lifted his chin into the air and took a deep breath.

"It is the last time before this site becomes unholied by the spilling of blood and the raiding of spirits that take away its absolute innocence. Its unspoiled virginity. It is an aura, a fragrance that must be appreciated, Vlad." Gideon looked toward me. "It is an essence that must be acknowledged for its impending sacrifice."

I had not heard him speak so cryptic during the preparations of war, for this was the time that he shined most. The fire within him burned so bright, it would be like staring into the sun. This was the time that Gideon rose like a lion, like the one on his banner, and roared louder than the two golden trumpets that crossed over it, which stood as his crest. This was Gideon's time to ignite that fire, but instead he remained calm, collected, and dim to the eye, as if something was keeping him from shining as bright as he normally did.

"Nothing has more significance until you are about to lose it, Vlad," he continued. "From an earthly possession or a mortal soul, life has little meaning until it is at stake. For when you have nothing to lose, then you have nothing to gain. A warrior knows this all too well."

I knew of what Gideon spoke. I had not given it much thought since the time I was roped to a stake and prepared to be burned. I too had smelled the river that day. I too had seen the skies and the clouds. I too appreciated all the things that the land had to offer for it was my last day, and I was so close to death.

Yet I wondered why Gideon would see this day as that above all else. Gideon was a master of war and he had seen so many battles; I could not dare dream this to be his last.

"A warrior feels every bit more alive when he is at war than any mortal who spends his entire life in labor," Gideon said as he brushed Re's mane, who gladly shook his head in joyous response. "A warrior knows what he has to sacrifice in order to feel that life, knows that he has to risk a certain death. A warrior knows what is at stake, always."

Gideon returned his gaze to the field, the massive lush field that seemed more alive now than ever before. Suddenly, a black spot sprouted on the green-hilled land, and it darted towards us. It was what Gideon so patiently waited for, what he was searching for; our scout had returned.

The man came barreling down, in sweat and concern, his face contorted with fear until he stopped in front of us, breathing heavily and giving his report in breathy spurts. The barbarian army was near, and it massed in the thousands like us.

Gideon nodded, unyielding, and eased the concern of the rider, who he then sent back to stand with the archers. War was to come and it was fast approaching.

This was always a marvelous time for me, the moment before. I had been a changed man since my inception into this new world, since Gideon took me away from death and opened the door of humanity to me. And from that night, from being such a monster, from days, months, and years back, I had grown and learned, become wiser and smarter, and became in control.

Yet, inside, I was still a beast on the field, just more skilled, more versatile, more assured. In all senses, deep within, I was still that raging, angry boar, although my shame kept it at bay. In moments like this, it tried to claw its way to the surface, and I could feel the cage door bulging out, ready to break open. I could feel its nails digging into my soul, scraping against my mind, trying to pry the bars loose that kept it. The more it did, the more I craved the battlefield. Yet as much as I felt that craving of battle, I felt an incredible worry as well.

It was a strange feeling to be alongside Gideon in these times, for every day up 'til my return from speaking with the King's messenger, he had been in deep thought. He moved about in front of troops, spending many moments in silence. He was not the cheery self that he was during usual times. It was as if his mind had left his body; it was a shell that wandered around the campgrounds completing the menial tasks that needed to be done, but the thought behind them, the wonderment, the spirit that was there, that spirit, that bright soul was gone.

Was he contemplating a great strategy, as he had always done? I had seen him in deep focus before, but this was something different, something uncanny. It left a bitter taste on the tongue; my actions needed to be cautious and more controlled, for I failed in reaching the King the way I wanted. From that moment on, I did not wish to fail him again.

* * *

Gideon raised his hand high into the air. In response, a soldier came forward and sounded the trumpet, signaling the army to be on guard, to set their blades in preparation, to ready their feet, and steady themselves for the oncoming war. Then, Gideon paused while he eyed the field once again, his eyes vacant. He stared at an empty hill as if he saw something fearful.

I looked, but I saw nothing.

"I rather like the sound of the trumpet," I said, trying to ease the tension that I believed to be on Gideon's mind. "A beautiful sound to welcome us into battle."

A moment passed as Gideon stared at that empty sight, and then finally moved his vision to the rest of the land ahead, pristine and still undamaged by the ongoings of man.

"Do you truly believe it to be a beautiful sound?" he asked calmly.

I did not respond, for in truth, it made no difference to me. I fed off the sounds of battle, whether it be drums, the clanging of swords, or a maiden's harp. It mattered not where the sound originated from, or what signaled its start. The only music I truly enjoyed was war.

That is what drove my blade in battle, but what drove me forward in all else and even to participate in battle was this man next to me—his thoughts, his dream, his goals, his desire, and now they were in plight. Yet, I could not ease his burden, all I could do was stand by his side, and I could not tell him that.

"I do not see it as such," Gideon continued after sensing my reluctance. He looked towards his own banner and continued. "I see the trumpet for what it is. It is a terrifying sound, for the trumpet is the sound of death. A herald of what destruction is to come. Much like lightning follows thunder, so does death follow the trumpet."

Gideon moved his eyes back to the empty hill point where he saw that invisible danger, seemingly searching for something. "That is why I carry it as my symbol," he said, "for when you hear its call, it is certain that death is around the corner, and that it will soon greet you."

I had always wondered what the symbolism of the trumpet was on his banner. I had thought the significance to be of glory and of royalty, and nothing more. It was one of many symbols used for that trivial purpose, to be put on flags, on seals, on painted uniforms that were to be tattered in the fields later. I had no idea what the true purpose was, or what it meant to the men who followed underneath it. I should have known better since I knew Gideon; there was no action he took without a purpose, every move was coordinated, calculated and precisely put on the board.

"It brings fear to man, and ushers in an unwashable stain." He paused and stared at me. "I know you do not feel the same, Vlad. Although all this time has passed, the call of blood and death still lives inside you, I am certain. But you are not alone, in a way it lives in all of us. Death can be a wondrous thing. Death can be beautiful; the clench of it near you, wandering around us, viewing our actions and taking its course. It is the way of the soldier, but we should never forget that death is still very frightening. It is a vengeful beast that is ever powerful and always hungry and it will consume all that do not expect it."

"Yes, I know of its hold on people. It is strange, I have never truly feared death. I have always felt near to it, comfortable in its presence."

"The men would not agree with you, Vlad." He glanced over his shoulder at his readied army, standing in frightful anticipation of the battle. "And you are right. I can see that you are very fond of death," he said as he examined me.

My demeanor was calm on the outside, but inside I was sprawling with activity. My heart was racing—not in fear, but in sheer joyous excitement. It was obvious to him what I truly felt even if I hid it with my actions, just as his current quandary was clear to me.

A nice calming air passed over the land, a gentle breeze that took away our worries for a brief moment. In that small moment, rays of sun pierced our thoughts and the wave of luscious of green sent scents of spring towards us. In response, we all felt a little less burdened.

"To tell you the truth, Vlad," Gideon began, enjoying the brief moment, "I do not value death as much as you, my friend." He closed his eyes, letting the memories of the breeze fill him again. "Instead, I wish for peace. It is peace that I fight for. It is peace that I hope to attain from all these battles, all this bloodshed, all this rage, war, and death, even if it costs me thousands of lives," he quickly opened his eyes as if he saw something fearful in his mind's eye, "…which it does."

"But those deaths have meaning." He turned to look at me and did not let his gaze go; he spoke as if he was trying to convince me as well as himself. "They are a payment, one that will pave the way for millions thereafter."

He unbuckled his sword from its straps and pulled it from its sheath as if with some sort of unworldly intuition. His sword gleamed in the sunlight and afterwards, the ever-dawning sound of war from the barbarian's march was heard.

"It is a payment that the world asks for when it needs to change. A payment that only the most willed man could bring to light and understand."

Moments later, I made out the first signs of the monstrous opposing army, which revealed itself coming over the green hill.

"It is a payment by blood, Vlad. A payment that I am willing to pay," Gideon said as the opposing army raised their banner as high as ours, with a following just as great, armed, ready, and determined as we were.

"And a payment that is most harsh, but a payment that will lead us into the future." Gideon returned his gaze to the opposing army. They readied their weapons, set forth their front lines, and came forward, ready to fight an endless assault.

"A payment that I am willing to pay," Gideon said as he reared up his horse, and held up his sword to the heavens. Our trumpets blew in response, and he shouted his battle cry as the heavens listened in silent wonder. Then, he rode full force towards the opposing army.

He rode like the wind, carving a path in the newly touched grounds. He was ready to make his dream a reality, ready to pay all costs with blood, ready to wager his life, and so did we all. We followed Gideon into the heat of battle like we had done many times before, in many places before, and many situations before, and we placed the same bet, ready once again, to play the game of death.

CHAPTER 30
The Demons We Create

"

I am sure you have heard of battle before, have heard of actions

taken before, have maybe even seen a battle in your mind.

However, that is not battle; that is a lie. A battle does not

involve just action, a sword thrust, or an axe swinging from

one being to another. A battle involves all that is with war, all

actions before, all actions after, all actions, all ideas, all thoughts

and fears. Because after you have warred, true war, there is no

end of the battle, for it rages within you unending, and you

are doomed for eternity to live the battle over and over again

whether you wage it in your mind or in your soul. Each time

you wage this unending war, something different occurs, and

that difference is something that you always feel remorse for. The

only thing that occurs from war, is regret.

"

I HAVE NO OTHER WORDS to describe it to you but gruesome and hollow, for that was the battle we fought. That battle was the toughest one I had ever survived. Yet we felt no glory or fulfillment. They had hit our numbers hard and many of our brethren had fallen victim to the enemies' sword. That was the way it was supposed to be. The life of the sword, to live and die by it, all on a game of chance. That was the game we played that day, and no matter how well we organized, strategized, used our skills to weigh the odds in our favor, there was still a price to be paid. There were still lives put on the table. Souls staked before the war even began, destined to be lost, and Gideon knew this all too well.

He knew what this battle would truly cost us, and what toll it would take on us, and now I understood why he mentioned what he did beforehand. He spoke of what he was willing to do, what was necessary for progress, all to make me understand that when this time was to come, that I would know why. Now that it has, I hate the fact that I actually understood.

Before the battle, Gideon had stared into the fields as if something watched us. His eyes were in terror of its awesome might. I think he knew that a deal with the devil was needed to win the war. A deal that set the reaper loose on the lands, and now I know, a deal was indeed struck. In payment, Gideon lay the bodies of men on the field, from both sides, allowing them to gather before the great reaper until it had its fill. For surely it was hungry and had an abyss-like appetite, for the slaughter that occurred there must have meant it had truly enjoyed its feast.

Although Gideon was distraught, ridden with guilt, and it toiled heavily on his mind, as would the act on any decent, sane man, Gideon showed one thing clearly. He showed that he would do what must be done no matter the cost, in order to benefit a better world. He showed that he was a man that did not cower down, even in the face of death. Against overwhelming odds, he stood tall in order to do what was right. He showed that he would risk it all, his life, his men, even his soul for his purpose. And as he said, he showed that the cost was great and he was willing to pay its price in full, and he had.

He was a man that I would follow to the ends of the earth, for I believed that was the deed of an honorable man. It may not seem so to many, but it was. For I, as he hoped, actually understood that cost.

It is a fool's thought to think no reward can be gained without any sacrifice. It is a fool's thought to think no glory could be attained without any bloodshed. It is fool's thought to think that there can be peace without war. A man like him was no fool. No, he was a sage.

A sage who knew of the dilemma and did what he said he would do. He was a man of his word. He would walk a path to righteousness even if it was going to be made of blood and bones, which it was. And with each life, with each piece of dying flesh, he stepped forward, ready to pay any sacrifice. And like he, I was prepared to do that as well.

I unsheathed my sword once again to the job that was at hand. For the war was over, and the fighting done, the battle even won, but the end had not arrived yet. For there was a final motion that was at hand, that comes with any battle, with any war, which was to examine every fallen body on the battlefield and put a blade through each and every one.

This was a dreaded act that was given out. In normal times, it was given to a squad of men to accomplish, usually picked at random or chosen by straw from a number of men with the deepest stomachs, and toughest hearts, for this was a gruesome act, a spineless deed, a sinister action. Still, it needed to be done.

Yet this was no normal time, for the battle had disheartened every warrior. I volunteered to take this task alone, to carry this burden on my shoulders so that the men could ease some of theirs.

It was now my responsibility to secure the field, to secure the dead, to make sure that the fallen were indeed fallen, and no one else would aid me in this strife. The men had seen enough bloodshed, enough misery, enough pain and gore for one day—any more and they would break. I would let no man hinder the footsteps of Gideon, no man question his action, no man to stand not at their strongest in his wake, even if it cost me my soul.

I see why Gideon truly took in the beauty of this once virgin land. It was strange how it had so quickly changed, from the rich, clear green fields to the one I stood now. Even the air had turned heavy, with a rich, musty smell. It must have been the sudden cold shifting over the lands that created an afternoon mist that took hold of the area and mixed itself with the smells of blood, steel, sweat, tears, human remains, and dirt all together. So thick was the stench that it tingled the tongue and gave it that iron-like flavor, which was evidently from all the blood that was scattered on the field. It would be prudent to say that it was a very familiar smell but this was stronger than anything I could have imagined, for the loss on both sides was so great that it brought victory, familiarity, and pain all at once.

I walked that day, through the aftermath of the bloody battle, accompanied by the sounds of ravens, which had swooped down, amassed in hundreds, and plucked at the dead bodies below as they tore into the flesh. I could hear the crunching sound of my own footsteps walking through the field, a field of broken bones and broken dreams, covered with tattered and mangled bodies as far as the eye could see in the ever-thickening fog.

Each step I took only revealed more horror, a visage of all those massed in one grave, piled on top of each other, discarded without thought, one after the other. Brother and enemy lay side by side in the harmony of death and a cauldron of dismay. Some arms embraced each other, some arms were cut off, some still clung to their weapons and shields as if it were their protection from the forces that would come after.

I wondered then what it would mean to truly die like these men did. I had thought it peaceful, even pleasurable perhaps. The serenity of it was what allured me, but the men I saw did not have a peaceful image. They were twisted in wretched pain, and their eyes were struck frozen in a state of fear witnessing the heavens above, but was it truly heaven they saw the moments before? For heaven would deem a sense of prosperity and happiness, this was something else. Was it hell? Or something that reached from far below?

I wondered, O how I wondered, but the time to think was not now. I did not want to dwell, for it would weaken my already shaking resolve. No, a job was at hand, and a deed that must be done, and I had taken on the responsibility of my own accord. Now, as with all men who walked the path I walked, I would have to accept that inevitable outcome, and face the demons—even if I was the one to create them.

CHAPTER 31

Tears of the Fallen

"

If you thought it as easy as walking away with a simple thought

of a readied blade to clear the field, then you are mistaken, for

the act continues to a depth that is hard to hold in true sight.

For what I will speak now will be quite gruesome, will be quite

detailed and hold into account of what had happened on that

dreadful night, when I proceeded to clear the field. The sun was

away, the skies were grey, the air was drenched red with blood.

I will be the diviner of death about to engage in a foreplay of

dementedness, and what you will read will not be pleasant.

"

I PLUNGED THE TIP OF MY BLADE INTO THE FIRST BODY. The sharpened steel went into the light colored brown, passing the fibers of the neck and into the red muscles underneath until it slid across bone, through the meat, through more of the flesh, and out into the bloodied, muddied ground beyond. That was the first death at the blade assigned for this task. But it was not the only location I could strike, for the neck was covered at many times, and I would have to bear through much to get that blow. No, I had to take a quicker route at times, but far more unpleasant.

On those occasions where the neck was not visible and the heart was hidden behind a breast of armor, I went through the only visible part to any man looking onto the field—the eye.

I rested the tip of my blade right in front of the eye. Lifeless and soulless they were, but they stared at me the same. They looked and I looked, and even though I knew the men to be dead, I felt them watch me.

O, how they watched. I could not forget those eyes. Blue, green, grey, brown, each as distinctly individual as their face. There were all sorts of hinted colors inside, a vibrancy of yellows, oranges, purples, and colors of the seas and the skies, but they all stood pale in comparison to that of the utter darkness that stared at me from the middle. That abyss-like hole that looked upon me and would not stop. It was that as if I felt the dark come from within those eyes and into my own.

I drove my blade straight through in order to end that darkened stare, pushing against the eye until it bulged and expanded and strangely would not pierce without pressure. Suddenly, it embraced the tip and let it slice through. It was an effective and efficient way to kill, but it was frighteningly horrid in its action. For when the blade went into the eye, it did not just die. No, it cried.

Whence the blade entered, it let out all the liquids inside, and they were mostly clear. The fears and tears that followed filled me with disgust and sorrow, and I felt as if it could still feel my blade. And it would not stop, it cried as I went through the socket and into the skull and through the brain until I could feel it stop, but that was not the ground that I felt. Unlike the neck, the head was different—the pressure I felt was the inside of the skull. And in every eye that I pierced, there was also pressure on my heart because every empty stare teemed with life while I took it from them.

I did this to every man on the field. Every man that was felled, I took my blade to and it was strange. For I knew them to be dead, but I felt that I killed every man on that field myself. The feel of each man was different, the body unique, the skin and armor diverse, the pressure changed. When I went into the flesh, they wept blood. When I went into the eye, they gave me a look of horror and stared at me while they cried.

O how horrid it was to witness that sight. Beyond that of any war, any fight, any misery that can be brought upon by simple pain, this was a tainting of the soul, but not that of being drenched in a veil of evil. No, this was an exact science, an art of evil. Each action was a small brushstroke on a large canvas; once placed, the mark could not be moved again, it could not be painted over. It would be visible and it would stay forever, and it moved swiftly. Each body that I struck was a further deepened mark.

O, this act brought a nightmarish revelation to me that I had never thought of before. A revelation that I did not wish to know, and that was that this reality that I faced, was what I always wished for. That this is the path I set myself on, deep down inside, one that I craved, one that I lusted for, and one that I felt empty and hollow without, as if I was a shell with no seed. I was an empty man destined for bloodshed, torment, pain, and misery, if I could still be called such a thing as man.

O, how disgusting my actions and my desires were. It was evil indeed, and it was not over. The field was many, and my deed not yet done. In the midst of all the countless bodies in the field, my destiny had only begun. I had to toughen my heart, hold my own tears at bay, my trembling hands steady, and take heed of my resolution. To do that, I had to let the monster out, for there would be no way to complete this task without an inhuman presence at hand. One that does not feel, one that does not worry, one who believes that death is the only answer and one that shows no mercy, whether it be friend or foe. If I needed to be inhuman to follow in Gideon's steps, then inhuman I would be.

As soon as my condition was at play, my mind set, and the monster to be set on its way to exit the cage and henceforth be my hand, I would again be scoffed from the heavens. Pulled back, and tested, and my sanity once again judged.

For I would be asked to be hold to my ideals, my memories, my beliefs, my contradictions, and the very idea of reality in question, because when I came to the next set of bodies something very strange happened. It sparked a sense of familiarity, as well as that of premonition, because I heard a voice call out for me, and it referred to me as, Dracul.

CHAPTER 32
The Dead Talk

"

I have talked about the power of a name before, but I don't

think you quite understand. A name is the essence of humanity.

In fact, humanity itself is a name. It defines who we are, what

we become, what we think, and how we think. So to name

anything gives it meaning and sets its destiny on track. If one

gave you the name of protector, you would aspire to become one,

if one assigned to you the name of murderer, you would become

one, and if one gave you the name of the devil, then...

"

"DRACUL, MY ANGEL. COME TO ME!" it called, but I could not see where that voice came from.

An enemy soldier it must be, for it called that name with such sincerity, such familiarity, that it sounded as if he had known that name for a lifetime, that name was a friend, a friend that he had bested and shared memories with. But why did I feel familiarity with it also? Why did I feel it as if it were calling me from a womb into the light? Why did I feel anything at all about the name?

I searched that grave of flesh and bones to witness the sight of the call, but I could not detect where it came from. Whether it be ally or foe, I needed to find this meaning. That was my need, my compulsion, and it consumed me most deeply.

O how angry I grew. Vengeful and wrathful in nature, hearing that name call but not knowing where it came from. I took my sword and reaped my vengeance on the ground beneath my feet that was made of flesh and men, armor and steel. Hacking and slashing bodies left and right, sending a rain of blood and flesh into the air so much that even the ravens had left the field in worry of my fury.

There I stood enraged, sweat-ridden and blood drenched, breathing in the heavy air of the dead, taking all of my darkness into the light. Even then, surrounded by the mess of humanity, I felt alone. Mourning and pained, scorned and standing in vain and in silent misery. Was it in my mind? Was it a call from afar carried through the winds? Where did it come from?

Then, in the midst of that turmoil, I heard that voice once again, that familiar sound—the call of death. It did not shine from the heavens, no, it came from the ground.

So it was true that it came from the field, but why did it not sound like what is expected from dying men? No, this was something different from that, for it was not pained, it was not in mourning or worry. No, it had no concern whatsoever but instead, held a tone that I did not expect to hear. A voice in a mass grave of a battlefield should not be a voice full of joy, excitement, of hope and light, but it was, and for some reason it was directed at me.

O how I dug, through the valley of bodies that I had created, my hands and feet soiled in mangled festering flesh, but I could not stop. I did not stop. I dug and I dug until I saw the source. The answer to my prayer, to the sight of where the voice came from and the sight shocked me more than the voice itself, for this man was not a man, but a corpse.

When I saw him, I dared not think it was him, for he was armless. He was legless and seemed to be ripped apart, half his body here, most of his body there, and the rest of him someplace else.

I thought perhaps I had truly gone insane, for in a place like this, in the state I was, insanity would be a sane conclusion. What I dealt with was not that of reality—a man so brutally decimated, so viciously torn into pieces, so horribly mutilated, could not live. The man was surely dead, yet he was not.

Suddenly, his eyes darted towards me, blue and clear with hope and love. His jaws moved, speaking though he should have not been able to do so. Instead of anguish, remorse or hate, he thanked me.

"O thank you, my angel! How sweet it is to see your face once again."

I held the man with relative ease in my hands, for he was light as a child, even more so without all his parts. It was as if I picked up a sample of a man and not a full one. But his eyes he still had, and they were different from the crying dead I had been condemned to witness. No, his eyes were still blue as the heavens, full of bright light, his bloody hair stranded on his face stuck as a spider web in a corner. I thought how great a miracle it was, that he kept those very eyes open, but even more so that he had the strength to call out to me, for every breath must've been the essence of pain, yet he looked at me with divine hope.

"I am no angel, fallen one. I am death and I have come to claim you," I responded with a grim statement. I did not want him to feel hope in me, for there was nothing I could do to ease his pain or burden, besides giving him the release of death.

He smiled a most brilliant smile. His eyes spread wide with excitement from my words. "O my angel, but you are what you are. Death or not, you are the angel of the field. An angel of war. My angel! And I have been waiting to see you again all my life."

This was a shock to me, for only one man had ever looked at me with such excitement, such pride, such hope as this man did. Only Gideon had the same appreciation of my presence, but this man reciprocated it and more. It made me uneasy.

"I think you to be delirious, warrior. I have never met you and soon I shall never meet you again," I said, trying to break this man out of his delusion.

"O but you will, my angel, and we have. I have seen you a thousand times in my mind, a thousand times in my dreams, and I have seen you now in reality and that has pleased the image of you within my soul." He beamed again, and his radiant smile tortured my soul.

How strange it was to have this man speak so highly of me in the state that he was in, in a state that I may have caused. He was so full of hope, when there was none. I wondered this man's intention, whether he was close to death or not. "I tire of this, fallen one. I will end your pain and give you rest. I am sure that is what you want." I readied my blade.

"Yes, my angel, but first, I beg of you to do something for me."

I laughed a hearty laugh to think this man to ask me a favor. My inclinations had been right from the very start. I was there to do him a task and that was all he wanted, nothing more. How dare I compare him, even in thought, to a man like Gideon, who strived and performed acts without selfish thoughts but for the greater good. This man was not anywhere near Gideon's caliber of righteousness; he was just the same as the rest. On top of that, he was an enemy who had attacked our very own troops and I had not inclination or incentive to help him. Yet, I must say, it was a marvel that he had come to this point and escaped Death's great reap when all others failed. I thought it fair to humor him by listening to his words.

"Very well, what is it that you ask? But first, I tell you that no act that I can perform will save you from your death. Whether you taste my blade or not, you will surely die."

"O yes, my sweet angel. I would not ask for such a thing. And I know that

I am soon to be dead and this is my final bed on this earth. That I realized a long time ago. But I must ask you to do one thing for me so you will believe my words."

"And what is that, fallen one?"

"There is a man in this pile of graves, in this stack of bodies laid out from the edge of this circle. Twenty-three bodies in total, thirteen bodies to my right, and ten below," he said.

"What of this man?"

"My angel," he whispered to me quickly, "he is not dead and he will try to kill you."

In an instant, I dropped this man back into the pile he came from. He let out a pained grown showing that he was a man still in pain, and he could still feel. As he dropped, I had drawn my weapon and looked about.

But the heavens were not kind, if the heavens were there on that day at all. No, the fog had rolled in, and the darkness around was thick and deep, like so many days when I was at my weakest, the darkness and thick mist were always there. And it had done so again, it had snuck its way in and surrounded from all sides, waiting for the moment to be at hand. A hand that would dictate my life and its course, whether the hand be of hope or doom, a course I was going to soon find out.

CHAPTER 33

Assassin

I COULD SEE NO MORE than a sword's length, which only stemmed a few bodies away because of the infernal incessant fog. I was perplexed by my actions and what the fallen man had said. It was a riddle of the time, a gamble with my life again to either heed this man's word, or to end his life and continue on my task of clearing the field. Yet, I did not have the answer or know the true odds that I faced. I thought it wise to at least explore his warning, even if it were a ruse, for the fallen one was surely destined to die whether I was there to deliver his death or not. The true question was, was I also destined to lay in this field?

I started to count in the direction the fallen warrior said, still not knowing if I was sane or not, or if the fallen man was even real or just in my head, brought on by my torment from the heinous task. I did not know if there were any truth to this supposed assassin. or even if it was some sort of last effort trap to spring onto me. I had not the right of mind to do anything else, so I followed his instructions and proceeded.

I was careful to examine each body as I passed, poking with the tip of my sword and watching to see any grimace of pain on each face. Seven bodies I passed, three to his right and four below and I saw no movement, and no expression on any of them. That gave me comfort that maybe it was all a lie, but that comfort was short last since the concern of the truth and his warning also rung in my head.

"He holds in his right hand a hidden dagger that he will spring into your neck when you approach. You must stay out of sight. You must kill him before he kills you," the fallen one had said.

There was a great chill in the air now, yet oddly my brow sweated profusely. My arms were heavy and my heartbeat raced as the tension mounted as I continued forward. Twelve bodies I had passed, seven to his right, and five below—still no movement, no action.

The fog was thickening with each step and I wondered if it a great trick from the divine to only add to my nervousness and anxiety. Perhaps it had all been a great setup of events to get me to a state where I was at my most uneasy, to get me to a point where I had started to value my life, when I had not ever before, when I had gained respect and a name of my own, and when I chose to be a human instead of the monster that beckoned inside. Life would always bring its wicked plan into play, waiting patiently to send my hopes and dreams tumbling down, exacting its strange revenge.

That would be most ironical indeed, to be unable to die when I wanted to die and to die when I wanted to live. O, what a sick sense of humor the world had. That would be true to the way life worked and if only it were that easy, but life that day did indeed have a plan, and it was far more devious than I could ever decipher.

Twenty bodies later, eleven bodies to his right, and nine below. I had come to my target just ahead, two bodies more to the right, and one slightly below, just like the fallen one had said.

I could make out the left arm of the supposed assassin. The body lay there in complete silence, no movement in sight. He looked like all the rest, that I was assured, but there was a hint of color in the exposed skin on his arm, or it could have been all in my mind. I did not know the truth. I did not know a lot of things then.

I didn't know if this was to be it, the complete and utter end. I did not know that I had possibly fallen for the fallen warrior's last joke upon the victor of the battle. I did not know if I would die before the fallen warrior did from his stark and fatal injuries. I did not know if I would see Gideon again or my precious Illyana, both which I longed to see. All those things I did not know and much, much more. Those thoughts wrought heavily on my mind, twisting and churning, and increasing in strength with each step that I had to take.

Suddenly, I felt a sharp stinging pain on the side of my boot, a pain that could only come from a blade. In that instant, the mass of terrifying thoughts I had feared sprang into my mind. I had indeed fallen for the trap the enemy had set out for me. I was done for, and this would be my final resting place. But life had another trick, and as I stared at my foot, it came to light.

I realized it was a just a mere axe's blade that slid past my boot and carved a cut while I was too focused on the target up ahead. Most terrible luck I thought, or perhaps a most gifted boon, for it was rather sharp and could come in handy if a trap was actually sprung on me.

I picked up the axe, squatting below, never losing focus on what was ahead. I perked my ears to all the sounds, any noise that scuffled about, but there was none other than my lone rapid heartbeat. With both weapons in hand, I proceeded to my target until I could make him out in full.

He lay there in silence. A young man with soft rounded features, but he was not fat. Instead, he seemed fit and in shape, and held a childlike innocence and was in his prime to experience the greatness of life. Surely this boyish man could not be an assassin for I would have thought he had not experienced much on the battlefield unless he started to war at the age that I did, which was unlikely. For it would be a boy most desperate to seek a path such as this, and I would not want any boy to take the path that I took.

No scars were on him, which I also found odd, for war has a way of marking the body with its stain even if no wounds were shown. This man had none that were visible, but still, that didn't mean his heart wasn't scarred, maybe as scarred as mine. And if it were true that he was a murderer such as myself, I thought it strange that my scars showed on the inside as well as the outside, my darkened arms and legs a constant reminder of my murderous sin, but this boy had no such wounds whatsoever, no marks, no paleness, no sorrow. How odd, that he had not faced the burden that all others did. It was also odd that he was so young, unscathed even in this brutal battle, only dried blood on his clothes and no sign of visible mangling or wounds.

For anyone as immature as him to take place on this battlefield must have had some harsh lessons and experience of reality. What also caught my sight was that he was stationed differently; he laid on top of the bodies and not buried below like the tapestry of broken men that were stitched together in this horrifying visage.

I wondered all these thoughts and I wondered even more of him being not what the fallen one claimed him to be; surely he was a benevolent boy caught up in the horror of war. Then, a strange thing happened. I thought I saw a glimmer of steel below his right hand. Maybe it was the fog playing tricks with the light of the moon, or maybe it was something else, but I would not take any chances.

I stood a few feet away from the top of his head, looking at his body, in such a way that he would have to twist his head to see me in full sight if he were to suddenly awaken. To make matters worse, he would have to spring upwards without any knowledge of what was there, giving me even more time to strike. All this I thought ahead of time due to my experience, to my control, and my love for the art of death.

I set my feet shoulder width apart and stood so that I could twist around to capture an attack from the back if it were to come from that angle, for the thought that this was a trap from the fallen one had never left my mind. I also set my right shoulder lower so that I may charge forward with a weapon in hand if an attack sprung forward from a hidden assault. I did all this in preparation for this man's supposed attack, or an ambush, and still never lost sight of his left arm.

That cursed left arm might come to rid me of my life that I had only just begun to care for. Was the fallen warrior telling the truth? I wondered and wondered, and if I killed the man before he acted, I would never know, and I had to know, so in all essence, I could not kill this supposed assassin without knowing the full truth. I had to find out, so I did what I must.

I raised the axe high above with my left hand. With a final deep breath, I brought it down with such great swiftness, speed, and strength that it cleaved the man's left forearm cleanly off. In an instant, blood sprayed into the air like a geyser from the earth. Because I had such fond knowledge of blood, I knew that the only the way it sprays like that is if someone is alive, rather than the darkened, clotted type that just spurts out. No, this man was alive, at least for now.

The impact sent the bottom of his left forearm flying into the air, revealing the dagger attached as proposed by the fallen one. With the cleave, the butchered man's eyes burst open as he screamed in unrelenting pain, raising his head just moments before my sword struck its way through.

He was now dead, truly dead, laying on all the bodies, now an honest part of this mass grave. That beautiful color I admired drained quickly; the blood spurted into a clotting, congealed pool that I had seen so many times before.

He lay there like he did before he met me, but now his body was broken, his eyes and face frozen and twisted in terror, like so many eyes I had seen before that stared at a grim terror that I could not see. His plans had been foiled and added to the horrific painting that was war, but he did not come to this fate because of me. No, he arrived to this fate because of a dead man that talked. A dead man that told me of what was to come before it had arrived. A dead man that wanted and could tell me much, much more.

CHAPTER 34
A Conversation with Death

THE FIENDISH FOG that had so quickly grasped the land had scurried away to the dens from where it came, and in doing so revealed the grisly field of dead in its entirety.

It was a sight that I would like to forget, but never will. Gone were the clouds that helped block the light from any source, a strangely reddened sky left in their wake. Gleaming stars reflected like twinkling lights in the gathered pools of blood and mist.

Yet it was no time to wonder, it was no time to be distraught. It was no time to be broken, for I had a mission at hand; I had to find the strange being that guided me to safety. He had warned me of death and helped to save my life, when my allies or I had taken his in the war.

I quickly made my way through the butchery of men back to the fallen one, convinced that he was surely dead or unable to speak by this point. I knew that the answers I sought would not be granted to me, because of my dire concern of his warning, because of my approaching the victim in a most careful manner and untimely way. But when I returned, I was surprised to find that the fallen one remained awake and in a wondrous mood to see me.

"Did I speak the truth, my angel? I heard the scream and I knew it to not come from you," he said as I climbed up the defeated bodies.

"You spoke the truth, fallen one." I kneeled in front of him so he could see me fully.

"Excellent! I knew it to be true." He cheered most gleefully, enough that he toppled into the pile that he once came from. I quickly dug him back out once again.

"O thank you, my angel, that was most kind of you."

"It is the least I can do for the deed you did," I said to him, "but there is much we need to talk about."

"Yes, my sweet angel, whatever you desire. I shall tell you all that I know."

"Very well."

I placed him on top of a nearby body, propping him up by setting another body behind him and underneath his mangled portion. I positioned another to the side of him so that his head would not stray. Instead, he stayed staring in my direction, for he had many tendons missing, and had lost the use of his neck long ago. It was as if I had built an altar of death with a talking head, but that was what needed to be done, for I needed to view his every response.

After he was propped up I sat close to him, putting a pile of dead bodies behind me as well so I could lean back in comfort. I laid my sword down next to me, for I had no more reason to fear this dead man or any that surrounded me. He had been speaking the truth so far, and would warn me from another impending assault. That fact both offered me comfort in my seating and left a most serious concern on my mind.

"What is it that you wish?" the fallen one asked eagerly, knowing he had little time to spare. His blood was running out with each beat of his heart and soon he would not be able to muster enough strength to even close his eyes.

"I wish to know the truth," I said, settling into my cove of dead.

"My angel, do you not believe my words, even now? Was I not right about the bladed man? What is it that I can tell you so you can finally believe my words?" he asked with saddened eyes.

"Yes, you were right," I assured, relieving him of his concern. "Yet I am uncertain how you knew, for I could not see anything beyond that of a few footsteps in front of me, but you saw far, further than I, all the while buried in a pile of bodies. Unless you staged this from the moment of your demise as a plan to be rid of me or someone who came, then I do not see how that is possible.

"And I am puzzled as to what benefit you would attain at the end of this with my survival, and your brethren dead. I also do not know how you knew that I would be alone in this task to clear the grave, for this is a task always done by many, not just one, and your plan, if it were a plan, would have required me to have been alone to have any effect.

"So for all those reasons, I need to know how. Tell me fallen one. How did you know this?" I commanded.

The fallen one took a long stare and a deep breath as if it were his last, while never averting his eyes from me, and then he spoke with a most pleasant smile.

"I have told you, my sweet angel, my dearest friend. I have seen this a thousand times. I have seen this field a thousand times. I know what will happen here in great detail, for I have lived it a thousand times," he said. "I saw it all in my dreams each night I slept. That is the reason that I came here, to fulfill my dream. I have spent my whole life waiting for this moment, and now, finally, the time has come."

The only thing I knew for certain was that this man believed that he declared the truth. He spoke with such sincerity and hope that I had no other thoughts but to believe his spoken words, whether they be true to him or me.

"It is most strange indeed that you have seen what you say you have seen," I said, curious about his knowledge. "I would have thought it all a ruse if it were not that I had actually lived through the dream that you foretold."

I thought of the strange dealings I had with the lanky man at the kingdom, what Gideon spoke of him and how he could forecast the future. Did this man have that same gift?

"Tell me, fallen one, is there more to your dream?"

"Yes, there is plenty more to tell, my dear friend." He spoke with so much excitement that he almost toppled over from his perch.

"Easy now, my warrior," I said, trying to calm his enthusiasm. "First tell me, in your dream, did you die by my blade?"

There was a most serious pause, but it was not the frightened terror that I expected. Instead, anticipation. "Yes, I did," he replied, with a most intriguing smile.

"Then how can you call me your friend?"

"Because you have come to take me away from my pain, and a man who does that is surely my friend. But more than that, you have given me something far greater—a gift of peace, tranquility, serenity. A blessing. For that, I am very thankful."

"Then you wish me to end your life? Is that the payment you seek for your advice?" I asked.

"O yes, I am sure you will, but that is not a payment I need to ask for. That is what you do and will continue to do for all your life. You will bring death to others, and death will be brought to you, that is destiny," he said with smile.

"How can you say that with such joy?" I questioned, wondering how someone could relish my monstrous nature.

"Because it is the very nature of man to kill another," he answered with a most wicked smile.

A chill ran down my spine.

"To end one's life continue another's. It is a cycle and a cycle that must be continued for the world to live on," he continued, "and you, O you have such a marvelous role in this cycle. A great, magnificent role that will inspire legends from your acts. It is a most glorious privilege to be seated near to you, my angel."

"So if I am this cycle of death that you speak of, would it not be best to rid the world of me? Of my nature, of my destiny?"

"No, my angel! My sweet angel of death, you must not be mistaken," the man cried with deep concern. "As I said, you are part of a great cycle and the cycle needs death as much as it needs life, and in so you are part of birth as well. To live is just as important as death. They both serve a purpose and are a necessity of life, such is the way for plant to wither and die to give root to another."

I thought of his words for a moment. I imagined myself being part of something beyond the role I thought I played. "I do not know, fallen one. I do not think it to be true."

"But it is true!" he cried. "It is truth in the utmost. You are Dracul! The Dragon! The darkest one! The De…"

He suddenly stopped himself from his excitement and quickly whimpered, as if he spoke words that he was not supposed to say. But those words brought forth such stark familiarity that I could not ignore them.

"Tell me, fallen one, please! What am I?" I pleaded. "Who is this Dracul?"

The man remained silent.

"I feel not a man. I feel not a monster anymore. I am a clash of thoughts, desires, and regrets. There is a hunger, an unrelenting hunger that burns deep inside, a dark hunger, a lust, a burning, a vengeance." Words fell from my mouth with no effort or consciousness on my part. "Have I gone mad? Have I lost my mind? Am I insane?"

"No, no, my sweet angel!" he screamed. "O no, you are not insane. That is the very essence of humankind, you should be glad to experience it. We are full of flaws and regrets. We are monsters and men, the same. For we are warriors, all of us, and we were made to be as such. We are at constant battle with ourselves. Each battle we win, we also lose, and each battle we survive we also die. That is what it means to be a man, to be confused and enlightened all at once, to be in joy and pain, to embody all conflicts in the universe within our own hearts is what makes us human. That is what you are, my angel; a human." He whispered something after that I could barely make out, but I could swear it sounded like, "At least for now."

I thought of what the fallen warrior said, for he spoke the truth. Every war or action I won, I suffered a loss as well.

"And what of you? What are you? A seer? A prophet? A madman?"

The fallen one's head slowly rolled to the side as the body below him caved under pressure. His face now hung with a saddened expression, but he still rolled his eyes to the corner to look at me, as if he never wanted to lose sight of me.

"Truthfully, I do not know what I am. In fact, I do not know what I was until this day," he said, sounding as if he was lost in his own thoughts. "I too had thought myself insane, just as you have, and I had lived a life as a servant. I had not even picked up a sword until this very day."

His face started to gleam with excitement once again.

"But every day I dreamed of this day, and I knew the time was fast approaching. When the war came, I volunteered. I have waited for this blessed day all my life, for I could no longer live a life without finding out if my visions were real, even if it cost me my life to do so. And it has, which I knew it would."

Suddenly, he brimmed with a glowing smile, and his eyes began to tear. "I must tell you that I am relieved to know that my life was not wasted, for here I am, living my dream. For that I am ever thankful, and that is why I speak with such joy. I cannot help feel any other way. You have given me purpose, my angel." He sobbed with joy, but even those tears were quickly mixing with blood and draining away and I knew my time was short.

I knew this man, a former corpse, waited near death's door. If I were to get any more answers, I would have to act quickly.

"Tell me then, fallen one. Tell me of your dreams. Tell me of all that you see and have seen. Tell me of what will happen and has happened in your mind. For your payment, as you have asked, I will give you what you wish for—the peace of death."

The fallen one's face lit up with excitement once more, for this was his chance to live the rest of dream through, and so he did. He sat there with that strange smile on his face, that strange glow and talked to me as if he were living his dream once again, as if he had all his limbs intact, and he acted them with his eyes while he watched me. He told me of strange things, of strange happenings, and of very strange predictions and premonitions. He spoke, and spoke, until his words ran dry as blood no longer dripped from him and he toppled back into the pile he came from, never to speak again.

CHAPTER 35
Destiny's Chains

"

To know one's destiny is not a gift but a burden to fulfill, for

actions become meaningless and lack the luster they once had.

But to know one's destiny and to change it, now that is an epic

undertaking that will pit man against the heavens, and the

entire world will feel the rumble from its repercussions.

"

THAT HELLISH DAY, unending and long lasting, full of contemplation, misery, and sorrow, had finally ended. We rode to the next camp, to the next site. The battle had greatly reduced our numbers and although struck with much sadness, we had become far more mobile, and this kept us hidden from the remaining barbarian army's scouts and lookouts.

The men we had were now few enough to have horses of their own and no man needed to be on foot. If perchance a barbarian scout or lookout was spotted, we moved quickly to squash them before they had the chance to react. Those who did not or could not ride rode in wagons and carts behind us. We passed through the fields and paths that lay in front of us in silent melancholy.

There were no words exchanged of the battle, no words exchanged of victory, or what was lost. It was what it was, an event that happened, an event that needed to happen to open our eyes to what was ahead, and an event that everyone wanted to forget but no one could. We were all changed. We were now stained to our very souls and that blemish could never be removed. Being Gideon's men, we were man enough to accept that sentence, the sentence of sleepless nights and a restless soul, the sentence of a warrior.

My mind was a blur as much as the scenery around me as we galloped forward. I was lost in thought just as much as the remainder of the men. They had their own concerns of the war, of the battle, of fear, of life and death, but I had not a single thought of the war that was in the past. I feared the future.

No, I had different concerns, different wonders, different fears, and it was all about what the talking corpse, the fallen one, had said to me. I must say, it felt mysterious and wondrous all at once. I felt a deep sense of privilege, and yet a deep sense of despair for being in the place I had been, to have had the opportunity I that I had taken advantage of.

I thought about how strange it was to talk to the dead on their way out of existence. It was as if he had stopped on his way to the light, only to look back and tell me all the sights that flashed before his eyes. And even stranger was that during all of this we were seated in a field of graves that I helped create, talking to a life that I helped take, so that it could in turn save mine.

It was if I had entered death's chambers and death had sat down and spoken to me himself using that strange man as a vessel to congratulate me of my murderous crimes, as well as reward me with my life. How strange was that man? He was dead yet alive, and had spent his life in its entirety searching for me. He was a corpse but still lived. Was he real, or was he just in mind, playing a trick on my senses?

I thought of what he had told me. All his dreams, all his predictions, all his riddles made little sense, and yet nothing but sense. I wondered and wondered so much that Gideon took notice. For the first time, I had spoken nothing to him about my concerns.

"What is on your mind, Vlad?" Gideon asked as he moved Re next to my own horse. I had easily learnt to ride after my brief time with Re, but my horse was nothing as glamourous, just an unnamed beast that trotted forward.

I wondered if it would be prudent to tell Gideon of the happenings, of the strange mystical nature of the conversation I had. I wondered if he would think any differently of me. If he would act any different. If he would change his plans that had already been set out, that were supposed to be set out. Would he still see me in the same light, instill the same trust that he had in me? Or would he see me for the new person I was, and no longer the person I had been before? I felt weak and tired. I had a heart full of regret, a soul buried in wonderments, and a discombobulated mind, all meshed together into a broken man who used to rage with all his heart and now could not mend it back together again. So I did what any man would do when he had not an answer to give, I lied.

"Nothing." It was the first time I had ever spoken anything but the truth to him.

He saw straight through my lie, as I knew he would. A moment passed, as if I had caught him by surprise for the first time, but that moment was quick and vanished in an instant and he gave me a narrow smile with a response that soothed my soul, as he always did.

"Very well, Vlad. We all have our secrets, I shall let you keep yours," he finished in a whisper and gave a clever smirk. "By the way, you are doing very well on the horse; you have taken to riding quite well. I'm pleased to see Re had such a good effect on you." Then, Gideon rode off back to the front leading the men forward.

He was right—I had learned many things from this man when I was lost. I had quickly mastered riding, after riding on such a majestic beast as Re. I had even been in the castle, walked the grounds and stood in the throne room. So many things he gave to me without even my asking, as if he brought onto my plate a feast of knowledge when I hungered and every time I thirsted for a drop of water, Gideon brought forth an ocean.

That was the man that I was destined to follow. He was brave, honest, vibrant, and ever glowing as the sun. That was the man that the fallen one had told me of before his ability to speak was forgotten. But before the talking corpse's eyes went empty and he could not see any more and was not able to utter a word, he told me of Gideon's importance.

He told me that I was his moon and he was my sun, and that when worlds collided we would stand as one. He told me how I would one day harm him, to shun his glow, and the flames from that act would burn ever so bright. That was what the fallen one told me, the one who was right in all the things he had said, but this I dreaded most.

For if it were true, then one day I would commit a treacherous act. I would break his trust and crash his world, and it would launch an event that would set all those strings of fate to be cut and a binding chain put in its place instead. It would lock the hold of destiny that was to be at hand, open the gates that were meant for us, so they would never close or even budge again, and it would also lock us into a fate beyond my current understanding.

Of all those words, I had no idea, no notions now than ever before, no theory or impression on how it would take place, but the day would come when that act would happen. I would be the one to haunt his dreams in a traitorous nature that I did not want any part of, yet that was my destiny.

When I heard those words I decided that I would leave his army and never return, that the moment my deed to clear the field was done I would be no more than extinct to Gideon and his men. Even that I could not do, for that was denounced from me by the fallen one's words.

There is no way to elude a man's fate, and that was set for me as well. Although I was given a choice in this dream of the fallen one, a choice where both outcomes led to doom. One of self, one of my heart, but both of my soul.

The choice held two harms that I could not allow. One was for me to commit the treachery and the diabolical act that I could not stomach and hurt the one man that I befriended in all the world, or the other which was something even more disdainful, which was to run and leave his side, which I hoped was the cure. But if I were to do so, were to leave him still a friend, then the repercussions would be thousand-fold, and it would be as if I drove a stake through my heart, for Gideon would never attain his dream. He would never reach the path he set himself on, and would walk an endless journey in misery. His men would leave, and he would die a lonely death, unknown, forgotten, stuck in misery, and taking my heart with him. That was the other path, the other tip of the scale that I was given. They were both dreadful circumstances with no hope on either side, but I could not afford to make either one.

I knew that the answer is never simple, and the choice never ours to make in the first place because truth is always hidden in a paradise of lies. It is because fate is a trickster, a gambler and a puppeteer that works its ways on the common man, playing and moving the strings, tying them in such a way so that they could never escape and the way out only entangles them even further.

Yet that is life, and it is what was destined and that is what made me angry. We have such little control over our actual lives, because another being or power is setting everything in motion for us. I could not accept that. I would not accept that as my answer. I would make my own destiny. For if both paths I had in front of me led to such an unfortunate outcome, I would make a path of my own. The heavens and their plans be damned.

No, I would create a new reality, a new path that was unseen, untold, unwritten in the great book and it would lead to glory on both sides, not doom like they promised. I refused to believe that there was no outcome where Gideon and I could not remain friends. I would make certain that he would reach his dreams, for that was my purpose. I would stay at Gideon's side until his destiny was set. Even though it would change Destiny's strings into iron chains, I would use those very chains to wrap around Destiny's neck and wring it until it gave me what I wanted, an ending for both of us, one not of misery, but of glory and everlasting friendship. That I vowed, even if I had to snap Destiny's neck to achieve it.

CHAPTER 36
A Gift of Misfortune

AFTER SOME TIME, we arrived at our destination—a village near the location of the passage that the invading armies of the barbarians used to gain entry into the King's otherwise impenetrable realm. It was a valley that was as much as a canyon, which only had one path through from the side of the desert lands into ours. The barbarians used that passage as a gateway and overwhelmed the defenses originally fortified there. The barbarians had split their large army into separate troops, acting like fingers clawing into the area. Each troop traveled on their own into the region, each one on a separate path to increase their reach. When all was set, they would grasp and pull the land from underneath us as a magician performing a trick. That was their plan.

We had met one such army, a mere finger of troops from its iron fist, but we took it clean from the hand. However, it had cost us a great deal, and diminished our numbers greatly to do so, but it also showed that we could win. Yet to war with the rest of the armies would mean similar fates and we had not the numbers to do so. Gideon knew this all too well, and to make matters worse, Gideon only had enough forces left for one final assault, for without the King's aid we were greatly outnumbered. The spoils of war only traveled so far, rations were low, and not enough men left to be gathered, for the invading barbarians destroyed every village, every town that stood in their path, and left piles of rubble and burned ash in their place.

For that reason, we could not replenish our numbers and the immortal army that we once were was withering away. Still, Gideon was a man not without a plan. His plan would mean making our opposition suffer the same challenge that we suffered, but to a much higher degree.

He would do to them what they had done to us. Gideon would use our remaining men as a final assault to hit the army's main supply line coming in at the passageway, effectively cutting off the hand at the wrist, thus giving the King's army a chance to squash the rest of its barbarian fingers that reached inwards. That move would remove any chance from the barbarians to gather any more strength than they had already attained, as well as remove any communication from the heart of their lands into ours, and removed all further supplies from their side, only leaving them the ones they had already. This was something Gideon had learned from experience.

Gideon knew very well the difficulties of running an army without any help from the mainland, something he performed in all his days in service of the King. If a general were not accustomed to it, he would suffer greatly in morale of his troops. In war, it is the heart of men that actually determines the victor in war, and not that of steel.

Without supplies, without support, they would lose that heart and be stranded in a foreign domain. They would have to swear fealty to the King or suffer a massacre from the people, for when one has no place to go, then he is lost, and when he is lost, it is easy pickings for the bold.

Yet this was not a plan without risk. In fact, it was rather a large gamble, for if the invading armies gained knowledge of our plan, they would gather back and attack from all sides, closing that iron fist with us in the center, easily wiping us out.

Nevertheless, the chance could not be ignored. We had already paid the cost of the ante with the lives of our men in our first battle, all to open up a pathway to the barbarians' foothold. This assault was planned by Gideon from the start, and if we retreated now then all those lives were for nothing. We had no choice, no matter the losses we already suffered—to conquer or crumble was all that was left to us, and we would not crumble for as long as Gideon stood by our side, that I would make certain.

We had arrived at this quaint village; it was slightly less than a town, but it roared with excitement—partly because they were stricken with fear with word of the invaders nearby. However, said invaders had little use of such a small village, as they ventured to hit big towns and villages that were on their way deeper into the kingdom. Any detour to them would have cost them valuable resources as well as time, and the more time they spent, the more they were at risk.

The barbarian generals knew that well, even many of the men of war understood that well and that alone was what kept this village alive. The village did not know of those strategies, the complexities of war, or even the common sense of knowing that this village, to many armies, was not worth the hassle. Instead, they were riddled with fear, filled with anxiety and concern, and blinded with such ignorance that they saw us as their saving grace when they had no need of one.

Gideon knew of these concerns, knew of their hearts, knew of their fears, as well as their ignorance. Instead of neglecting them like all others had, Gideon made a conscious decision to visit each village, even if those decisions cost us days of travel and resources in the process, an opposite to a common engineer of war's thoughts. For every village that was forsaken, forgotten, or forfeited, Gideon would save and take unto his shoulders. This is what made Gideon a legend amongst the people.

Gideon saw greatness in the common man, ability in the most soiled soldiers, and even gave time to those that would cost him more than it was worth, because he knew one thing. He knew that the hearts of men were worth more than any amount of gold, any amount of supplies expended for them. This was the very reason why we traveled from place to place.

We went to different regions, different sectors, and different towns, all to show a presence. A presence to towns and villages that were not touched since their inception, to towns that had been decimated, to show that we saw and that we were there for them. Even though we would not be able to turn the wheels of time back to reverse the tragedies that we came across, we made it shown that there was one in the land who knew what happened, saw what happened, and would rise and seek retribution with such devastation and sheer absolution that it would never happen again.

We traveled to show that we were the sword of justice and would strike down those accountable for their actions. That no one could escape the horrors that they created and that there would always be someone who would avenge the burnt villages, lost homes, murdered family members, destroyed souls, and all the horrors of war that are far too real for one to handle, once they have encountered them.

This act had a twofold effect. One was to raise the morale of our current troops who placed their lives on the line with each battle, reminding them what they were fighting for, what they bled for, and what the men who had lost their lives had sacrificed for.

Yet there was another reason, a great reason that I understand now more than I had ever done back then. That was to gather forces, but not to just gather any forces, but to gather forces of the ones that had been personally hurt, victimized, assaulted, and distraught, because those forces came with a special talent. That talent was the gift of misfortune, a gift that at one time I had also—the gift of fury.

However, those men were few, for many were murdered so they could not retaliate or attack. Those very few that survived, the ones who saw their children taken from them, who witnessed their wives and loved ones raped in front of their very own eyes, the ones that were too ashamed to take action, or too afraid—they burned inside for redemption and would move heaven and earth to redeem themselves, and Gideon's army gave them that chance. It was that light. It was that fire that burned the soul clean. It would take those tainted, devilish men to make that sword of purity, and that is what made Gideon great.

We were welcomed into that village for those traits that made us famous. That we were valiant warriors, that we were the pinnacle of an army led by the greatest of tacticians, and the most famous general in the lands, Gideon himself. With Gideon's legacy guiding us, we were welcomed and cheered into this village as we were in every village. With his legacy, we had picked up a few warriors here and there. The pickings were slim, but our numbers did increase slightly. Even so, to suffer a battle like what we fought would still mean certain death.

I knew that Gideon had a plan, but I did not know what. I, like all the rest, had put my trust and heart into Gideon's choice. Of course, it was far too great for someone, anyone other than him, to handle. Yet I wondered if I did him a favor by giving him that burden alone, for he carried much on his shoulders, and I could not believe how they did not break.

That night I rested in the lodgings that the townsfolk made for us. I rested an uncomfortable rest, but as it is with time, like with all things, I finally slept. I dreamt a strange dream for a strange night. Dreams that appeared to make no sense, but seemed far more real than reality itself. Dreams that pulled the very essence of my heart out and unfolded it within my mind's eye as the muddled mess that it had become. I dreamt of my greatest desires, my deepest loves, Illyana my heart, Gideon my brother, my rage, my shame, the usual wanderings of a lost soul, in the usual way I do when I tend to drift into my violent tendencies. But that night, I also dreamt of something else.

I dreamt of the man in the graveyard of broken bodies, in the aftermath of the bloody battle. I dreamt of the mutilated corpse of the fallen warrior. I saw his face staring back at me but I could not recognize it any longer. I heard him speak as he did that day, over and over again, like a bell ringing through my skull. I heard him say those words, repeat those words that kept ringing in my mind until I was forced to open my eyes. "My sweet angel of death."

CHAPTER 37

The Riddler

IT WAS AN ODD AWAKENING FOR ME—the day was crisp and bright, yet I had not felt that nature inside of me at all. Instead, I witnessed the morning with a darkness, even when there was none. I felt the sun faded when it rose, and warm air to have lost all its warmth, the brightness of the day lost of its luster and full of gloom. It was if the words the fallen one had said to me plagued my mind and rid me of the joy of the day. I had been so close to being someone worthy of being on that battlefield, but I had lost that now. Is it true that one cannot escape his fate? I wonder that to this day.

He had told me that I had become who I was because of the acts and deeds that I would commit, but was I truly to commit those acts and deeds if I had knowledge of them? I did not know the answer, and every time I thought of it, I was only left with more confusion. Every answer raised brought forth even more questions.

For example, the death of the assassin on the field was something that was not to happen, had it not been for the foreknowledge of his attack. If it were not the message from the fallen one, I would have lost my life instead. But with his warning, I was able to rid myself of the burden and change my fate.

However, if so, and one is able to change one's fate, then what course did I now walk on? Or is it already destined to unfold in a series of events that can only be prolonged but never changed? Or is it that we only have control over actions that affect very little in our lives, where there are some things we can change yet others are set in stone. And if so, then I wondered what action I was to follow next that would lead me to my new fate that I created, or deeper into one pre-destined to me.

How odd it is to think of the future. No true thought reveals any answers and leads one only deeper into mystery, yet I still do. I say them to myself, repeat them in my mind, and dwell on them in my spare time. Is it true, that there are no real answers to any of life's questions, but only riddles that leave the mind as puzzled as the riddler who asked it?

I am such a riddler, one who ponders and asks these questions, these thoughts, without knowing the answer. It must be the very nature of man to think up things that he cannot solve, to delve into matters that he cannot understand, and to tease thoughts that need not be thought of.

It all must seem foolish to the logical man, but I am no such man. I am driven by feeling and emotion, my past and present, my heart and desire, my lust and rage. My logic is gone, for no logic can describe the life I lived, and no logic could make all that pain worth having endured it. That is the man I am. Foolish it may be, but I am one who wishes to have answers to my plight, and I walk each day in hope of finding them.

I thought of those wonders when I woke up that morning. I thought of those wonders when I traveled the streets. I thought of all those wonders when I visited the town's blacksmith, who endlessly toiled on my sword that once did not belong to me and yet now functioned as close to me as my arm. A sword that had been dulled from various battles. The sword whose clang rang through the air, reminding me of the war that I could not leave behind. And just as the sword, war and battle had become a part of me as much as my own blood. The sound of metal clanging was so familiar to me that it was as if it were my very own heartbeat. I could hear it thump in my chest. I could hear it push war through my veins. It was what I was now, a symbol of brutality, and of my pain.

I walked aimlessly in that apathy, hearing my fate in my head over and over again. I wandered in misery as I picked up my sharpened blade from the blacksmith and toured the town until I found myself at the town's edge. I stood in front of a little lake, a small dying lake that had waters collected from the far trickles of the mountains surrounding the area. Staring into the water was the only peace I could find, for every place I went, peace was the last thing I felt.

Instead, there were constant reminders, for every place I went, the children revered us as heroes and welcomed us with warm, bright smiles that I did not wish to see. Every smiling face brought a stark reminder of the role that I truly played. The role of death dealer was a role that I could not escape. Every smile brought forth another torment, one of wondering and one of also longing.

To see children happy was as foreign as the ground I walked on now.

Those smiles reminded me of how I grew up, and raised questions on how they lived. I wondered how they survived the way they did, unbroken, un-weathered, un-pained. Their mothers and fathers that held them surprised me even more. They held them with love and attention, the likes of which I had never felt from mine. I envied that moment, even now, as grown as I was, aged from traveling with the army.

I still yearned for that touch, for that hand, for that heart, the one I was long denied. On many days, I have wondered what it would be like to see the world through a child's eyes. I had never been a child, so how could I know? I wondered what magnificence I would see, what hope I would witness, what dreams I would be able to paint in my mind with the brush of innocence. Alas, I had grown too fast, in too little time to frolic with those ideas now. My canvas was already painted red before I had the power to see color, or even know what I was doing.

That was my destiny and it has come to fold. The only hope I had ever seen was from the three things I cherished most— vengeance, Illyana, and Gideon.

I thought of those things when I stared at the water that day. The gathered water had stood still for days because little water traveled into it. As a result, without the movement from water, no ripples were present and it left a pristine mirror-like surface showcasing a reflection of everything that peered inside.

I stood there that day, staring at my own reflection, which had so greatly changed through the years. I had not known, and had even forgotten the way it looked. I could see details that before I had not seen. Although my eyes still remained the color they had always been, there was something about them that lost had its warmth, and now was cold and steely. My soft features had been replaced with sharper, harder features without my knowledge. I had not even felt the lines that had crept on my face; they must've sneaked their way while I was asleep one night, and with time had become deeper and darker because of lost attention. My hair had grown quite long. Although it was still as black as the night, as it had been from my very first day, I had a strand of grey, and my hair now traveled down to my back. I had not taken the liberty of maintaining it, but the blood-ridden battles must have been nutritious for it to grow to this length.

I wondered how many years had passed since I first joined the army. It all happened in a flash that I did not have the fortune of counting. We traveled for months from place to place, spent days on the fields preparing, countless afternoons just thinking, and all of it I had not noticed. It had went so quickly. I was a mere child when I came to be a student of death, and a young man when I became a student of war. Now, what was I? Was I a master of pain, or of regret and sorrow? Why had I aged so? Had truly that many years went by without my notice, without my attention?

To me, everything stood still. New faces appeared and left through recruitment and death, and I had only seen the face of Gideon as my stamp of time. From when I first took this journey up until now, I still saw that face everywhere I looked. That is how I determined my age, but he still seemed like the man I had seen on the first day, stuck in time, youthful in nature as well as his attitude. He had not one wrinkle that hadn't been present before. For I had seen his face many times, enough to have it burned into my mind and its image, I could never forget.

I thought how strange it was that a man could remain the way he did without any change while everything changed around him. It was as if he was a force beyond that of time, a force that I needed to know as well. Then all of sudden, a voice woke me from my thoughts. The voice was unfamiliar and pleasant, but trembled when it spoke, and it simply said, "Excuse me."

CHAPTER 38

Men and Monsters

THE VOICE I HEARD BELONGED TO A CHILD. I turned to see him watching me from far away. He trembled from within and out, but spoke anyways with uncertain words, and an even more uncertain behavior. He looked like a desolate boy, full of wonder, fear, and an emptiness that was about him, unlike all the other boys in the village that I had seen before. He looked alone, covered in dirt and filth, no owner, no ruler he had, just a boy who wanted a soul to speak to, much like I was when I was at that age.

"Excuse me, sir," he repeated.

"What do you want?" I responded coldly, staring at the boy, but he was unable to meet my gaze.

He instead looked onto the ground, put the tip of his toe on the dirt and nervously looked for the courage to speak up, until finally he found it and spoke again. "Are you part of Lord Gideon's army?" he asked coyly.

"You know I am, boy. You are just wasting words. What do you want?"

Again, the boy hushed from my response and stood still, trying to find his ground again for he was lost. It was as if he was not on this earth but lived in deep sorrow that only another sorrowful soul could see, a sorrowful soul like mine.

"Do you not have parents?" I asked.

Yet again, the boy was unable to speak, not due to the timid shyness he had already showed, but because of true loss and deep emotion. I had struck a deep cord and it echoed through him loudly.

He stood there, gritting his teeth, and fought the tears back so he wouldn't show weakness. To his credit, he only let one escape. He was extremely prudent in showing his strength, and quickly turned away and brushed his hand against his cheek, trying to conceal it. "I am alone, now," he uttered those resilient words. Words that I would not want to hear from a child.

"We are all alone, boy. We just don't know it," I told him. "Again, you are wasting words and my time. What do you want?"

He did not waste any more time, for the boy spun around quickly to meet my gaze, tears still sneaking from his eyes. "I want to join your army!" he cried out.

The words took me aback, for I did not expect them to come from a child. From anyone else I would have thought it a fool's promise, the imagination of a child going astray, but this boy was different.

He had an intensity in his eyes that I had only seen on the battlefield. I knew he was a boy who had witnessed death firsthand; he was a boy far less ignorant than even the men of this village.

"Where are you from, boy?" I asked. "You are not from this village, I am certain. From judging the look on your face, this village has not seen what you must have seen. Otherwise, they would have a different exterior than what they hold."

"I'm from the village of Muhi," he said, "the one near the lake, with the tall windmill on top of the hill."

I was surprised to hear that. Muhi was one of the villages we had visited on our travel to this village. It was completely and utterly destroyed. The barbarians had been extremely callous and lived up to their barbarous name. They had even tied bodies of the villagers to the blades of the windmill, the very windmill the boy spoke of, and then used them as target practice as it spun. Yet, I could not tell the boy of this for that was a gruesome outcome to hear of one's own people, and too harsh at any age to absorb.

"I visited your village, boy. I saw what happened. Your windmill is gone. There were no survivors."

The boy instantly disconnected once again and tried to hide those tears that kept creeping out. The memory must be still familiar, and his shoulders dropped down as if a heavy rock was just placed on him. In fact, so much was his body defeated that he could not bear to meet my gaze anymore.

"There was one. I survived," he said.

Had this boy really seen that sight? Really witnessed the horror that was war? How could he decipher such acts?

"If that be true, then why didn't you show yourself when we approached?" I asked. "Our army was there—we rode tall and high, and you must have seen or heard us."

The boy took a while to respond, then kicked his feet into the dirt. "I was scared," he said in aggravation of himself. "I didn't want to show myself because I didn't know if you were there to kill me or not." He raised his eyes to me burning with anger, and spoke with great courage. "I don't want to be scared anymore."

What a wonder was this little boy, brave enough to die. Surely, he must know death firsthand, the way I did. I had always told Gideon that I was not afraid of death but Gideon knew better because I had never truly seen death until the day I cleared the fields. That was death and it was hauntingly frightful and full of remorseful terror too great for anyone to ignore.

"How do you know we won't kill you now?" I questioned.

"Because you are Lord Gideon's army. You are heroes."

"Heroes," I laughed.

I scoffed at the idea of being thought of as heroes. How could we be called such things after the devastation we brought onto others? The truth is we were as vile as any of the other criminals that walked the land, only we had directed it towards our enemies. Our wrath was set with a purpose, but we were very much murderers, I could see that clearly now.

"There are no such things as heroes, my boy," I told him. "You will eventually learn that."

"Lord Gideon is," he objected.

Yes, it was true. Amongst us, he would be the only man I would consider as such a thing, if such a thing actually existed, but the recent dealings had even tarnished that.

"Yes, he might be the only one. And now, you want to be like him? You want to join us?"

"Yes! I want to be like you. I want to fight evil. I want to make sure those men pay for what they've done! To me!" he screamed. "To my family," he cried. "I want to be a soldier." He clenched his fists so tight that I thought blood would pour out any second.

The boy had such determination in his eyes, such ability. He stood unwavered, even when I approached him. He had the look of dedication, of intensity and solidity, of fire that raged like an inferno, much like I must have when I was a child. For a moment, I thought that this boy was the epitome of who I was when I was just a mere child. Alone, lost, unknowing of his next actions, and filled with fury and nowhere to use it.

"Very well," I said as I approached him and patted him on the shoulders. This revealed a change in the boy—a smile.

It was the first smile I had seen in our entire conversation. One of those smiles that reminded me of all the other children in the village. What a beautiful, innocent smile it was. So pure and full of hope that everything will be all right, that all worries will go away, that vengeance, death and murder is the cure for his blight, and that smile made me angry.

O how quickly that smile quickly faded as I moved my hand from his back to his neck.

I grabbed him by the throat and lifted his light frame with one hand as he started to choke from the pressure. His legs kicked violently at my stomach but they bounced off in vain and only made my grip tighter.

I could see his face quickly start to shift color and instead of kicking me, he started trying to loosen my grip from his neck.

I thought how easily I could wring his little neck. How easily I could snap it with just a motion of my hand. How I could easily slit him across the abdomen and watch his insides spew out. How easily I could do all that, but that would be too easy. No, this boy needed to be punished.

So I took him to water. I must say, he had some spirit, for he did almost muster enough strength to pry one of my fingers loose, but still, my firm grip remained. Before he could manage to loosen any more fingers, I plunged his head into the pool of water enough so that his face was buried below the surface and he could not breathe, but his ears were still out and he could listen.

He still squirmed for some reason, trying to rid my fingers around his neck, not realizing that even if he had gotten my fingers off of him and he was able to breathe, the only breath he would have would be a gulp of water that would fill his lungs.

What a stupid boy I thought he was, as his body floundered around, his whole body shaking violently, unable to get free, unable to scream, only able to listen, only able to hear words of death.

"Do you want to be like us? Do you want to be like me!" I screamed, and that moment I felt a tingling sensation throughout my body as a hold of furious anger took over me. I could feel my eyes bulging out of my head, my arms getting stronger, and blood rushing through my veins. O, the beast was out and he was hungry.

"Come on, boy, answer me!" I screamed.

Yet he did not, for he could not. He was still struggling with my grip and the necessity to breathe, knowing that death was just seconds away. This I could tell, because his spirited kicks that were so ready to fight before had faded into meek taps into the muddied water, and those restlessly toiling hands that had tried to loosen the grip around his neck became slow pats on my hand.

Finally, when I felt the last bits of life starting to leave him, his soul ready to open the door to another world, I pulled him out and threw him onto the dirt.

O how pathetic the image of that boy was, uncontrollably and violently coughing, trying to remove the water from his fluid-filled lungs.

"This is what it means to be like one of us, boy," I roared as I made way towards him, unsheathing my blade. "We walk close to death. You must be prepared to die, and give your life. There is no fear in a soldier. There is not a 'perfect time' for you to be ready." I held my sword out.

As soon as my blade was pointed, another blade flashed through the air, striking my newly sharpened blade in such a way that it sent it flying out of my hands and into the air with an emphatic ringing sound. In that moment, all other sounds had halted, and my sword struck the ground, still vibrating from the hit.

A blow that quick, that precisely struck, that unseen, and with such a powerful aura could have only belonged to one man, and I knew that man well. Gideon.

Gideon looked at the boy and looked back at me.

The boy was frightened, shivering. He still stared at the blade that Gideon held in between us as if it was not a weapon but a protective shield from my assault, which it was.

"What are you doing, Vlad?" he said, looking at me with wonderment.

I looked at Gideon for I knew exactly what I was doing, but did not want to offend him, so I told him the truth. "Teaching the boy a lesson, my lord."

"What did he do to offend you so much?" Gideon asked suspiciously.

"I did nothing, my lord!" the boy screamed in a defense not needed. "I just asked to join you, that's all!"

The boy scampered on all fours to Gideon's side. Yet, the boy's eyes were locked on me, unblinking, worried of my actions at that time, even though they were none.

Gideon looked me over for an objection to the boy's comment but I looked away. I was ashamed. The boy had spoken the complete truth, and I had not wished to let Gideon know of my regrets of the path of blood that I now walked.

The boy finally stood onto his feet, still with those tears streaming down his face, the tears of an innocent. He latched onto Gideon's legs like a boy does to his father. Gideon was his only hope.

Gideon sheathed his blade and smiled a great smile, embracing the boy. "That is excellent news, lad!" Gideon said, comforting the boy. "We would be honored to have such a brave little warrior such as yourself in our ranks."

The boy looked stunned. He looked toward me and stuttered in unbelief, "But he, he..."

"What? You're worried about Vlad? Do not worry about him. He was just testing your courage, your resolve," Gideon lied as he bent his knees to kneel in front of the boy, eye to eye, and stared at him with that steely stare, just as he did upon my recruitment into his army.

"You will be an excellent soldier and we will personally make sure you will be looked after." After a pause, he looked at me. "Right, Vlad?"

I had no words to say to the boy, because I knew all was already lost. This boy would no longer have that gift of innocence that I once was not permitted to have. A gift of innocence that was far too precious to lose in war, just to be traded in for a sorrowful life of death and dismay.

Gideon rose and smiled. "Why, there is no sense in being all serious. These are good times. Relax and rejoice, for the time of concern will be upon us later. Today, we will welcome our new friend and new soldier."

With that, Gideon patted the boy on his back and turned to leave.

"But, sir!" the boy objected.

Gideon halted his steps and without even a turn said, "Vlad, I presume you will leave the boy unharmed."

"Yes, sir."

"There you go, little one, nothing to worry about."

Before leaving, Gideon turned and examined me with his eyes as if seeing into my soul, like the way he did so well, unveiling all my inner, dark, hidden truths with his light. Then he looked at the boy once again and smiled a most sincere smile.

"I trust Vlad with all my life, little one, and one day you will also." Gideon's words ushered in a smile from the boy, and then he proceeded to walk off.

Left alone, the boy turned his attention to me, unsure of my next actions. I only had one, the one that I had grown to learn, the one that he needed to learn before it was too late—the truth.

"There is no good or evil, boy!" I said. "There are just men and monsters, and men are prey to the monsters." I turned my back to him and stared at the dying lake that just moments before I had plunged the boy's face into, nearly killing him. "But you must understand, to kill a monster, you have to become an even greater monster. Else, you are already dead."

I did not need to turn to see what happened next, for I already knew. I knew the boy ran, ran like the day he did when he first saw us, ran away because he was afraid of the tough fight, ran away from the fingertips of death, ran away because he was afraid to die. One cannot be afraid of death if he is to survive in war, one cannot have any humanity in he is to succeed in war, and one cannot have any hope if he is to keep his mind in war.

CHAPTER 39

Gods No More

WE RODE OUT OF THE TOWN THE NEXT DAY towards the mountain passage, a week's ride at best. Gideon rode upon his mighty horse Re like usual, but he didn't lead the army. Instead, he rode in the midst, surrounded by his men. His scouts were sent out ahead to make sure the way was clear. I rode, watching and wondering when would be the time, the time to change all things that were to come. The time when I would commit my treacherous act to this great man, and I thought of how much I hated myself that I would do it.

Before I knew it, Gideon had brought his horse trotting next to mine at a pace comfortable for the both of us. His mighty white beast, who was at ease with me, snorted in a way of saying his hello as it approached. It was almost humanly, as if acknowledging our time together.

The beast that I rode was a rather powerful horse as well, which I had taken from the village. It was black as night and strong, but held no comparison to the beauty and grace that Re had, and did little to show any sign of intelligence other than that of following simple commands. It ran when it was asked. It slowed when it was told. It ate when food was put in front of it, and that was the extent of this beast. It was a follower of commands, there to serve another and that was all; it was simple, as much as I was. Re paid no mind to his lesser qualities and snorted a hello.

Gideon sat perched above, watching the horses bicker away with each other with short snorts back and forth. Then he looked at me before staring at the horizon and out of nowhere asked a startling question. "Do you think less of me, Vlad?"

I could barely mutter a response, for it was a shock to hear Gideon say those words. "I would never..."

I did not expect Gideon to ask such a thing. To my dismay, I wondered if I had done anything to hinder his trust in me or my reverence towards him. My actions towards the boy were towards the boy, not towards Gideon. I hoped he did not think I did not respect him, for I did, with all my heart and much more.

Gideon stared at his army that traveled ahead and the trees surrounding us. There was a peace about him, even though the subject we were on was disheartening to me.

"I know I have caused great mischief and the decisions I make are sometimes harsh and unexpected," Gideon said. "It is a lot to take in for a man to follow without question, but you never asked any."

Again, I was taken aback. It was if he sensed the disloyalty that I would commit one day. Yet that day was far from today and I would do my best to not allow it to happen. But he spoke as if he knew so well, knew every detail that I wondered. It was as if he had overheard my conversation with the fallen one, but I know that was to be impossible for there had been no soul in sight when the fallen one spoke, besides that of mine.

But there he was, apologizing for his actions when he had no reason to, for I knew them to be just and necessary regardless of the harshness.

"I believe in all your actions. I would never question them, my lord," I said, pledging my loyalty once again.

Gideon leaned back and let go of his reigns, balancing himself with his hands on top of Re's hind legs. He leaned onto them and let the mighty horse take control and follow his own wishes, which were still straight ahead but more of a casual approach.

"It is alright to question someone's actions, Vlad," Gideon said as he stretched his neck muscles and then loosened up his shoulders, getting out all the kinks from the long rides we had endured.

"I question my own actions sometimes as well," he said. "I do not have the foresight of the future. If I did, I could bring great wonders to the world." He paused to look at me, which unsettled me because of my dealings with the fallen one.

"No, instead, I make actions like any other man," he continued, "with great thought and great concern. That is why I do not wish for such blind obedience from anyone. I just hope that the actions I make are worthy enough for the lives of the men who follow them."

"I would have never thought you to question your actions, my lord." I watched Gideon finish his stretch, and the ease with which he rode on Re, maybe his oldest friend.

"Why not?" Gideon laughed as he brought himself back upright. "I sometimes have strange ideas; I am sure that most men would think them rather insane. You have never wondered what I do at times?"

"I have faith in you, my lord," I said as I stared back at the very innocent and inquisitive demeanor Gideon wore.

But that time was short, for his face became sincere and his mind was away for a moment before he came back to me.

"You know, you don't have to call me, 'my lord' all the time," Gideon said as he shifted his attention back to the route ahead. "I would like to think us as friends. Title only puts distance between that. You are as equal as I, Vlad. I told you that on the very first day you took arms at my side." He grabbed hold of the reigns once again.

"I'm sorry," I said.

"No need to apologize, Vlad. It's just a suggestion," he said with a warm smile. "As I said, you are free to make up your mind and do as you please. I value your mind as much as your blade."

That put a smile on my face. I still could not understand why this man treated me as a brother, but he did. For a moment, I forgot what the fallen one had said, and my mind and body were once again at ease.

"I am sorry for what I did back there," I said, "…against the boy."

It was true, for I was. I knew not why I took those actions, maybe genuinely trying to save the little boy from this life. Maybe I took those actions to drive Gideon and I further apart so he would not trust me when that day of betrayal came, so he would not be so hurt.

"There is no need to apologize, Vlad. You did what you did for your own reasons, which I understand quite clearly." Gideon stared at the road ahead as a warm breeze welcomed us through the passage of trees. He took a pause and breathed in the air deeply. "You know that you are not the monster you used to be, Vlad," Gideon turned to look at me with that steely gaze. "You are more human than anyone I have met."

"Me? What is so human about me?" I laughed.

"Emotion," Gideon said with a smile, "humans are humans for the emotions that we feel, the regret, the shame, and even the rage. With it, all there is a sense of understanding. That's why we humans feel emotion. Why we need to feel emotion."

There was a pause as I rolled that thought in my head.

"Sometimes I wish I did not feel," I said. "I wish to be as ignorant as an animal sometimes. It would be so much easier to be a dumb animal like this," I gestured to our horses.

"I think you offended Re," Gideon laughed. Re had picked up a little speed after glancing a strange look, as if he understood my words.

I laughed and said, "Re is the exception of course." It seemed to confirm my suspicions that Re could understand, for he eased back again to his trot.

"You see, even animals feel and that is what makes them connect to us. They are, in part, somewhat human," Gideon said joyfully. "Emotion is very strange, Vlad. When one cannot feel, that is all one wants, and when one feels, all he wants is not to feel. That is the ridiculous irony of it all."

We moved together through the road as the army moved ahead, keeping rear guard, going at our own pace.

"I have never told anyone this, Vlad, but it is a difficult chore being a leader," Gideon said with sadness in his voice, a sadness that I had never heard before. "Because when you are a leader," he continued, "one does not have the luxury of feeling anything. You have to be strong and calculating, always calm. You cannot let your troops see you waver. There is no rage. There is no contempt, even if that is all you want to feel. You have to block it out and focus, and the more you focus, the less human you feel. You do not see the world with your heart anymore; everything is a plan. A step to the next, a rung on the ladder, and when you get there and you accomplish what you need to accomplish, then there is no joy because you only see what is still ahead, the next rung up, and the hard climb ahead, even if that climb is eternal. And if you spend a lifetime doing that, then you spend a lifetime without joy, without love, without hope, without any human feelings whatsoever."

Then Gideon turned his attention to me. "That is what I love about you, Vlad. You are as pure as emotion can come," he said with a deep craving, "and even when you don't speak, when you don't say a word, your actions speak a thousand-fold. You speak with your eyes, your face, your hands. Every move you make speaks, but not only speaks but roars, and it roars loudly."

Gideon calmed down and spoke with a soft sincerity. "It reminds me of something that I cannot have but desperately crave, Vlad. Something beautiful that I sorely miss and that I cannot attain. I go through life fulfilling tasks that are set in front of me."

"That is not necessarily a bad thing," I said. I knew we were different, but I never knew him to value me in such a way. "You have accomplished more than most men dream. They would be happy to attain half of what you have fulfilled."

"Yes, I am, but those men do not know the costs. If they did, they would not pursue this route. You see, Vlad," Gideon said staring at me, "you can have fulfillment or you can have happiness, but you can never have both. For fulfillment is a lifelong hunger that always grows and never gets full, and happiness, well, happiness is the absence of fulfilment."

Gideon looked back to the path ahead and continued. "I know you think of it as a burden having all that emotion, but do not be willing to throw it away so quickly. Some men would be glad to have a chance to express it like you could."

"I have never thought of my emotion to be anything less than a nuisance," I said. "I would have never thought that you would have these concerns."

"See, I am so focused, Vlad, that I think you do not see me as human," Gideon teased. "In fact, I think half our army thinks of me as some unworldly, supernatural creature." His tone was one of fascinated amusement.

I had no words left in me, for I was embarrassed to think that deep down, I too thought that .

Gideon sensed this immediately, leaving us with an awkward silence.

"And no, I am not, Vlad," Gideon said raising his hands in playful defeat, "I am as human as you, no great or divine power resides within me. I take my actions as any man does. I follow the desires set in my heart, my experiences that I've learnt the hard way, my own beliefs that I have come to understand," he glanced at me, "...as best as I could, and nothing else."

Gideon continued as he returned his eyes to the road. "I am just a mere man with a dream, nothing more, and one day I will die like any other. Death will finally come to take me. Hopefully it will be after I reach my dream and not before. That is all I wish for. That is all I struggle for."

We rode silent for a moment without any words exchanged as I absorbed the notion that I had misled myself with. Each moment I spoke to him I hoped would lead me into understanding the greatness of this man, his ambition, his nature, his honor. Every time I learned more, I was left astounded.

This action showed Gideon in a light that I had not seen before, even when I thought I knew all of him. How foolish I was. He was a man that I knew so well and stared at but had never seen. I had held him in such light, in such reverence, that the glow blinded me to his true self. I had put him perched on such a high pedestal that I did not think any man to be able to reach him. But he was far different than what I thought him as. He had the same concerns, the same remorse as any other man. He was not a god or an ethereal being, or some creature of light, like I wished him to be, or as so many of the other men in the army also wished for. He was simply a man.

A man that walked and breathed like the rest of us, that truly wondered of his actions and what would happen next. A man that made mistakes and had faults, and a man that did not know what to do next, but still followed his heart. A man who was just as alone as I was, just at opposite sides of the spectrum—him in glory and myself in shame.

Up ahead, the forest started to clear and the barren land started to show itself. This was a clear indicator of the mountain pass coming near. Gideon had already lost his playful nature, his face had become stern and void of emotion, just like he said it would when that ladder of life would come into view.

He properly sat himself back on his mount and held the reigns tightly before letting out a sigh. "I guess it's time for me to be off, Vlad," he said. "I must go be a leader once again." He rode forward, heading to the front lines once more.

"Thank you...Gideon!" I yelled, for the first time taking his name as he started to move out of reach.

Gideon leaned back and yelled, "You said you were a monster back there to the boy."

I was surprised that he had heard what I said to the boy.

"You're wrong, Vlad!" he said emphatically. "A monster does not regret! A monster cannot be ashamed! And a monster cannot love anyone besides himself." He smiled a most bright smile and pointed at me with one hand, the other still on the reigns. "You do!"

Then he turned back and went full-fledged ahead, ready to lead his army forward into the new territory. Unfeeling like he had seemed, confident and un-showing of concerns, inhuman and godly as he had to be, all because he must appear that way, all for the love of his troops.

CHAPTER 40
The Field of War

"

I have heard many depictions of what it feels like before a battle. They tend to simplify it to pleasant talks and comparisons, such as butterflies in one's stomach and unease. How simple and arrogant these thoughts are, and far from the truth.

For the truth is, there is no feeling before war that can be described by simple words and terms. It is complex and perpetual and in constant change. War is not made of one thing. No, there is hope, failure, possession, fear, anguish, love, faith, terror, and rage, and it happens all at once and changes the very moment you feel it. All I can tell you of it is that at first, there is a stark emptiness in the body, that part is true. But not for the reasons you imagine, no, it is because the body does not know what to feel, for war is too great of a presence to be felt by anyone alone, and too hard to be comprehended by the sane, for war is insane and chaos incarnate. That is the only truth about the feeling before war. And for those wondering how it feels to be in it, should imagine plunging into a raging volcano

and surviving, for that would be the only way to do justice in

comparison to war.

99

ON THAT EVE OF BATTLE, the one that would change all things that came before and all that resulted after. On that dawn of the new tomorrow that would lay the foundations for destinies to be carried out. On that new frontier that no man had traveled and would change all inevitabilities for the future to come, we stood strong and ready. This was the ground where laws of nature and man were to be broken, and plans of gods to be tested and molded, and it would all happen from the fallout of the oncoming assault, the oncoming doom, the oncoming storm that was to be our making.

Our armies gathered on the crest of the hill, watching and waiting in anticipation and malevolently eyeing the enemies that had been prepared for our coming.

Despite our best efforts, despite our best tactics, they saw us coming and were ready. They waited in arms, weapons ready, armed for an assault that would decimate those that stood before them. They were instructed and lead by their General, a rather large man with broad shoulders and powerful thick arms, an axe the size of a man mounted on his back. He directed the orders to his fellow barbarians, who eagerly waited for bloodshed.

They were ready, for they knew what was to come. Desert life had taught them that much, I was assured. It had taught them that strength and brutality can be powerful weapons when combined with confidence.

However, this would be a much different battle than they had expected, for we were a skilled bunch and just as much brutes, trained by various battles. He were experienced and weathered opponents that had warred for all our lives. If brutality was what they knew, we were born from it.

Yet, they had great advantages at their side. Their raw numbers outmatched ours. Their fortifications made their position on the field an immensely difficult task to overtake, if not nigh impossible. They had an army ten times our size, allowing archers and spearmen from their wooden ramparts to strike our horsemen down before we even reached them. Then there was the size of their force that dwarfed ours—if met on the open field, they would overtake us by the fact they could easily overrun ours. The terrain offered little use of anything strategic but dirt and rock, and if a battle ensued upon it, it would be a fight to the death for neither army would be able to retreat except to the perilous mountains that rose into the heavens so high and were so vicious that no army had ever survived the journey across. The only way to escape would be the passage that they now controlled; anything else would be complete suicide.

It was to be that once this battle was started, that there would be no second chance, no retreat, not even a surrender, not to a brutish bunch like these animals. There was not much that could be certain in the outcome of battle. The only thing that was to be certain was there would be blood, and the grounds would surge like a river of it, and there would be much death. That is what excited me, for no matter how much I hated myself for it, the beast still lurked very much within and it was getting hungry once again.

We stood at our end, out of the reaches of the ramparts, out of the reaches of the arrows. We were ready for our final battle, for our final act of defiance from the invading barbarians. We stood waiting in the cold dawn of the new day, a day that would be the dawn of hell on earth, and we the demons that walked it, torturing each other for the sake of a right that seems laughable in the memory of time.

It was then that Gideon, as the man he was, rode forward to make his speech, in the way that he always did before our battles.

He rode in front, put his back to the barbarians and faced his troops so that they saw what he saw—strength, courage, and a life at risk. Gideon did so that day, the way he does on all days.

He sat perched high on Re in his usual ritual, taking in all its surroundings, all the smells, all the sights, and all the feelings, for he knew that this might be the very day that was his last and he would enjoy every moment of it if it were. There is no greater honor than fighting for your dream, even if it is unachievable and insane.

He took in the smell of the dry, humid weather that weighed the body down. He took in the sound of the silence that was only interrupted by the wind blowing through the mountain pass like an instrument warming up. He took in the feel of the warm sun that gleamed off his armor, creating a shimmering display of brilliance on the field. He took in the energy of uncertainty and anticipation in all of us as we waited, unknowing of what would happen next. And when he finally took in all his other senses, he took in the sight of his troop.

We were the ever-ready troop that would stand with him to the very end, the troop that would sacrifice all they were for the purpose of his dream, the troop that were more than mere soldiers but instead, an army full of brothers and sisters. It was this sight that lit the fire in his heart, that lit his ambition and brought out a warrior and leader that had not the luxury of emotion, but a calculated godly symbol of strength and perseverance that was unmatched. As the fire burned in his heart, he spoke to light the fire in ours.

"Welcome, brothers, to the field of war. A field that we have visited before. A familiar field that we have bled to sustain, that we have struggled to rebuild, that we have seeded so that others may prosper. This field that you stand on is that very field, as the ones that all those before you had stood on in their times. Stood and maintained like we did before there was a kingdom, before there was order, before there was law."

"They stood on this field and planted the first crop. They stood together and farmed this land, took dirt and dust and transformed it into a kingdom. They took away the disorder, misery, and chaos and formed an empire from this field that after all those years, we have still maintained.

"But those men behind me have brought back the misery, the chaos, the disorder. Those barbarians who are not from this land, who did not build this place, who did not struggle for their place on the earth, and who have not bled what we have bled.

"That is what we are here to fight for today. We stand against an army of barbaric men that have greater numbers than ours, who want nothing more than to burn our fields, after stealing the fruit that we planted, taking away the harvest that they have not earned. They want to take blood from our sweat so that we would weaken, so that we would fall and give in, allowing them to steal our bounty. They want us to watch as they pillage our lands, murder our men, rape our women and make slaves of our children.

"Those are the men that stand behind me, an arrogant band of barbaric men. They are barbarians—uncivil, unkind, and full of contempt. They sit and watch, waiting. Right now, I say to you, they are arming themselves, mounting their fortifications, readying for the assault and asking their gods to grant them victory on this day.

"Well, we will not do the same. We will not ask for victory today, men. No, today we will earn it. We will earn the right to live where we live, live the way we want, the way we have worked so hard for, and everything that we have built for. Victory is ours. That is a fact and we do not need to ask for it. We need to show it.

"I say, let the barbarians behind us do the praying today. Let them ask for forgiveness, for blessings, for anointment in battle, for today, we need none. We do not need to ask for these things, because we already have them. We have earned those rights, and those traits, all those honors, all those favors, because of the road that we have traveled, and the road we have bled on to be here, so much and so long a road, that even the Gods cannot touch us on this day, because we have traveled past them.

"In fact, it is the Gods who ask a favor of us, they ask us to fight for justice, to show light in the face of darkness, to vanquish evil with the sword of good because they cannot. Yes, I say that is the truth!

"For I say that the Gods are watching today. They watch in great envy of what is about to take place, for they will not have the pleasure of this battle. They will not have the luxury of experiencing this war, this want, this glory, this unattainable wonder of what we will accomplish today. They will have none of it and they will want what we will have in abundance.

"So, I say to the Gods in the heavens, and those in Hell, to fear me devils, fear me, kings, for we walk amongst the earth, untouched by holy and unholy alike. We are the blessed! We are the anointed! We are the unbroken! We are the unattained, unwanted by worlds above and those below, for we belong to a world of our own, this world, this world of war.

"We stand amongst the greatest of men who have stood on this field, the greatest of champions who have ridden their way to victory, to tell a story to the Gods, a story beyond sheer mortality, sheer conscience, or sheer belief. A story that will rain through the starlit skies at night, a story that will bring the dawn of a new kingdom, and a story that will never be truly understood except by those that stood here on this field and felt it! Such is the glory that we will achieve on this day.

"We are no mere men! We are no mere soldiers! We are not even mere humans! We are much more. We are the darkness and the light that roams the earth. We are the terror and the hope that travels from one's mind. We are the dream weavers, who will take our enemies' ambitions and twist them into a tapestry of their own nightmares. We are the scholars of this story and not that decreed by heaven or hell.

"We are here to create that destiny that we willed into existence with our blood as the ink, and write with our flesh as pages. That is what we must do today. We must protect what we have made. We must tend to these fields that they have tried so desperately to spoil. And tend we will!

"We will be farmers who will raise our swords as death's scythe, and rid the vermin that has infested this field. We will do so for the sake of the people. For the sake of the poor, the ever hungry, the wronged, the sinned, the massacred, and all those who were victimized so they could steal our soil, so they could stand on our land, so they could sit and watch us as we suffered from their wrath. Well, no longer. For their violation ends here. It ends now!

"There are no manner of walls, no manner of shields, no manner of flesh that will hold us at bay. We are the gods of war in this life. We are the rulers of the land, and we will reap and reap until the fields are cleared, until we have soaked the fields with their blood and poured it from the vessels they call flesh, and their blood will pour until they stand empty, until they can stand no more.

"That is the truth, men, and I shall tell you another truth. I tell you that today I am afraid. I shiver in my boots as I see them, standing behind their walls, covered in an array of shields, mounted with weapons that can skewer any man that comes near. I am, in fact, terrified of this battle—but not in the way the enemy hopes.

"No, I am unnerved at what I will do to those men when they step onto this field, onto our field. I am terrified that I will not be able to stop myself from hurting them, from claiming our victory. I am horrified that I will not be able to be knightly and show mercy when they ask for it, which they will as they bleed on our field. They will beg us to stop as we annihilate them. I am mortified that there will be no power on earth or the heavens that will be able to stop us as we take their heads.

"For that is what we will do today, men. That is what we are here to do, so I say do not fear the army in front of you. No, do not even fear their number, or the walls that they stand behind. Instead, fear yourself.

"For they are just men, and we are much more, beyond anything they can imagine. When the stories of this day will spread, and they will, they will know that you stood strong and stout and resolute. They will know that you stared into faces of the opposition, and they shook in their boots, because you are the men that will not stop, that will not waver, that will not let death grasp at you, because death will be too busy tending to the enemy.

"So, my brothers, be ready, which I know you already are. You are ready, waiting for the chance to strike at our enemy and you will have that chance and that desire filled soon, that I promise you!

"For the time is now for us to do what we have done, what we have always known, what we have seen, and what we do best—we war. We war greater than any storm that is to come. We war greater than any might that can exist. We war because we are war. So I say onto you, my men, my brothers, my arms, to move now onto the field, our field!

"It is time to show them that war that we wage so well and deny them their God's words when they beg for them, for we will give them ours, and it will be a blessing that they would most desperately crave after we get done with them. Their death will be a blessing. So now, let us show them how we war!"

O how well those words traveled within us. It was if Gideon breathed the flame of the Dragon from his very mouth, and if fire be what Gideon hoped to churn in our hearts, then he caused a volcano to erupt instead. It roared as a towering inferno; the men gathered their arms and set forth to march across the barren field to wage that very war he spoke of, and to give them that death they so desperately deserved, a death that we all deserved.

CHAPTER 41

First Assault

THE FIRST WAVE OF THE BARBARIANS could only be described as a stone wall, a stone wall of force that came crashing towards us, that obliterated all those in its path. Impenetrable and unbending, it moved across the field, grinding up men and leaving them mauled. It trampled over them as they marched across the field.

Such was the force of the enemy when they attacked us. No matter the strength that we showed, the desert forces had much more and in spades. They moved far more precisely and were better organized than I could have imagined.

Even Gideon made no advance and retreated to aid the men that were severely suffering from the blows of the unending barbarian horde. There was no retreat on the other side, for they advanced and advanced, taking out all those stood in front of them. They moved towards us like a deadly animal, with their strongest warriors leading the way. Our preliminary troops stood little chance when engaged with these men. Each man of theirs was a hulking specimen of a warrior, built for war, an executioner in their own right, fuming with rage, foaming at the mouth, and undaunting in their task of killing.

All our expertise in combat, all our training, blocking blows, parrying and striking when it was opportune, were of no use to our men. Once the horde's large axes came crashing down, it took our steel, flesh and bone away with each swing, whatever type of matter stood in front of it.

When we made a rare kill, it only made them more enraged, more infuriated, and they moved faster and pushed us further back until we retreated. They moved as a block of death, chopping its way through, pushing us and pushing us until we could not be pushed back any more.

What a wonder, they were true berserkers on the field. It was as if I saw a whole army of me running towards us. The very sight, the very thought, brought out something in me that I had been hiding, keeping caged deep inside. As their force grew and grew and that wave of death became a tidal wave of destruction and wiped away all that stood in front of it, it only loosened that tightly held cage door.

I bit my lip and held my blade's hilt tightly. The beast within was awakening and how he hungered. I breathed in all the scents of war—the blood, the fear, the entrails, the discarded flesh. I took in all the screams, all the rage, and it was O so magnificent.

O the darkness, the beautiful darkness, and how wondrous the souls flew in the air. One after the other, the line of men in front of me fell, and the stone wall force of the horde drew nearer.

My sinews were fuming, my body pulsing, my blood rushing. O the energy that traveled through me, just waiting to be unleashed, but I could not let it out. I had to wait. I had to wait until it was time, until I could show them what I truly was, what we scarred men of flesh could truly do to an unstoppable force such as this.

Then I heard the call. Gideon finally gave the word and the trumpet of death blew. The trumpet that I knew meant so much to Gideon now meant the same to me as well.

I stood waiting in front of the horde as they halted at the sound, and they saw the smirk on my face. It was at that time that they knew something was wrong, but not what or where they erred. And in even more confusion, they wondered why I was not afraid, why I smiled the way I did.

I was not afraid for I had been what they were, for I had seen what they could do, for I had done it myself. I had seen better, was shown what I could truly be. More than all that, I was not afraid because I knew Gideon, and they did not.

They did not know of any man who would be willing to sacrifice what needed to be sacrificed. They did not know of any man that would be so emotionless, so cold, so calculating, but still a marvel of a man. On that day, they would learn of his greatness and his ruthlessness, and his unbending will and might.

It was then that the horde's stone wall of force started to topple, as brick by brick our archers plunged their wooden poison into their exposed backs. In midst of the battle, in the heat of the war, they had not noticed that we had no bowmen, we had no slingers, we had no missile troop whatsoever. We had only the lightly armored who thrashed and thrashed until they could not thrash no more.

No, our forces were weak and that gave them advance, that gave them strength, that gave them confidence, and that gave them a reckless behavior that would cost them dearly.

I smiled, gritting my teeth in wondrous anticipation, for they had just realized that this was not a war, but a hunt. And in this hunt, they were to be the boar, and we the hunter. As I ran towards them with my eyes widened, my sinews tightened and my blade drawn, they realized in utter terror that the hunt had just begun.

CHAPTER 42

The Cost of War

THE FALL OF THE BARBARIAN'S FIRST WAVE had severely hindered the outpost's defense and angered their General immensely. For the men that were lost were to be the predominant front line for all attacks the outpost had to offer, and now they were stripped back to their core defensive troops. At one time we were outnumbered, but our strategical victory left us on even ground, troops equal on both sides, for every one of ours we lost they lost four. This was our trade and it was barbaric, but such is the cost of war.

Still, even with our prominent victory, it would take a lot more to succeed in this battle. The outpost still held great advantage, for their fortifications, while not at their peak and hindered from the initial assault the barbarians took to gain hold of it, still gave them great defense that would hurt as immensely if we were to attack full front. Also, they were blocked by the daunting perilous mountains on both sides, and in doing so were also blocked from behind, so we could not flank them. Climbing those mountains would be a futile assault since the mountains were so jagged, so high that not even trees dared to sit at their peaks, rather grew from the sides to avoid the treacherous ascent. This only left one choice—a front assault from our army. If we were to engage them, that would be doom. Our army, on the other hand, was open to attack from all sides and with swift action from a keen General, could be taken advantage of.

However, our victory over their front lines also gave us a second advantage, which was to add fear and uncertainty to the enemy, which prevented them from taking hasty actions, even if it would benefit them. This supplied our troops ample time to rest and recover from the fierce battle that left many men drained. One thing was for certain— this was a battle that was not to be fought in a day, but days or even weeks if the heaven's permitted. The men needed their full strength if it were to be a victory, but as it is always in war, nothing is truly certain.

That night we rested in a field, with full view of the outpost as well as the dirt-ridden, blood-drenched battlefield where the dead bodies of our enemies festered. Such was their caution—the barbarians dared not send a funeral man out to drag the fallen back to give them a proper burial, so they were prey to the vultures and wolves that roamed about. After a full day in the baking sun, the bodies had rotted. They emitted such a great stench of decay that it appeared as visible steam coming from boiling water, and a foul, nauseating odor that rose high into the air. So fetid was the stench that even the predators of the night left the rotting bodies untouched. Yet, fortune was again on our side, since the wind carried the smell towards the outpost. It only added to daunting fear of the barbarians to not take military action, which gave us further reason to rest undisturbed with ease from concern.

That night, the moon had risen in full view. The sun had taken a bow early in the day and the night was filled with brilliant moonlight in a star-filled sky that would let many men see far beyond the campfire.

Gideon and I sat near a campfire, our clothes covered with dried blood and our limbs tired from the day's labor. I had grabbed a piece of timber and threw it in the fire as Gideon rested, drinking his ration of water that he had boiled to kill any disease that might be carried with it from the war.

We sat for some time with no words exchanged between us—Gideon was occupied with the plight of overcoming the outpost—but our serenity was broken when a voice of a boy was heard.

It was the same boy who I had menaced in the village, and he had appeared out of nowhere. He showed instant concern when he looked in my direction, but Gideon welcomed him anyways. He looked different from when I first saw him; his eyes were hallowed, his skin was pale. War had changed him, yet I had not seen him on the battlefield and was even surprised to see him at the campfire.

The boy quickly came to Gideon. In return, Gideon whispered something to the boy that I could not understand. In an instant, the boy went off with a look of determination, disappearing quickly into the night as mysteriously and skillfully as he had come.

Gideon went back to his drink, staring at the fire that crackled in the night, but it bothered me deeply to see the boy still involved.

"What can that mere boy do? He is no warrior," I said.

Gideon smiled and said not a word. Instead, he stared at the flames that traveled and engulfed the piece of timber that I had thrown within.

"He is very naive little boy, a coward at best," I continued. "He hid from sight when the barbarians raided his village, and even hid from us when we reached the ruins of it."

Gideon calmly sipped his drink. "Yes, but the boy is a survivor. He has his use."

"What purpose is that?"

"Everyone has a purpose, Vlad. Besides, what is the point of living to just exist and occupy space if there is no purpose to it? There is no point to survival if you don't apply it to something, even if it be war."

A moment of silence again traveled through our campsite as I threw another log into the fire. Gideon watched.

"War will change him," I said, "like it did me."

"War has changed us all, some parts better, some parts worse. I believe you have changed for the better. Don't you think so, Vlad?" Gideon looked at me. "Maybe the boy will change as well."

I was aggravated at the comment, for I did not like what I had changed into. "I have not changed much, Gideon," I said as I took my sword to the fire and turned the piece of timber over to bake the other side. "I was born a murderer, and I am still a murderer."

Gideon paused as he examined my answer. "I like that," he replied.

That was a response that I had not expected. Gideon had never encouraged the practice of death, only shown that it was necessary in war.

"I mean," he looked at me with a smile, "I like that you are finally using my name."

He stared back into the fire and laid on his back.

"I cannot promise that death will not be part of our lives, Vlad. That would be a lie. All I can promise is that it has a purpose and it is a very heavy burden. What makes us worthy warriors is the ability to walk with its burden on our shoulders, no matter how much we do not want to."

Gideon stood up, stretched the kinks of his neck and turned to me.

"I see the conflict within you, Vlad, no matter how much you try to hide it from me. As I said, you show your emotions quite easily and I understand your reluctance. The war that rages within you is as great as the battles that we fight."

Gideon put his hand on my shoulder.

"You have done me great service by being with me on the battlefield, as well as being my friend. I cannot ask you for much more. The decision you make I will respect, whatever that decision is to be."

With that, Gideon got up. He brushed the dirt and dust off of his clothes, and walked off to his tent, leaving me by myself, wondering what actions to take next.

How calm Gideon was, I could not understand. Had he just given me permission to leave the army and leave the life of murdering and death behind, something that I was, in a way, desperately craving? Yet to stand by him was also what I wanted, and I did not want to leave his side before he accomplished what he wanted to accomplish.

Then, I thought of what the fallen one had said, that I would commit a treacherous act. Would this be that act? Or was the act that of leaving him and dooming him to live a life that would fade into obscurity, failing to achieve his dream. That would harm me greatly as well—I had followed his dream for so long that now, it had become my dream also. Or could this be both of those outcomes combined in one, where I destroyed all chance of any peace because I would doom myself to commit a treacherous act and be pained from a guilty conscious, at the same time increasing the chances of a man that I loved and admired to be plagued with misery. Was this the new destiny that I had created for myself because I failed to submit to the one that had been planned and preordained?

How malicious a creature is destiny and how ruthless it is in its doings, for when I took up arms against it, it struck back tenfold. It had me at the brink of madness and dismay, and had torn my mind into pieces of worry and concerns. My concerns were further enhanced from the fear brought on by my enlightenment of Gideon's humanity.

It was a fear that I had not known before because I had been blinded by ignorance. I had made Gideon stand in the place of gods, a supernatural being that could not be harmed or damaged in any way. In the stable of my life, that had been my foundation of sanity.

I was at risk of losing it all, simply because that false sense of reality was gone. Instead of a rock, that I imagined stood safely and firmly on the ground in the garden of Heaven, now stood a wooden plank on a creaking bridge over the pits of Hell. One misstep, one blind move could take that very foundation away and send us both hurtling below to the blazing, tormented purgatory that I had created.

It was certain that I could not leave at that moment, for I could not let any of those outcomes occur. If I did, then I could not protect Gideon when he was at his most dire need, for he was at more risk than he had ever been before and I needed to be there for him. That was a task I would commit to, for that was the strength of my love for this man. He had given me all I ever asked for and more, had shown me mercy, compassion, and time when I was in need. At this time, when he was in need, I would not abandon him, no matter the cost I had to pay.

CHAPTER 43

A Patient War

THE SUN SCORCHED THE GROUND and the skies were blinding to stare at. In that blistering heat, we readied ourselves for another assault, another attack, another victory. Only when we stood directly in the outpost's path did we feel the gentle breeze come from the passageway, but it was mild and barely made the hair tingle on one's head.

I had made up my mind that I would not leave Gideon, no matter what happened, and this I had fully absorbed. It had kept me late and I had dozed off rather later than usual. I woke up to see the army had already mounted and Gideon already set.

I quickly grabbed my blade and headed to the front lines, past the men, past the lines, and near Gideon, who stood eagerly waiting with two shields on the ground in front of him.

"I am glad you chose to stay," Gideon said with a vibrant smile that was unfitting for war. "I was beginning to wonder."

"I will never leave your side, my friend. I owe you for all that I am."

Gideon smiled one of those most sincere and innocent smiles that made him seem childish in nature. "You do not owe me, Vlad. It is I that owe you for your trust."

I hesitated but found it an opportune time to ask what plagued my head. "Then I must ask a simple favor of you."

"Ah, well planned, Vlad. I give in." Gideon smiled, raising his hands in defeat. "What is it you desire?"

"I ask you to leave the boy out of this."

Gideon stood, puzzled at my request. "The boy? He is that important to you?"

I took a deep sigh and responded with reluctance. "I have caused much pain and destruction in my life. I wish to do something good before my time comes, before I expire. If there is one life I can save for all the death that I have brought onto this world, then let it be his. It is the one thing I desperately desire and want to do before I die, and this battle may be my end."

"Oh, quit being so gloomy, Vlad. Not every story ends in misery and despair. You will not die this battle, I can assure you that," Gideon smiled and placed a hand on my shoulder like he always did when speaking from the heart. "And if this boy is important to you, then he is important to me as well. I will send the boy home. I promise." He picked up one of the shields and held it towards me. "But right now, you need this."

"A shield?"

"Yes."

"I am not one who fights with a shield."

"Trust me, Vlad. On this day," he said with a smile and placed the shield in my hands, "you will need it." He grabbed the other shield and pulled the straps tightly.

Another gentle breeze came from the outpost, and I wondered what plans Gideon had in store.

"So you have decided what we will do with the outpost, I presume?"

"Yes, Vlad, I have." Gideon looked sternly to the mountainous pass where the outpost so formidably stood, untouched by our assaults.

"What will you do?" I looked at the shield that I held strapped onto my arms.

There was a moment before Gideon responded where the air around us felt changed, where the very feel of our pleasant conversation had taken a turn and became very serious.

"They will burn," Gideon said rather coldly. "Like a fire that burns in hell, I will make them burn."

Before I could ask what Gideon meant, he smiled a most wicked smile and raised his hand for the archers to draw, and so they did. Each had an arrow adjusted to the height of the sky, pointed in an arch that seemed far above the outpost. Each long laced bow mounted an arrow with a flaming tip that sizzled in the air. It took all the strength they had to maintain the pull.

Then Gideon's hand sliced through the air, and in instant later the arrows sliced through the sky, releasing a harmonic wisp of hundreds of wooden rods flying through the sky all at once, accompanied only by an orchestra of twangs from the bows releasing them.

In the meantime, the barbarians at the outpost took up their shields, raised them high above their heads and ducked down, setting their feet solid to absorb the impact. The remaining barbarians entered the roofed buildings that our arrows could not penetrate, in full security away from our assault.

They watched us as I watched the arrows fly. They flew higher and higher, into the sky, soaring like fiery birds, moving so fast and rising so steadily that it appeared that they would miss the outpost entirely, which filled me with concern. It was not until the first arrow struck, that I realized the outpost was not what they were aiming for.

No, they had no need to hit the outpost, for the archers had aimed for the hanging trees high above. The trees could not travel up the steep mountains and hung sideways, providing much relief of shade and shelter by jutting from the mountain walls, blocking the barbarians from the attack of the sun. As each arrow struck, it was snuffed out by the might of the trees. The thickness of the trunks absorbed the blow with just a little spark of light before they absolved into nothingness. I wondered what Gideon had in mind, but I could not decipher it, for I would have thought he knew the trees to be too thick to be able to do any damage to them.

The barbarians must have thought the same, as they roared in heinous laughter and riddled the air with disparaging remarks at what a lousy shot our archers were. Yet, as always, Gideon had a strategy at play. Even though I knew not what it was, I knew not to question him.

Gideon searched the skies, emotionless, without any reaction, undaunted by the remarks from the outpost. He was looking for something, and it was not until he saw a flock of birds leaving some trees that he smirked.

He pointed towards the trees that birds flew from. With another raise of his hand, the bows were loaded with flaming arrows once more. Then, as before, the moment his hand came down, another volley of fiery arrows flew through the air, all targeted at his mark—the tree the bird was nested within.

The arrows once again sailed through the air. The barbarians readied their shields, and the arrows once again struck their intended mark. Each disappeared into the tree that the birds came from, and snuffed out once again.

Immediately after, Gideon told the archers to retreat and take cover, and so did we all, for Gideon was well prepared and knew what was coming next.

As soon as we had raised our shields, the barbarians released their arrows in response to ours. They were not precise, and in fact, appeared like ours, set to miss their marks. They had little training in long ranged combat—their hulking size was meant for close quarter warfare. Even with that, they made up for the lack in their techniques, for all their inaccuracies, with the sheer number of arrows that flew. They blanketed the sky in darkness as if it were a speeding cloud of shadow that grew bigger and bigger as it neared us, until it struck its mark in a wildfire of strikes.

The arrows went onto the field, powerfully striking the ground in thwacking sounds one after the other as if a hammer hit the dirt with each one. Each arrow struck a spot and left a wooden spike, its shaft embedded into the dirt. Such an abundance of spiked sticks stuck out that it made the entire field appear as if it were a giant bed of nails, so vicious that even an armored horses foot would have been pained to cross it.

Yet, that was only a mere fraction of arrows that were launched. For then the other half was released, the half that actually reached us, one after the other, hitting in our mass of gathered flesh and armor. Despite the shields we held, the arrows still broke through.

In that time, I saw men fall, those who stood next to me, those who stood behind me, all injured. Each of them toppled over as arrows passed their shields and hit their marks. But it was not over, for soon as that volley was done, another set was launched from the outpost.

Again, I heard the grunts and the quick death of men all around, and they fell one after the other. And before any of us could move to prepare, another rain of arrows struck in an unending assault until the ground around us was covered with spiked ends. One would have thought that no arrow would have remained in their outpost, for the multitude they expressed were that of a forest undone.

Finally, when I was satisfied that no arrows could reach us any longer, that no arrows were in flight, and there was no sound of any wisps in the air, I took down my shield to see the carnage around me.

I saw the fallen men, the tortured souls, riddled with pointed sticks. They were permanently stuck to the ground, for moving them would sever their bodies into pieces. And then there were the men, like Gideon and I who had survived the assault, with arrows stuck around us in such mass that it appeared as a cage of wooden bars holding us within.

One by one, we stood to view the turmoil, and saw the ground towards the outpost riddled with a pathway of broken pieces of wooden death.

Gideon waved his sword, and his horsemen took flight and moved the long way around to avoid the wooden spiked carnage. They traveled to the right of the pass and to the left, but oddly, they did not attack.

They stood well out of reach from the outpost, and well out of reach from their own assault, and in no danger of arrows being launched, for the outpost had none left. They waited for something I did not know, but eagerly waited to find out.

"What now?" I asked as we looked at the stalemate of both of our assaults. The outpost was still in one piece and our army, though reduced, was still standing strong.

"Patience, Vlad," Gideon said with the most brilliant of smiles. "War is about patience." He placed a hand on my shoulder to ease my tension and in that moment, my heart stopped, for everything changed.

For the outpost did have an arrow, and that arrow did fly, and that lone arrow came and it was precise. It struck, but it had not struck at my heart. Instead, it came howling death's song and struck right into Gideon's chest.

CHAPTER 44

Flames of Hell

I LEAPT FORWARD AS FAST AS I COULD, but I could only catch Gideon falling into my arms. His armor, magnificent as it was, did not hinder the arrows path, and only held the arrow in place while the tip dug deep into his flesh. Gideon's eyes had drifted to the sky above; the clouds raced by as if they ran from the sight. Finally, he shifted his focus towards me, and instead of agony, instead of pain which I knew he must have surely felt, he smiled without saying a word, and then his eyes closed, and I held him tightly in my arms.

The army halted in shock, for there stood our god, our guiding light, our beacon in the shadows. He was now beaten and broken, leaving us in complete and utter darkness, with no sight of a victory. All those talks, all those paths, all those hopes, all those sacrifices came crashing down in an avalanche of broken dreams, running towards us with a force that we could not fathom, that we could not stop as it overwhelmed our hearts.

In response to our misery, our anguish, our pain, the outpost roared in victory as they achieved their mark, their victory against an opposition that had bested them in all ways, up until now. They roared in victory, they roared in undeserved glory, they roared and roared for they thought it was over, but they were wrong, dead wrong.

They thought it had been done, that the war was close at an end, that they had injured our morale, that they had taken out our spirit, because they took away our hope. They had. That was for certain, and I cannot deny it, but in its place was not defeat. No, not despair, or fear, or retreat. No, it was something far different, and far more devious and twisted. It was unquenchable anger.

O how I raged, I felt my veins pulse with fury, with vengeance and strength. I would not, could not hold my anger any longer, and I screamed. I screamed a most atrocious and loud heinous roar, such as the lion that sends the jungle animals scurrying out of danger when it is angered, so did my roar. It hushed the cries of the outpost. It calmed the wind. It alone spread across the land for nothing else dared stand in the path of my ferocious cry. If I was a monstrous beast, then I had become injured in the most dire way. They had taken from me everything that I held dear, and I had nothing left to hold me at bay. I would be the most dangerous opposition that they could ever have imagined.

I gathered my blade. I put aside Gideon's body, and I walked to the tattered path of broken wood, and past the remnants of the battle that had stained the ground red. No arrow came my way. No man stood in front of my path. No friend nor foe dared walk beside me as I walked.

And I continued to walk. Past the blitz of arrows that stuck in the ground, past the decaying bodies of the dead, past the incessant smell of putrefaction, I walked. I walked and walked to the outpost to wage war as Gideon had pronounced, to wage vengeance like he had promised the first day I met him, to battle and take on an army by my lone hand. To take the hand and guide the way of death to its next target, for in that moment, I was death, I was fury, and I was the very flames of Hell.

There was no response, for no man could fathom my claim and the anger that my exuded from my flesh, my muscles, my bones, my breath. No man had the ability to perceive that one man would take this feat on himself but I did and I did not care who stood in my path or how great the obstacle was, I would reap my vengeance. My hate would not be ignored.

The outpost waited as I approached, for they too were alarmed at what had conspired from the change of events. Finally, one dared to take lead and got up to stand in my path, for it was his honor at stake, and his legacy to break.

He was a brute of a barbaric nature, broad shouldered and wide, but a man that towered and appeared as a mountain to all other men; it was the General of their army. Fitting, for they took the General of ours and it would be his head that I would take.

Yet he was a mighty behemoth of a man, who rose from behind the ranks and walked out, parting his men to the side as he took his large, hefty steps. He carried little armor on him besides a long, flowing cape of leathery bearskin. He showcased his immense muscles and the scars that plagued his entire body, from head to toe. He carried only one weapon, a two bladed axe, but it was not just any axe—it was a titan of an axe. It was the length of a spear, with blades that circled in half-moons, one on each side. This powerhouse of a man, a mass of humanity, a behemoth of brutality, had one thing on his mind, which was the same that I had on mine—death to one of us, no matter the end.

Any normal man would halt at such a sight, would run as they heard the brute's stride that was large and heavy and thudded the ground like thunder with each step. Any normal man would be sane to do anything but fight, but I did not care for I was not sane. No man, or mountain, could stand in my way. The world was weak against my will, my fury, and I burned with such ferocity that thought was little in the way of action. In that moment, it mattered not if I made my actions as a man, for I was not a man. No, I was an animal. I was the boar. I was the monster that clawed its way trying to get out, and now it had. It showed, and all men cowered at the sight, for they were right to fear a monster such as I.

But the brute was different. He was a veteran of war, arrogant from his size, and as he walked, he made his claims and boasted his exploits of war, of battles won, heroes decimated, and victors of armies and crusades, all in attempts to break my spirit. I did not hear any of those claims the way he wanted—he hoped to instill fear, and to make me tremble from his exploits. No, I heard no name I cared for. I heard no death I feared. I heard no words that mattered, for only one word mattered now, and it was the name dearest to me, the name of Gideon, and I would not let him add it to his list of conquests.

It was not long before we met on the field, and the giant brute stood towering over me with his monstrous axe in hand. In an instant, he had raised that axe high to take a strike, raised steady, raised strong, and brought it forth with such might, with such momentum that it would cleave an armored horse in two, right through to the very bone. The only sensible thing to do was to dodge such a blow.

Yet I was not sensible; I would not budge. I did not and would not take even one step away. Instead, I stared into his eyes and knew that death would not dare to claim me until I had my vengeance. No might nor light would shine again until I had my score evened. I grabbed my blade and ran so close with such speed that I stared him face to face, straight into his eyes, so he could see my anger up close and know the pain that I felt inside, feel the fury of my blade that leaked blood for I held the hilt so tightly.

He had no time to react, as his weapon was still held high and I was too close to strike with a large weapon such as his. I took my blade and swung fast above my head in a circle of speed that resembled the shape of the moon. It severed the hands of the brute from the hilt of his gigantic grip, and sent the gigantic axe, with his hands still attached, flying down behind me with such speed, such force, that it embedded its blade into the dirt so deeply that only one side of the weapon was exposed.

The brute was in so much shock that he did not even scream, for his mind was so confounded with what had happened that he had no chance to react rationally. No, he stood towering with his missing hands, showering the air with red.

But no, that was not enough, for the pain was far from over, and I did not wish to end his misery with such swiftness, with such quick action. That would not do justice for the pain I felt. No, I took my blade and drove it into his left thigh, knocking him to his knees. He buckled down onto the dirt, and I twisted the sword so much that blade broke inside his flesh. It was then that the brute finally screamed, taking hold of the situation that his mind had finally unraveled. He started flailing his limbs about, trying to pull the blade out of his thigh, even though he no longer had hands to do so.

He screamed and screamed a most terrified and vile scream. The blood from his severed limbs had bathed us both in red, but it mattered not for that was all I saw in my head anyways, from the moment he had put Gideon's life in jeopardy.

O in my sight, in my mind, what terrors I saw and what terror I had become and what terror I would show. I grabbed the closest weapon I had, which was the brute's mighty double axe behind me, and pulled on the handle so hard that it broke from the head, leaving a wooden pole-like spear.

I raised the spear high above, the brute eyes and mouth gawking at the sight, and drove it through his terrified and screaming mouth. It severed his flailing tongue and gargled down through his throat, out the back of his neck. I did not stop my thrust until the end stuck into the ground behind him so quickly that his eyes remained moving for minutes, trying to see the weapon that pierced his head, before they finally lost their light and went dim.

The scene was a silent one after, for neither side made a noise. They just stood and watched in horror at the butchery that occurred in front of them.

The outpost stared as I left their General, their champion, in a mangled mess on the battlefield. I walked back to my own champion, the one that they had wounded, that they would never touch again, one that I would destroy an entire army for. I would take the head off of any man who dared to hurt him, and I would show fury of the darkest nature if they ever asked to see it again.

CHAPTER 45

A Prayer

THE VERY NEXT MOMENT, after I destroyed their General, I quickly pulled Gideon onto my shoulders. I heard not a beat of his heart for it must've been too soft, but I knew blood was still rushing through his veins, for it leaked immensely from his wound. The fact that I still saw blood gush was a fortunate sight, even though it might seem cold. It was good that it had not clotted or darkened like those of the dead, for it meant that he was still alive and his body in working order. Still, if he hadn't reached death's door yet, I knew he was running towards it. The next moments were dire indeed, but I had no idea on how to bring him back. I did what I thought must prudent and quickly retreated from the battlefield and took Gideon back to his tent.

Inside, I attempted to replicate what the healers had done when I was in distress, and from seeing other archer's attacks, which were usually fatal, almost always ending in death. I broke off the arrow at the shaft so that the tip was still attached and would not dislodge from the front of the stick. This was done because the sinews around the arrowhead would be wetted, and along with the heat from blood that would surely loosen the pitch, a glue-like substance that holds arrowheads in place. If so, the arrowhead would dislodge from the shaft and leave it astray in the body with no way to pull it out, causing even more damage. Breaking only half the shaft allowed the rest of the arrow to remain inside, without letting it shift, helping to stop blood loss, and kept the arrowhead's whereabouts until it could be properly removed.

I cleansed the area with water that had been boiled in the morning, keeping the arrow straight at all times. I wrapped cloth and leather pieces around the wound, fully circled around the body to allow as little movement of the arrow as possible, fixing it into place, for each movement would cause further tears and cuts inside.

Afterwards, I put a wet cloth on top of his head to allow the body to cool, for it would soon burn with a fever that could cause more damage than the arrow wound itself.

That was the limit to my knowledge for I had no guidance at bay. How

I wished the healers and medics were there to help. But they were not, for we had no men that weren't soldiers, and the ones that had knowledge of medicine had taken arms and fallen in the first wave of assaults on the very first day of the battle. From that moment on, all men knew that an injury could result in death and were prepared to take up the sword, but I had never thought that injury would happen to a man such as Gideon.

My attempts were to no avail, for the response I expected was Gideon burning up with a fever. Instead he was getting colder, and the color in his skin quickly faded. I was at a loss, for I could not decipher any other action to save this man's life. All I knew was that I would have traded a thousand of me for a single one of him. I looked about frantically for anything to aid his distress but I saw nothing, so I did what I had never done before, what I thought I would never do. I prayed.

I prayed to a being that I thought had not existed, for it had not been there, had not shown its presence in all of my life, in all of my days. But then, when there was nothing at hand, it was my only salvation.

I cared not what the price would be. I cared not who would grant me my wish, except that it would be granted. I cared not what outcome it would bring. I cared not for any of those consequences, for I had only one care in the world, and that was to see Gideon rise once again. To my surprise, something must have heard my request, for at that moment, Gideon coughed.

I quickly moved to him in hopes of it being a good sign. Miraculously it was, for soon after, he opened his eyes.

"Vlad," he said, his first word when coming out of his shock.

I smiled a most enthusiastic smile, for everything I had believed before was a lie. I thought I had been shunned by the heavens but they had granted my wish, the greatest wish that I could have asked for. What wondrous nature that had become, a moment of glory intensified into reality, one of which was unknown to me, for I was imbued with a faith that I had not before.

"Yes, Gideon, it is good to see you back," I said, overjoyed at the change of events.

"We must return," Gideon said immediately. His face and body started to regain some color.

"But you are still weak!" I advised, "It is best to sit this battle out."

"Vlad, I need to be out there."

He had with him a stern look that showed the importance of the matter at hand, and I could not object.

"As you wish," I reluctantly said, "but I warn you, the arrow still remains inside. Any movement can kill you."

"I do not need to fight, Vlad. I will let you be my arms in this war."

"Very well."

Gideon still had not the strength to walk so as he said, I would be his arms, and in that moment, I would also be his feet. I carefully pulled him back unto my shoulders, making sure that the arrow was not interrupted in any way.

"Thank you, Vlad," he whispered into my ear as I started carrying him out.

I did not know what power at hand commanded death to stand at bay, but I was grateful for the mercy that was shown. Whether it be from the heavens, or from the depths of Hell, it did not matter. For the deed I so desperately desired had been granted, but as with all deeds, there was a price. I did not know what that price was, for what I had exchanged a soul for, or what could equal the soul of a man so great. But that price would be great indeed, for I could not fathom what actions were to come. All I knew was that someone or something was listening, watching, and had answered my call. The question was, who or what had truly answered that call?

When I stepped outside the tent, I saw smoke coming from the battlefield. That should have been my first clue.

CHAPTER 46

The Creature

"

What is the price of a soul? To understand that one must understand that value changes from one man's perception to another, so the same item's worth can differ in the hands of one to another. The true value of a soul is the value that man is putting on it. It could be worthless to some. It could be monumental to another, and can vary differently with just a matter of opinion. But what is the value if a man regards a soul to be greater than any other soul, greater than any that had walked the earth before, maybe even greater than all combined? And what if that man regards that man's soul as a God? Then the question we should ask is what is the value of the soul of God?

"

IT WAS A STRANGE SIGHT INDEED because the armies were still at a standstill. Even so, the smoke came from the outpost. There was a fire that flew above the heads of the men as if it were a moving blanket of crimson light waiting to be dropped down.

It came from the trees that hung from the mountains above the outpost, which were now burning steadily. They were the same trees that Gideon had fired arrows at. Although it had taken time, they were engulfed in a blaze that was spreading from one tree to another and releasing a cloud of black smoke into the air. Yet the outpost was not dark, for the light came not from the sun but from the fire that roared dangerously overhead.

Soon, burning branches and scorched limbs fell down on the outpost, but mostly behind, blocking any retreat into the mountain pass, which was the only escape left to the barbarians in the assault. Now that had been taken away, we were on common ground. It left them stuck with little sense of any safe, viable direction, and they were cornered by a flank of fire. The only route would be to clash with us in a full-on assault that would decimate both our numbers, for running away would mean a burning death.

I placed Gideon back on the frontlines, seated against a shield that I dug into the ground so he had a rest for his back. Gideon groaned as I moved him into place, but he only said words of thanks.

I looked at the outpost, wondering how quickly the flames had spread above, causing mayhem to the men below.

"The birds," Gideon said. "Thank the birds, Vlad."

"The birds?"

"Yes. The trees are normally too thick to burn with a flaming arrow. But this is a harsh terrain and birds in these parts would not have any place to nest but those trees. So when they flew, they showed us the trees that were riddled with nests. Nests that made perfect kindling for a fire to be lit." Gideon moved himself carefully, readjusting his back to see the outpost as he continued. "All we had to do was find out where to expose it to the heat and then wait."

"What happens next?" I asked.

"What happens next is what always happens with fire, Vlad. Such is destined for all things, natural, man-made, or even humankind—everything burns, Vlad. Everything burns."

I had known Gideon for some time at that point, and in all his days he was a benevolent, giving man, who showed compassion and kindness, always giving what he had to give, but on the battlefield, he was different. There was never any escape.

He was cold and calculating. He showed no mercy to his opponents, no moments of weakness, and no sign of hesitation whatsoever. For when any warring battalion collided with his armies, it always ended in their death and destruction. It was not just any destruction, but utter decimation, so that when the stories were told no man would take arms against him and his troops again. For he loved his troops, and to show that love he had to show unadulterated hate in the most sinister way to those that opposed them. This was to be the same.

A stark and unreal silence spread as the barbarians panicked, but they were too scared to know what to do. Instead, they waited in uncertainty and eerie silence, with the fire burning above. Their leader was gone. Their retreat had been blocked with a raging fire, with only us standing in their path. But as always, Gideon had a plan, a plan that even I could have not prepared my mind to grasp that day.

For it was in that eerie silence that I saw my next strange sight, one that I would have imprinted in my mind forever. Another stain that would never leave, for it was the end of my innocence as a man of faith, of hope, and of dreams.

I saw from the outpost, silent and daring, a figure walking of blackness and decay. It walked towards us, staggering its feet forward and forward, over and over, making its way towards us by leaving a trail of darkened footsteps and clumps of liquid blackness in its path.

Was this a trick of the mind, or the barbarians who had dreamt a horror of a creature to unleash on us when things became dire? Perhaps this was my dream that came into existence, strange and unreal but living now in reality. Was this the being that I had brought into the world from the wager I had made for Gideon's soul? It was as black and dark as the night itself. I did not know from whence it came. Yet the figure still moved and no action against it was taken from either side, since both sides watched in astonishment.

"Grab the bow, Vlad!" Gideon ordered quickly.

"What is it?" I asked, wondering if this was the creature that Gideon looked for before battles.

"Just grab the bow, Vlad," he said again.

I did what I was told, and the figure moved and moved. Although it moved slowly, it made its way past the mangled mess of the General that I had left behind, still stuck to the ground. All I could make out of the dark creature was that it had limbs, that it was small, and that it had two eyes that were white and starkly bright in contrast to the darkness of its blackened body.

The creature trembled and had not the strength that I would imagine such a creature to have, but it still walked in slowed movements, leaving a murky blackness in its wake, as I and the rest of the army watched it, confounded.

"What is it?" I asked Gideon again.

"I am sorry, my friend," Gideon said with a pained sigh. "I cannot give you what I promised, Vlad."

It was only then that I realized what I saw, what I had feared. It was my dream brought into reality. In fact, it was much more; it was a nightmare that I was being forced to face. It was the surviving boy from the town.

The boy that Gideon had saved, the one I tried to show what a monster was so that he would run and not fight in this war. The one whose freedom I had asked for, and the one that Gideon had emptily promised to let live.

That boy was supposed to be my salvation for my murderous and treacherous ways, my barter for the last bits of my soul that had I asked Gideon for. There it now stood, blackened, dirtied, tainted, and distraught, as much as my was heart inside. Yet he was covered in a murk that I could not decipher.

"Do not make me do this, my friend," I said.

"You must, Vlad. For I cannot."

"I cannot!"

"You are to be my arms, remember," Gideon reminded.

Was this the debt I said I would pay for Gideon's life? My soul and the boy's for Gideon's, because his soul was so great? No one life could make up for his, that I must have known. I had promised anything and the time for repayment had come far quicker than I expected. If that was to be it, then I had no choice, no matter how I felt. The moment that I had been so grateful for just moments before now pained me dearly, and filled me with immense dread. Still, I raised the bow.

The boy's eyes widened and filled with shock. They seemed so pure and so pristine, surrounded by such black darkness that it made his eyes clear even from our distance, and they stuck out like two full moons on a dark, cloudless night.

"Light the arrow, Vlad," Gideon said.

I finally knew what the murk was and I looked at Gideon, shocked at his words. "Not like this!"

"I sent him to break the oil pots within the base so they could not use them against us. The black murkiness on him is that very same oil, and so is the black trail that you see behind him. You know what that means, Vlad. It leads straight to the enemy's base. The trees above have not yet hit their mark, and need aid."

"This is wrong, Gideon."

"You must do this, Vlad. One life is not worth the cost of many."

I stared back at the boy, who did not understand why such outcome had come to this. He expected nothing but help, salvation in this time of need, and now we stood there as his doom. O how my heart burned.

"Do not make me do this, Gideon. I cannot take his life. Not this way." I was reluctant to make even a move, and a tear trailed from my eye without my control.

"You must, there is no other way. See the way he walks, Vlad. The boy is already injured, he would not survive," Gideon said. "I told you before, to be a leader requires tough decisions, inhuman decisions sometimes, Vlad. This is one of them. I am sorry to have to ask you to do this but only you can, for you are my limbs."

The boy raised his hand, yet I did not know for what. Then he reached for us in what was not vengeance or scorn but hope. Hope so powerful and direct that even from such a distance it felt like it grabbed my heart and pulled on it so roughly that I felt it would tear out of my chest.

"Do it, Vlad, before we lose the chance," Gideon commanded.

I could see that the boy tried his best to come towards us, reaching for us in that moment of despair, in that moment of gloom, hoping that we could save him, praying for salvation from the misery that we had set him on. In return for that hope, for that faith, I launched the burning arrow.

The arrow flew in silence until it struck the boy, but it did not kill him, not the way I would have hoped. No, a gift like that from the heavens would be too graceful, too benevolent. The arrow struck the boy in such a way that he remained standing, and stared at us in confusion at what Gideon had promised to him. What he had promised I would give him, trust.

The flames lit soon after, and while I had hoped it would be a quick death for the boy, it was far from that. The flames rose and started to engulf him. It first traveled to his legs, as I imagined it would, racing down, taking his body. All I could think of was the moment I was on the pyre, the moment I was saved, but I could not save him.

Then I saw what made my heart sink deeper than I thought it could ever sink. It was as if the ground swallowed me up whole and then spat me underneath to the center of the earth. I saw the flames travel up, and the boy's arms flailed in agony, trying to pat out the flames on his face. The flames did not stop; they relentlessly bit him with their fiery teeth and grew into the demon that I had created. The demon of fire that I was all too familiar with.

The demon grew and grew, with such quickness, such evilness, such might. An instant later, it ate the boy whole, only showing a dancing silhouette of darkness moving in torment inside a bright light. But it did not stay for long, for the shadow grew smaller and smaller until only his black bones appeared moving, until it could not move anymore.

The barbarians stared in horror, for what we had done in the battle, for the sacrifices we were willing to make. For the monsters that they faced and the ruthless practices we took hold of. With all that fright they became even more afraid, for as Gideon planned, the demonic flame leapt from the boy and ran in his footsteps on top of the river of black, trailing towards the outpost. It moved so quickly, so ferociously, that the barbarians trying to stop its charge were no match for it.

The barbarians ran out to kick dirt on the boy's darkened footsteps and even smudge it out, but it did not work, for the demon was still hungry. Unlike before, it would not be defeated again. It ran and stuck onto everything that had been touched by the darkness. It touched what the boy had touched, and it burned and burned in a rage that grew just as much the one in my heart. But unlike the inferno, I could not let out my rage, for it was directed at a source I could not believe. It was directed at Gideon.

CHAPTER 47

A Heavy Burden

"

I realize now that we are not spirits or residents of a paradise in the sky. We are not above the dirt, above the trees of the earth, and in the clouds that rise high. We do not live amongst angels and winged blessed beings, all in a fantastic lie. We are not those who live in purity and in that desired light in an out-of-sight empire. No, we are something different, and it is a darkest truth of the darkest night.

We are the forest below that grows and matures, and overtime stiffens and cures. When we are ready, we will be cut down, and not for a holy reason like to build an empire for the holy town. No, we are fertilized with lies that they use as tools to make us grow from seeds into gigantic oaks, oaks that travel high only to be harvested, for we are mere fools. We do not know the truth, the truth that we are only here to stoke the flames.

Flames like those spoken in all those stories, in those tales, direct us to a path of aimless glory. Because the stark truth is that we are mere kindling to burn for the light above. Grown, weathered, and dried, perfect for the reaping of our souls. For

without our souls, there would be no fuel for heaven to glow so

bright.

99

THE SILENCE FROM THE MEN was haunting for no-one spoke, no one said a word, and the wind and the air remained calm the entire time. Yet the night was ablaze, and it was indeed not quiet, for the night was filled with screams of burning men, of our enemy, as the scarlet fingers of roaring flames danced in the dark of the night.

The flames had lunged onto to the earth as if a giant demon had burrowed its way from the pits of hell and exposed its hands to the un-expecting world. With a crimson touch, I watched the monstrous hands grab hold of men and burn them to cinders with screams that shrieked from the outpost and echoed through the high walls of the mountain pass to an infinite degree, that traveled through the lands as if blown through a trumpet to warn even the stars above.

Those lucky few who escaped the burning torment ran out of the flames and into the flanking horsemen that waited on both sides, cutting them down into pieces so they could not run anymore.

I could not believe what conspired in front of my eyes, for it was what Gideon had planned from the start. He had set the pieces so precisely, ensuring that everything fell into place. I wondered what monstrous vision would be in store to deem an act like this worthy of its doing, to take vengeance on this scale, unlike anything else, a massacre on earth. A massacre that I had taken full part in.

The outpost was a pile of scorched ash and bones, the wooden ramparts and the walled defense all burned to a crisp, serving as a reminder of what happens when the lands of the King are invaded. All men who would witness that site would know of what conspired in that place, and once they had seen they would know of all the lost souls at that place, those of the dead that bled on it and the living that helped create it, and they would know that they would have to enter hell and be changed for eternity if they chose to take arms. That was true even for us, for no man escaped that battle without a scar, no matter how visible or invisible it was. It was war and what war meant—to leave every man broken, whether he stood or fell, unrelenting in its reach.

I myself was in torment for my own actions in the assault, my own reminder of the occurrence, my own sinned hands, drenched in an imagined blood that would not leave my memory. I had seen the boy before, I had seen the boy fall, seen him hurt, seen him die, all in front of my eyes, with a single arrow shot from my bow. How I wished that I had missed. How I wish someone else had that burden, but it was mine and mine alone, and I regretted it inside and out.

I walked up to the remains of the boy, remains that were dark and grey, flesh that was a mere pile of ash, and bones that were charred to the core. I stared at the remnants of the boy, a boy who had sacrificed his life to do Gideon's bidding, who had given up everything and overcome his fear to bravely enter the outpost to set the groundwork for the victory, a boy who had saved so many of our warrior's lives with his actions. In return for his valiant deed, for his benevolent gift, what did we give him? We showed him betrayal. I betrayed him.

In all my actions, I had failed. I, who faithfully grabbed my sword to scare him off so that he would not fight, so that such a day would not come. I, who showcased a monster, so that he would not lose the innocence he still had in the inevitability of war. I, who failed in all those tasks because I could not save a single soul, for no matter how hard I tried to save his life, in the end of it all, I was the one who ended his, and I still lacked the courage to end my own.

I knelt down on my knees for I was powerless to do anything to bring this boy back. I could not say any more prayers, nor do any more deeds, for the act was done, and it had been done by my hand. It was yet another mark of darkness that I had to carry. One of many that painted my inside so black that I did not know if there was any place left untouched.

I grabbed a sword and ran the blade into the ground, punctured it over and over in anger, stabbing the earth until the soil was broken as much as I. Then I took my hands and started to dig, each hand full of dirt, scooping it out of the earth until I made a hole. I grabbed the bones, still searing hot from the flames, and gathered up as much of the ashes I could and placed them into the hole. I moved the ground back, covering his remains with dirt, leaving my sword embedded in that spot.

And at that moment, seeing that final spot, a place of rest for the restless soul I made, my eyes brimmed with tears. I would not let them out, for I would not have the pleasure to ease my pain. I did not deserve such benevolence.

No, I would walk with that heavy burden, that stain, because I deserved it. I deserved the suffering, the pain, the anguish that screamed inside. I deserved every minute of sorrow, regret, and remorse, for I was indeed a monster, indeed a murderer, and at that moment, I knew that I was not alone in my actions, in my deeds, in my sin. For that burden belonged to another man, and that man's name was Gideon.

CHAPTER 48

The Laughing Man

IN THE NEXT FEW DAYS, we made camp in hopes to recover our energies, to recover our mind, since we could not recover our souls. Yet those days were still distraught. Even though the battle was won, we had run out of rations, and spoils of the war from the outpost were burnt beyond retrieval. The men were tired, famished, sick and thirsty, and in the heated sun. We had not the supplies to even make the journey back to the nearest town.

Yet we had done what we had set out to do. For us, the war was over. No one would further dare oppose the King's lands after what we had done. We put a final mark on it to guarantee that, for once stories were told, once the sight we had left was seen, any further invading armies would do their utmost to run from the horror that would befall them. And for the current invaders, it would take them months to clear the debris and the wreckage of the fallen trees that blocked the passageway from the other side. It would take even longer to gather their spirits to attack again.

This would leave the others trapped within our lands at the mercy of those around them, unable to be supplied, unable to return, unable to win. The war was over and the truth was that there would be no more fighting needed, for no manner of words or speeches could recover us from the unremitting hunger and sheer exhaustion.

We were a decimated army, with many of us completely debilitated from the battle, wounded from the days before. Many more of us were dead from the journey of slaughter that was even before. The immortal army that we were was gone, our numbers were lost, and no number of recruitments from towns and villages nearby would make us recover for there were no villages left—the barbarians had made sure of it.

That was what we were, an army that stood in victory but was unable to stand. Through it, our leader harmed and straying in and out of consciousness, fighting for his own life. For despite our best efforts, Gideon's wound had become infected and he was riddled with an unending fever. We all feared for his life, every moment that went by.

It was then that fate played its twisted game once again. From inside the encampments, we heard the rumble that sent us scurrying out of our tents, as we felt the ground shake the earth with a grumbling, thunderous moan.

What manner of being was coming we had no idea, but it would soon be upon us. If it were the returning armies of barbarians come to band together again, then we would be doomed, which was a fate we had determined and accepted long ago. We would suffer their final wrath before they would die out in our lands, or be bargained off as currency to be spared for their lives.

Yet we did not wish for that to occur. We did not wish to submit so easily after what we had bled for to attain. For that reason, we gathered our weary selves and grabbed our weapons once more, loaded up our bows and arrows, which I dared not look at for the memories that still haunted every corner of my mind.

We set out our boundaries and flanks that were minimal at best and stood steadfast for the assault that was to come, for it would be a final battle. Even after the finale, even after the war, it would be a cleansing of the darkened souls that did not deserve to live on this land any longer. If that were to be it, then I would be happy to have ended it there. But that was not fate's plan.

Still, I thought of those things as I saw the first warrior coming over the hills. He rode on a dark brown beast fitted for war, held in his hands a lance and wore gold and silver armor that covered his entire body, and seemed like a true seasoned veteran. Moments later, I saw another, and then another, and soon after, many more. Enough already to cover the entire horizon with a line of silver, blue, black, and yellow, all mounted for combat, all ready for war. They would decimate us in our current condition. But then, another rider came over the hill, carrying a banner that I never cared to see again.

It was then that I fell on the ground. The men stared at me, wondering why their leader would fall, for I had inadvertently become their leader since Gideon had not the ability to stand, and all others of worth were dead. Yet I did not fall out of the exhaustion that I felt; I did not fall out of fear of what I had lost, for I faced my very own nightmares. No, I fell because I found it funny.

I found it humorous how the gods mocked us, even now when we had our hearts already lost. I found it entertaining that they would take that heart and raise it again just so they had the chance to crush it once more. For it was with strange irony and fateful hilarity that when the war was done, the battle won and the fight ended, our reinforcements had so quickly arrived.

An army of knights, led by the King's order, mounted on horses, supplied with arrows and weaponry that would have easily dispatched the opponent and held the barbarians at bay. Yes, it was an exuberant sight to see so many refreshed men that did not have a mark of battle on them, but were bright-eyed and virginal in every sense of the word.

It was an army of so many well-trained men, well equipped, unscathed, and untouched by any blemish on their pristine armor that was so wonderful that I would have thought it was just made. It seemed that they would blind those in front of them with the sheer brilliance of their unscathed display.

That is what I saw, and that is what I found amusing, that my sins, my acts, my pain, were irrelevant, purposeless, and pointless. All our sins and anguish were for nothing. If we had waited, then the barbarians would have been bested easily by the might of the King's army.

So I sat on the field of war and laughed and laughed. I laughed as a messenger came forward holding up the banner of the King. I laughed as a knight came forward and asked where the commander was. I laughed as the men directed them to me, for Gideon was in dire shape and could not attend to them, and I laughed as they asked me why I laughed.

They set their tents up and learned of the scenario from the other men. They learned that the battle was already over, and there was no need for them to war. And when the question came up of me, they thought me struck with insanity and full of madness, and they were right. I was struck with a strange calamity and I was not myself, because the only thoughts in my mind were of both extremes.

One was to laugh at the strange irony of it all. The other was to kill every soul that was on that field because the King had delivered an utter refusal when I was sent to see him and in doing so forced our hand into the war, only to change his mind and take action as we had suggested in the first place. This made me furious, boiling with a deep scorn for the living hell they had put us through.

So that is why I did what I did, because laughter in that most insane of situations was the sanest action that I had left, because by God, how I would have enjoyed killing every last one of them. Instead, I laughed.

CHAPTER 49

No More Heroes

THE FOLLOWING DAY, the King's men set up fortifications and made preparations to rebuild the outpost so that they would be protected from future assaults. Although the other men were grateful for their arrival, a chance to take rest in this unending war after we had raged for months and months on end, and spent days on fields such as that one. Even more so, they were grateful for the supplies the caravan of the army brought, sharing with us food, water, and rations.

Yet I did not feel the same. I still fumed at their unforeseen and unplanned arrival, in its untimeliness and unconcern. I was still angered by all the events that took place up until that moment, to that end that could have been avoided. It could have all been different, could have resulted in a different outcome, but it did not, for we were broke our backs to create this victory, no matter how hollow it was, and then they came riding in, untouched, unhindered and would make those sacrifices meaningless and steal our glory. They were the strong and we the weak.

The King's army gathered in varied numbers in many different tasks. After they acknowledged our presence and their arrogant commander made the almost forced formal introductions to lowly beings such as we were, they went about their tasks as if we did not exist. It was as if we had not made the ground that they walked on, as if we had not tended the fields that they harvested from. They went on, not knowing how much blood we had spilled of the enemy and our own to gain our victory. They did not know how tormented we were from the sights we saw. They did not know and they did not care to. They thought our presence as a nuisance to their undertaking and went about their routines.

Yet our presence could not be ignored. They finally inspected the outpost, and they saw the carnage that we had created, the fallen timber from the burning trees that blocked the passageway to the desert and beyond. They stared at the broken, burned, and tattered scorched bones that lay in the aftermath of the outpost, and witnessed the stacks of bodies piled high that lay rotting in the scorching sun. They could no longer ignore us. Instead, they stared at us, and talked in mutters and mumbles all around. They dared not look us in the eye, for they not only felt disgusted by us, but also feared us.

Like them, I had no concern of their company or explaining the on-goings of what they had missed. Instead, I retreated into Gideon's tent, ready to change the bandages of his grim wound once more. When I approached him, I saw his face, pale and grimaced with pain and I could not move.

There lay the man that I had so admired and still did, but there also lay the man that I hated inside, that I scorned for his actions and what he had made me do. Taking the life of the innocent boy that I had toiled so hard to save had killed me inside, as if he had pierced my heart himself. I did not know if it was the rashness of his actions that had led us to this path, or if it was the desire of prestige and fame that truly drove Gideon. I no longer knew. I wondered if all he spoke to me was a lie, muddled in his own mix of vanity and pride.

Nonetheless, I removed the old bandage, revealing the darkened, clotted wound that reeked a stench of death. It did not cause me concern like it did before. Instead, I recalled all the deaths that were caused on the journey and the pilgrimage of war.

I thought of them, all the murders on my hands, all the pain and devastation that I had caused with these stained, godforsaken, miserable masses of flesh. I thought of all the damage that they invoked with their mere presence, and maybe that was all that was needed to cause one more.

I reached for the new strip of cloth that I would use as the new bandage and thought that if I were to risk one more life, risk one more death, that perhaps I could save countless more. For one death, one life, is not worth the many, as Gideon himself told me on that day. Perhaps that was the omen for what needed to be done.

Perhaps ending the life of a man who walked a path of war would be the salvation for those standing in his path. Perhaps, if the light that burned so brightly was not there, then men would not be so blinded to follow in his footsteps and destroy innocence that is so precious and so pristine before learning its true value. For a moment, just for a moment, I held that new mass of cloth in my hand. I was about to place it near his wound, but I let it travel.

It traveled up to his neck, up his chin, to his mouth and I thought, how easy it would be to let him pass on this day. To let him go into silence, covering his mouth so that he did not suffer anymore, so that others did not suffer anymore. To let him travel to another world and be remembered in glory as one who fought and died because of his sacrifices for the King, to go out like the magnificent spark that he was. To escape this exhaustive life and live forever in the hearts of warriors, and no longer be capable of committing another murder or act that would stain his reputation. I thought and thought and I held the bandage to his mouth.

Yet I could not bring myself to do it, and moved it back down to his wound and patted down the area and placed the bandage in its rightful place. Then I slumped down next to him, tears in my eyes from what I was about to do in my moment of grief. I had lost much in the war, and I did not want to lose any more. It was then I felt a hand hold onto mine, but not that of a strong, valiant warrior. No, it was weak and frail, and it grabbed onto mine and it belonged to the man who had once been godly in my eyes—Gideon.

I did not know if he had seen what I did or was about to do, or if he knew of what I had planned, but he slowly opened his eyes for the first time in days and looked at me with a smile.

"It is good to see you, my friend," he said as he made effort to move further but could not, "my Vlad."

"Good to see you too…my friend. How are you feeling?"

"I have seen better days," he laughed, but instantly halted from the pain in his chest. "O what a wondrous world we live in," he sighed in amusement. "I have stared death in the face so many times. Yet the moment I looked away it was a stray arrow that took me back to its doors."

"No matter. You are awake, and far from dead. That is a good sign of your recovery," I said. "Although your wound looks infected and healers we do not have. I asked the King's men to take a look at you but they have not sent any as of yet."

"The King's army is here?" Gideon asked, perturbed.

I nodded.

After a long, turmoil-filled pause, Gideon finally responded. "How are the men?"

"They are fine, but we are reduced in numbers. Only seventy at best. Many have slipped away from their wounds. You are the only one that still hangs on."

"You say that like it's a bad thing, Vlad," Gideon smirked.

I paused before I spoke. "I am glad you are back, Gideon. There could be no other to lead our men but you. Still, you should rest and regain your strength. The road to recovery is long."

"Very well, my healer," Gideon smiled. "I shall do as you say."

I proceeded to leave the tent.

"…and Vlad," Gideon interrupted before I could exit. Yet I could not turn to look at him for I felt too guilty to see his face once more.

"Thank you," he said.

As I tried to leave once again, he spoke once more.

"I know you hate me, Vlad, for what I made you do. But I cannot tell you I am sorry, for it had to be done. I have asked you to do many things that were unkind, unjust, and raw but I did it for the sake of the army, no other. It was not for vanity or glory, but the nature of war."

It was as if he had read my mind and spoke the answers to my questions that dwelled inside.

"You see, Vlad," he continued, "to disturb the feared, you have to be even more feared. To invoke fear in the savage, you have to be terribly savage. To invoke savage terror in the inhuman, you have to be far more inhuman and horrible. And to strike horror in the inhuman, you have to be a demon on the earth. I was that demon that day, Vlad, for that was what was called of me. I cannot say my action was righteous, for it was not. I cannot say that my act was just and civil, for it was not. It was barbaric, inside and out, but only because it needed to be so. It was my savagery that saved the lives of those who now do not need to fight. It was because of my inhumanity that humanity was spared an inhuman sight. It was because of my demonic, sinful deed that no more evil deeds would even dare be committed for the horror that would be reaped on to them in return.

"That is what you try to do as well, Vlad. I know that. On that day, in that town, with the boy. You tried to save him from his fate. I did the same, but I do not scare the good from acting. That is their fate and they must follow it. I scare the evil, Vlad. I scare the evil from taking foot onto the earth, from ever conspiring. That is what I do. It is not what I like to do, but what I need to do, what I must do, and what I will continue to do. I am the man that will sacrifice anything and everything to save the world, even if it is his own soul, which I lost many battles ago.

"So I ask not for speck of retribution, not a shred of remorse, not a drop of sorrow to be offered to me. No, that is something I do not ask for because I do not deserve it, but I ask you to understand that was the reason that I did what I did, and what I will do again and again. That is the reason I made those plans, set those motions, made those actions. That is who I am, Vlad, and for that, I am sorry.

"I am sorry because I am not who you thought me to be. What I am is not a hero. No, a hero does not commit unjust acts. A hero does not take time to cause misery and torment. A hero forgives, and I do not. I cannot forgive, Vlad. It is not part of me. I am a villain, Vlad, but that does not do that word justice. No, I am more than that. I am a nefarious being. As much as you think it to be you, I am the true monster in this army, not you. As I told you before, monsters do not feel, Vlad. You do.

"So I understand the actions you have to take and I bear no ill will towards them, for I understand them. I hope that one day you will understand mine as well."

With that, Gideon fell unconscious again, into a sleep that took him to the brink of death again, fighting for his life again, and leaving me standing at the tent's exit with tears that ran down my face, again.

CHAPTER 50
The Night Attack

THAT NIGHT, I RETURNED TO GIDEON'S TENT after wandering on the grounds to clear my head. I watched him as he slept and checked his breathing, which was light, to be sure he still had breath. I stood there for many hours, staring at the figure who now rested in front of my eyes.

A figure had come out of nowhere like a whirlwind and scooped me away. It was a figure who had played such an important and integral part of my life. A figure who had led me on a life that was not just full of pain and dread, but one of redemption and purpose as well. My mind ran with all those thoughts, of all those things until finally, I needed rest of my own. I slumped over into the corner of the tent, next to Gideon's shield that bore that familiar symbol of trumpets blowing crossed over a lion's head.

I slept and slept, and then I dreamt. I had not known how much time had passed, or what other sights I dreamed, but I returned to the graveyard of red and black, the cloudless dark skies, and the shimmering stars above. I saw where I met that strange man, the fallen man, the one who had only a working head and the rest of his body mangled. I saw the sight of the piled seating area that I had made for him, that looked more as an altar than a seat.

And I saw myself, in and out of the body as if I was him and looking upon myself all at once. I saw that I walked up to alter of the fallen one. I do not know how long it took me to walk but it felt endless. When I came to the fallen one once again, his eyes suddenly sparked open and his blue eyes filled with a brilliant blue flame. He commanded words that rang through my whole body, words that shocked my senses, and sent a surge of energy and rattled my bones. He shouted, "My sweet angel of death, you must wake!"

I awoke to see a strange devilish looking man standing in front of me, fitted in light padded clothes of the darkest color of black, and barefooted as to make no sounds. His arm was raised, and in it, a sword ready to strike, but not at me. Instead, it was ready to come down at Gideon's head.

I had no weapon nearby and had no time to even pull the shield that I lay next to, for any moment lost would mean Gideon's certain death. So I sprang up as fast as I could, launching myself forward, using my body as a weapon and striking the intruder with my shoulder. The impact was so hard that it knocked him outside, through the opening of the tent.

I quickly got back to my feet and rushed outside to warn others of the intruders, but before I could even make a call to another soul, the King's knights were already there, fitted and ready for the assault and had the intruder fully surrounded.

"What unfortunate luck, assassin," I scoffed at the man. "Now you've done it."

To my surprise, the assassin did not show any sign of fear, but instead, contempt.

What befuddled me even more was that the King's guards took no immediate actions against the man. Furthermore, they had not even a slight bit of concern of their faces, but abhorrence, and towards me instead of the assassin. Not a single one raised their sword against the intruder.

"O aren't you a brilliant one," the assassin said as he lazily got up.

I was shocked as one of the knights picked up the assassin's weapon and handed it to him.

"I believe you are mistaken. For it is you who is the one out of luck," the man said.

I should have known. It would have taken them much time to adorn their armor. It would have taken much time to ready their weapons and gather in such a fashion, and it would have taken them much time to find the intruder, but they had done it in an instant. It was simple. The assassin was not the barbarians' doing, no, it was the King's men.

"I guess there is no need to hide anymore," said the assassin, taking off his mask and showing himself to be the General of the King's army.

With a flick of his wrist, his small band of knights pointed their weapons towards me, but before they could attack, he stopped them with another raise of his hand.

"Well, isn't this exciting. Two armies, the top men clashing at once. I thought this entire trip was going to be a bore, but well, let's make it fun. Now, I am not entitled to give you this chance," he said, "but I am a man of sport, so I will give you an opportunity to save your life. All I ask in return is that you leave Gideon to us and withdraw from this site. In return, we will grant you mercy."

"Never!" I cried out. "I do not know what you want with such a man as Gideon dead, but I will see that the King will hear of your treachery!"

The men laughed.

"You are brilliant! A brilliant buffoon," the General of the King's men laughed.

"Who do you think ordered us to do this?" one of the knights asked. "Why do you think the King did not offer you his support? Why did you think we came here after the battle? A withered army is much easier to annihilate than a complete one."

"It is true," said the General. "We had not expected you to survive the battle at the outpost and actually win, so we came with our numbers to deal with the barbarians if need be. If I had known that you had won and that Gideon was already so near to death, we would have brought far fewer men to deal with the likes of you, but what's done is done and here we are. Now, as I said before, we will grant you mercy, and the King will surely reward you for your act of obedience."

How laughable their deal was, I thought. "I have seen the way the King rewards service. I do not wish to take any part in it."

The general grew extremely quiet, and his jovial and arrogant manner became rigid and cold. "Withdraw now, I will not ask again," he said, "There is no need for fighting from the likes of you. You have played soldier long enough. It is time to put away your toys and go back home. This is a game for worthy men."

In all outcomes that I could run through my head, I saw no victory, only death in that situation. They were right—Gideon was already at death's door and I did not know if I could make him return from it. What he had told me and had shown me, clearly and cruelly, was that one life was indeed not worth those of many. If it were him, he would have sacrificed his life for his troops. So in his place, I needed to do the same.

"Very well," I said, finally standing down. "I see that there is no way out of this, but I want your guarantee that rest of the men are spared. That is what Gideon would have wanted."

"The rest of the men," the General laughed. "Yes, you can have those weak vagabonds' worthless lives. The order was only for Gideon's head; the remaining are no concern to me."

"There is only one more request that I ask," I commanded.

"Insolent fool! You are in no position to bargain." The General drew his weapon. "You are outnumbered, outmatched, and outsmarted. I will not waste any more time with you. Stand aside or die!"

"Please. The request is a simple one, and one that will not break your vow to the King, only support it."

The General stood staring at me for moment before finally succumbing to hear me out. "O very well," he said putting down his weapon. "For the sheer sake of my own curiosity, what is it that you request?"

"That I will be the one to kill Gideon."

The knights looked shocked; they started to murmur amongst themselves.

"If Gideon is to die, the least honor that you can give him is to grant him a death by one of his men, not another. That is what I ask. You may do what you will with my life but if he is to die, then let it be by my hands. I beg you."

The General stood there for a moment, almost gawking in disbelief at my offer. "What an interesting situation this has become." He smiled a wicked smile. "I had thought that I was going to die of boredom from this task once I found the outpost was already taken, but you have changed that, warrior." After a moment of further thought, he spoke again. "Very well! I will let you go and commit this act."

He said as he stepped back, but before he let me go, he continued. "I assure you that you will die instantly if you betray us, because there is no need for us to even enter the tent to kill you two." He pointed to the ready bows on the ground near the men's feet.

"I understand." I turned to go back inside.

"...and warrior," the General said, "I expect to see his head in your hands when you exit that tent."

"I have no weapon."

The General grinned a most wicked grin. "Then use your teeth."

CHAPTER 51

Teeth

I ENTERED THE TENT KNOWING WHAT WAS AT STAKE and what had to be done. No matter how much I did not want to take the task at hand, there was no other way. It would be horrific, brutal, and demented, but it had to be the way it was. Now, I know that it could not have ended any other way. The King's men were waiting outside and they would not rest until they had Gideon's head, a head that I had so easily planned to take earlier on. So I did what I must; I pulled Gideon up, his head resting on my shoulders, his neck next to my teeth as I held him.

I straightened my legs and raised him up, and then ran to the shield that I had rested on earlier in the night. I grabbed what was nearest to me—cloth bandages, the bed, sacks of rice—and I moved them to one side of the tent. Then, I sat in front of those and placed Gideon down in front of me, and then the shield in front of him also.

I waited for the inevitable to happen, which did not take long. I saw the first arrow fly through and strike where the bed had been before, and then a dozen more, all entering the tent from different angles. Finally, a few met their mark towards us, but were stopped by the shield.

Next, the arrows came from the side and I positioned my body to shield Gideon's flesh with mine, but none struck either of us. Finally, the arrows came from the back, which I knew they would. I could see them flying past me, could hear them hitting the rice sacks with quick thuds that pushed against my back. Quickly, my vision started to blur and I knew what had been done. The arrows had penetrated through the sacks and had sunk into my back, but it did not matter for Gideon was not hurt, at least not any further than he was before. Soon after, I saw the pool of blood start to spread on the dirt and collect near my feet; it was mine.

"There are no deals in war, boy. Only statements!" the General of the King's knights yelled from outside.

I knew that in a few moments they would enter and finish the job, so I waited patiently for what was to be, but that time did not come. Instead, to my surprise, I felt the presence of a very familiar friend, a very familiar feeling indeed. A being that had spared me once, took my hope away and now came back to claim its ultimate prize. O that demon was back and he brought with it that same smell and heat that he always did when he took what he wanted.

The King's men had lit the entire tent around us in flames. I started to laugh, realizing the fault in my ways. I should have expected to be met by a death of flames when I knew it was my destiny.

How magnificent a game fate played to put me in the same situation over and over again, no matter how much I ran from it. It surrounded me once more like it had on the pyre that day, looked at me like it did when it took the last bits of my soul when it engulfed the boy, and now it was there to claim me again, along with a bonus prize—the man that denied him his original meal that first day, the man who had the demon snuffed out with his words alone and now did not have the strength to speak. Gideon.

But as the fire burned, I realized one thing. I realized a most important thing that gave me hope. The heat I felt was from everywhere but not from underneath, because no life grew where I stood, only dirt. It would be this lifeless soil that would save the life I cherished most. Today I would once again bury someone I held dear, but not for the sake of death, but for survival.

I moved to my feet and grabbed the shield and drove the end into the ground, pulling it against the dirt until it scooped a large trench, and then I did this again and again. Each stroke pulled aside more dirt, and more dirt, making that grave larger and then large enough for a single man. The fires did not stop as I did this, and with each scoop it raged more and more, and with every haul of dirt it licked my back, my arms, giving off enough heat that my wounds no longer bled from the arrows, for they had seared shut. I would not let Gideon be taken by those men, who did not deserve to touch such honor.

Once large enough, I quickly moved Gideon from the ground and put him into the trench, just in time to feel a sharp pain in my gut. O how magnificent and awakening it was to feel such pain in the darkness of inside the flames. Then again in my side, I felt it as another arrow hit its mark.

Yet I would not stop. I was a selfish being. This was my fate and mine alone, and Gideon would not dare steal it from me. I would burn and I alone. If he had saved me from the fire once, then I would pay him in return.

So I stumbled around pulling the dirt in scoops and pouring the soil on Gideon, as the arrows continued to penetrate the tent's cloth walls as well as my flesh. It was then I started to laugh at the strange situation I was in. There I was, being burned alive and they were not satisfied. How much they truly feared as a man such as me, I thought. After the final scoop of dirt was placed and I could not see Gideon any longer, once my body was riddled with arrows and the tent surrounded in flames, I rested.

I collapsed onto the mound of dirt that covered Gideon and watched the flames that had reached the roof of the tent, the smoke blackening the edges of my sight. I stared into that roof and I saw my life. I saw my father. I saw Illyana. I saw Gideon. I saw the boy. Then, I saw the boar, and I saw red.

It was then that I had my taste of a familiar rage. As Gideon had said, the boar does not give up, it does not stop, would not stop until its rage subsided. So I needed to do the same, I needed to once again be that boar that lived so violently within me.

O how I raged. I took apart all the locks in my mind, all the hold in my heart, all my fears for my soul, all my sanity. I threw it all aside and let the boar take over; I let the raging monster that I held within come out.

Before I knew it, I was outside. I had run through the tent opening with the shield in front of me until it hit the first man. I knocked him down, whoever he was, but I did not care. O no, I was not in control then. Even if I had wanted to stop, I could not, for the boar was in control, and he foamed and fumed for everything he had been denied before.

I only caught moments as my vision cleared, for the beast was acting with furious haste. I had already ripped an arrow out of my side and plunged it into another man's neck, and then I pulled another and struck the nearest limb I could see and stabbed another through his foot, making him drop his sword. O what a marvelous boon it was, for the boar had access to his tusks and this tusk was made of tempered steel. I quickly grabbed the sword, swung it aside and decapitated the fallen man on the ground. I had swung so fast that I had sliced another man in two, all from the ground where I laid.

Finally, when nothing was near, I made my way to my feet, finally standing yet still hunched over, still in a craze. As my vision cleared of the haze that I was in, I saw the three men that I had already taken the lives of laying in a piled mess of armor and blood. Then, I saw the four remaining men, one of them the General, standing in horror looking at me. They were trembling to their very core, knowing that it was not a man they stared at, not even a beast anymore, but an angel of death. That angel of death stared at them as they quivered, and showed a wicked, toothed smile.

CHAPTER 52

A Statement

THE SOUNDS OF CLANGING WEAPONS and the thumping of blades against wood could be heard from a great distance. Yet they were not the sounds of war. They were not the sounds of battle, but that of a statement, a message that I was to deliver. They were the workings of my men and I, a very small number. We were all that remained of Gideon's army, all that remained during the slaughter—but it was not of ours, it was a slaughter of the King's army.

We were a small band that took on numbers that outnumbered us twenty to one. Yet we were light on foot and knew how to battle in a moment's notice, for it was in our blood, and how much glorious blood we took. Like ravenous beasts we went from one body to the next, taking on the entire King's army and only falling once our toll for life was met. The toll was paid by the countless bodies of the King's men.

It did not matter if they were not part of the plan. It mattered not if they had known or had not known of the attack and the plot against Gideon. It mattered not that they begged for mercy, or tried to side with us, for none could be trusted anymore. We hunted them all, for they were all guilty, every last one of them. Those who took up the sword and those who didn't, whatever their role was, they were guilty for just having a role. For that, they would all die, and they would die at our hands, and die they did.

After the brutal battle that we should have not won was won again, we stood silent and disturbed, for the men that survived were like me now. No longer outcasts, no longer scoundrels or vagabonds, but boars on the field, dead but not willing to die, not yet.

We took every last one of them, all fourteen hundred men, all but one. Yes, I saved one. A special one, just one to witness the aftermath of the King's plan. The one that I saved was their so-called leader, the want-to-be assassin, the General of the King's army, the man the army had followed.

We left him alive to see the disaster that he had brought unto his men, the destruction that was to come after facing against a man like Gideon.

"Please," he screamed, "I will reward you all if you let me go."

We did not listen to his pitiful cries. No, we were busy working, toiling. Every last remaining one of us, counting no more than forty, endlessly clanged their swords against the timber, knocking pieces off the wood, sharpening each of them, getting them ready for what was to come.

I slaved away as the skinless scabs were removed from my fingers and my flesh stung with any touch, but I did not care. I worked and worked until my arms had swollen; the boils on my back as well as my legs burst, and the blood in my wounds stopped leaking because I had need of it elsewhere.

I worked and worked, toiled and toiled, until it was done and the last of the King's men, the General, screamed as I dragged him to the sight of his destroyed army. I took him to show what it meant to take arms against us, to take arms against Gideon and his brothers in arms, for that was what we were. To strike against us would be to strike our family. Finally, when there were no more sights that I wished for him to see, I sat him down and looked him in the eye as he screamed and screamed.

"I beg you," he yelled and pleaded, "please don't! I promised to give you anything you want. I have fortunes beyond what you can dream of. Please, just don't…"

My response was simple. "There are no deals in war, boy! Only statements."

And then I stuck the last wooden spear through his mouth, slowly into his guts until it came out his other side, being careful that I did not kill him too quickly. While still alive, I lifted him up ever so gently, so that he was raised. Unlike the other soldiers that I impaled from the bottom up, I left the General choking on his own vomit, blood, and feces, upside down until he could not choke anymore.

Then, I grabbed Gideon. I pulled him onto Re's back and mounted the horse myself. I kicked off and headed up the forgotten mountains, our only haven now, for no man would dare to go there except us, as we were men no longer.

I stopped and stared back at the carnage we had left. It was a statement I had made clear to the King. It was not political, was not hidden in dreams and visions like a puzzle that he could misinterpret or not listen to, but was simple and easy to understand.

That statement consisted of his entire sent army, men that were sent to kill us, now all dead and impaled on hand carved wooden poles, displayed for the world to see. It was then that he would know that no man would harm Gideon, not while the Impaler was here.

EPILOGUE
A Message from Vlad

ALAS, WE HAVE COME TO THE END. Yet, this ending is only the beginning of my journey. No, as I have said before, my journey is long and cannot be told in one sitting, for it delves into aspects of all minds and all manners of ill intent. If you thought that the words I told you thus far were vile, disruptive, blasphemous, and disgusting, then I caution you deeply and advise you strongly not to go any further. Darkness is around the corner, and it only has to look at you once to steal you away.

Yet if you are of strong will and choose to listen for a bit longer, then I can tell you that a darker journey than this is still to come. What you have read was the start of me losing my humanity. I still have my sanity to lose, and then there is the matter of my soul. But that is for another time. For now, I bid you a good night, but not farewell. I shall see you very soon.

~Vlad

ABOUT
THE AUTHOR

THOMAS ARTHUR was born in Poland in 1946, during the aftermath of World War II. After growing up in extreme poverty, Thomas and his uncle, a cobbler, escaped to Brooklyn NY in 1961 where they both worked at a shoe repair shop. At an early age, his talent for writing was seen and Thomas took opportunities from local reporters and writers, ghost writing to make extra money and eventually helped his uncle open a shop of his own. After many years of notable work as a ghostwriter, Thomas became frustrated for not being acknowledged for his talent.

Thomas applied for various writing jobs and was denied due to his lack of educational merits. At a late age of 34, Thomas decided to change that and went to pursue his education, eventually receiving a Masters in English from Brooklyn College in 1988, and gaining acceptance into the acclaimed John Hopkins University Ph.D. Writing Program. But after the sudden death of his uncle, mounting expenses, and the unrewarding obscurity of ghostwriting, which he continued to do to pay for college, Thomas decided to take over his uncle's shoe repair shop instead and stopped writing altogether.

Being retired now, and with much push from his long-time writing friend, Professor Ron Lovell, gave Thomas a unique chance to return to his long lost passion. *The Book of Vlad: The Impaler* is his thirteenth novel, but first under his own name, as well as the first work he has written in over twenty-five years.

CPSIA information can be obtained
at www.ICGtesting.com
Printed in the USA
LVHW040333170120
643847LV00002B/34